THE BROTHERHOOD OF RAIN AND CINDER

THE BROTHERHOOD OF RAIN AND CINDER

Book One of The Brotherhood Trilogy

S.C. MEGALE

The Brotherhood of Rain and Cinder

ISBN 978-1-964715-16-2 (Paperback)
ISBN 978-1-964715-03-2 (Hardback)

Library of Congress Control Number: 2025909786

Published by Night Song Press. Centreville, Virginia.
Copyedit by Madelyn E. Dulle

First edition.

Cover design by Neslihan Yardimli. Map illustrations by the author. Interior illustrations by the author.

Printed in the United States of America.

For the men of my life. You know who you are.

And specifically . . .

To John Flanagan

Fellvren
Misty River
To Ghil Dor
Fort Rilke
Hillswallow
Cathair Mór
Fort Myrth
Galeduen
The Shrine
Southton
Welshire
Grave of Lare de Sille
Endraft
Calder Glen
Arluian Sea
"Sea of Mercy"
To Port Loch
Mt. Vestevor

t Vendar

= Ten Miles
= Emperor's Alarm Gongs
* Illustrations not to scale

Sille
Ford Pull
Kroikcher
Darson's Ford
Skerholm
Wulfhurst
Highland of Kings
Darvica
Calamus Mountains
Rookville
Durv Keep

Narun
Calsepheus
N
W
E
S
Dralus III
Dralus II
Dralus I

Breath
of
Durvoth
Polar
Easterlies
Niordeibith

CHAPTER 1

Adam's light floats at his wrist. It is a deep, purplish-blue orb that clings to the small hairs on his skin, slowly revolving around his hand. Emily watches as he stands there next to her. His eyes are closed, his head bowed. His hands are crossed in front of him. Colors from the stained-glass window above muddle the hue of his green forester's shirt and disguise the wrinkles at the corners of his eyes. He's in his forties—but sometimes, in the right light, he looks younger.

"If the women would extinguish the men's light . . ." Druid Parr says. He leans one elbow on the altar carved out of peryx, a glassy, dark blue marble worth as much as the village. The cleric wears plain grey robes that fail to hide his bandaged foot. In his free arm, he grips a wooden crutch, and he eyes the steps in front of the altar with trepidation as he straightens and prepares to move down.

His own whitish blue light accompanies him as he heads for a pair of altar girls awaiting him at the bottom step.

Around the pews, only the blue spheres, orbiting like planets the men's hands or wrists or fingers, illuminate the small room. Adam flutters open his eyes with a wry smile. His short, reddish-brown hair looks violet in the blue light, and he meets Emily's eyes with gentle anticipation.

"Would you?" he whispers, offering his wrist where the light rests. Emily smiles. Of course, he would always ask her.

She steps over to him, and he leans in as she lays a soft hand over the blue light. It shrinks under her fingers until there's nothing. She glances up at Adam's eyes, and his golden ones linger on hers with affection before he straightens and lends his gaze around the temple.

The dots of blue light extinguish under the touch of females around the room, until darkness falls. Only the stained glass glows, the panels behind them showing vivid-blue spheres dancing through emerald-green leaves or riding over pearly waves.

The forceful stomp of Parr's crutch kicks dust from the floor. The altar girls have removed his orb, and he winces now as he makes the arduous journey back up those two stairs.

The congregation waits for him. Emily raises her eyes to the large, circular window above Parr as he struggles beneath. This window does not spill in deep blue, or purple, or green like the ones behind them—but red and orange and bright yellow.

This one depicts fire.

The fire struggles in the picture, suppressed under legions of light and water. It is a beam of lava streaming onto the floor.

Each window in the church tells the story of the blue light replacing the fire—or what little there is to be sure of.

In the east window towers the first emperor, Myrril. A halo of orbs—all different shades of blue—glows around his head as he raises a sword triumphantly. Under his foot is the broken crown and body of the last fire-ruler. That happened almost a millennium ago.

In the west windows are the burning villages in the era before Myrril's time. The melting skulls. The magma slipping with the ground into a dark abyss—and carrying men with it. Words of ancient Vicars ring the walls between the windows, warning of the horrors of the flame. One of these windows is broken out, and Druid

Parr once said, "Probably for the best" in a tone Emily was never quite certain of. He sounded weary and cautious.

The last window shows the mystery: the final breath of fire before its permanent banishment. No one knows who or how, only that fire vanished sometime around when Myrril Braelius founded the Braelian Dynasty. Fire's mystifying death is shown through simplicity that is somehow profound . . .

Smoke.

A thousand tiny triangles of glass, all different shades of grey, depict smoke. The collage covers the entire window—there is no subject, no hint of sky at the edges. Only countless pieces of grey. It conveys an intentional feeling of chaos and mystery.

Parr's hand trembles as it reaches the peryx altar. But he grabs it hard like a sailor at the wheel and looks at the churchgoers.

"A beautiful day lies before us," he speaks, "in which we celebrate Celestial, the..."

Adam's hands gently cover Emily's ears on either side of her head. She gives a small jump and looks up at him. He is gazing ahead, but the corners of his mouth are lifted. This was Emily's first observance of the rural holiday, and Adam had wanted the festivities to be a surprise. Emily chuckles as she feels the pressure of his steady hands against her ears, hearing only her own blood rush now against his skin. Far be it for Parr to ruin Adam's surprise with his sermon.

So instead of listening, Emily studies those flames in the window once more and wonders if there's something wrong with her for it.

Adam's hands slip down. It must be safe to hear Parr again.

"Go forth," Parr says, "and celebrate the Celestial in *safety* tonight." He pins a bright eye upon a trio of rowdy-looking teenagers shoving each other's shoulders. They stop and look up at him when they notice his stare. "The camouflage of festivity is ripe for enemies of the church."

There's a collective sound of distress among the pews. Emily thinks she knows why. There have been rumors that those enemies live among them. But rumors are all they are.

The druid sighs and stumps over to an oversized stone chalice of water on the floor. Its reflection dances on the ceiling like silvery snakes.

Everyone forms a line to the altar. Adam and Emily make up the rear. They walk in rhythmic steps forward, but the laughter and playful screams from teenagers outside the church walls make the pace quicker than usual.

Emily's older companion approaches the druid and the stone basin. She watches Parr dip his fingers in the water and bring the drizzling liquid to Adam's forehead, where it dribbles down his lashes and nose. Most close their eyes respectfully during this ritual. Emily notes that Adam's eyes only stare across the room and blink away the water. He turns, and Emily takes his place. The druid dresses her in the same water, and she closes her eyes, unsure if it's instinctive or something more spiritual.

Water extinguishing fire.

Do they expect to find fire in her?

She breathes deeply. The water does not sting. Most druids in Galeduen fill their basins with seawater—and perhaps the stinging in their eyes, for others, is spiritual. But not for Emily. To get such water all the way to this secluded village would be expensive. She remembers Druid Parr pouring a pitcher into the basin and saying, "The water here will do." He seemed confident.

Each leave the wooden church, and Emily follows Adam's silent step towards the door. He squeaks it open with one long arm and lets her pass. Parr wipes his hands on a cloth behind them and watches fondly the last of his people depart in good spirits.

Sun hits Emily's eyes and she squints. Dark, murky water glints off rays around her. The dock she stands upon, though sturdy as earth, darkens from recent splashes. People must be active in the water today—a rare event.

Adam closes the door behind her and inhales.

"Are you ready for tonight?" His voice is gentle, level. But Emily thinks she caught just a tint of amusement behind it, which annoys her.

"Why is it so entertaining that I don't know what Celestial is?" The statement intended to be defiant, but she finds herself laughing. "I've only been here a year." She'd moved from Cathair Mór, the capital, where the Emperor's throne sits. It is on the opposite corner of the map, hundreds of miles away. Although she is only sixteen, Emily's mother had sent her here to make money—and eventually to purchase a shop for them both to move into and work in.

Boards creak beneath their feet as they walk down the dock to the row of shacks on stilts ahead of them, where other boardwalks connect. Mildew gives the wooden walls a green patina, but the buildings of

Darson's Ford are almost all identical boxes, including the church they just left behind.

"City folk," replies Adam in a low, neutral voice again. "I don't like to think of you missing all those Celestials."

A sentimental smile creases Emily's lips that Adam, walking just behind her, won't see. Her voice is softer now, though. "I'm sad I missed them, too. I love it here."

Adam is quiet at this, contemptuously, as they reach the rail-less dock way along the first block of shacks. She knows what his silence means. He doesn't approve of her being here with no guardian, nor of the work she needs to do to support herself. Whenever Emily reads letters from her mother as Emily and Adam sit together with their feet in the water, his whittling knife seems to dig a little deeper and scrape a little louder. More shavings seem to float in the water below them than usual.

"Are you working tonight?" he asks now, trying to mask the displeasure in his voice. Yes, their thinking had gone through the same process and ended up with this question.

"Just until eight," Emily replies, her casualness a little too obvious. In reality, a muscle in her stomach tightens. But Adam is rarely in need of being defused. He has a knack for nodding until the problem goes away. And he nods now.

A loud splash sounds ahead—someone must have dived into the water. They both stop, amused, as a wave sloshes against the poles.

"It's hot, but not that hot," says Emily, shaking her head. Adam grunts playfully as they resume their step. The waters of Darson's Ford, though nostalgic and iconic to the small, secluded village, are also none too clean.

Eventually, the screeching footsteps behind her stop. She turns to see Adam standing there with a regretful pursing of lips. The fine-chained silver necklace resting against his forester's shirt catches a glisten of sun. The brown leather sheath of his short sword hangs along his belt and is so worn and faded, it barely holds the blade. The smile wrinkles around his eyes are weary rather than joyful as Emily blushes.

"I just passed work, didn't I?" she says.

Adam watches her with his honey eyes, a hint of phony rebellion behind them. "I almost wasn't going to stop you."

She smiles and brushes past him for the door, but his fingertips catch her arm before she opens it. "I'll wait for you here at eight?"

“I’ll be here,” she promises. She has never celebrated the holiday before, but something tells her the Darson’s Ford regular standing next to her never truly has either.

Adam watches her, eyes heavy, as she opens the door.

○ ~ ○ ~ ○

The soldier removes his helmet and sits on the log bench, spitting into the ground. Crickets chirp in the forest edge behind him, and the grass is soft under his feet.

A dark-skinned guard is sitting on his right and turns at his arrival. His own helmet rests on his knee. He frowns. “Shift time already?”

The other shrugs. “Come on, Maron, I gotta get home!” he says with mock enthusiasm. “It’s Celestial!”

Maron gives him an unamused look. “The peasant holiday?”

“Easy. We really did use to celebrate it back home.” The falsity drops from the other’s voice, replaced with reminiscence. Maron looks forward.

“Sorry, Wes,” he says at length. “Educate me. What does it mean?”

Wes unbuckles a strap holding his pauldron on his shoulder. “Goes back to fire again. Doesn’t it all . . .”

“I can take a little more detail.”

Wes’ armor jangles as he tries to shake off more of it.

"It's . . . I don't know, a heavenly celebration. We're told the stars do this every year to celebrate the banishment of fire from our world. The stars celebrate that only they hold fire now."

"That doesn't sound like a peasant-only holiday," says Maron.

"It's called that because you can't see it from the city," Wes chuckles. And he's right. In the city, the blue light orbs of every fallen emperor encircle the city walls, floating there for eternity. There are so many now that, for decades, the night sky has been washed out.

"Too bad my transfer isn't sooner," Wes continues. "It's dark as hell where I'm going—the skies would be even better than here."

"Where are you going?" says Maron.

"Darson's Ford. Rumor has it there's a Brotherhood chapter underground there. The Emperor wants to lock the place down until we find it."

Maron huffs. "You'll find nothing. Just as I found in Rookville, Port Lochlan . . . the old man is paranoid."

Someone closes a door in the fort behind them. Another watchman going to bed. Maron doesn't question the transfer—or the Celestial lore—further. Most ceremonies revolve around fire. The absence of it. The banishing of it. The replacement of it.

"Thing is," says Wes, looking up at the sky, "Celestial should have started by now . . ."

Maron stands. "Enjoy your holiday."

"Flame perish . . ." says Wes as Maron trudges off into the forest behind the fort, shoving on his helmet. But Wes' eyes were still to the heavens as he'd spoken the words.

Blue light grows from Maron's fingertips and he directs the bright orb into a glass lantern. The glass dilutes the light into a soft glow as he clicks the lamp closed.

The ground is spongy under the silt of the forest—mushed leaves and twigs. The air is thin and rich with oxygen. Trees seem to go on forever in column after column of grey. Maron's walk is sleepier than the time last he patrolled the border. A mouse scurries under the thickets of bush and catches his uninterested eye.

The *snap!* of a large branch ahead jolts him to a stop. He drops the lantern, and it shatters against a stone, spilling out his light.

Before he can pull his sword from his sheath—

Wham! He's pounded in the head and thrown to the forest floor. Mud against his face. The welt from the strike is already throbbing on the back of his head.

Heart racing, he splutters away leaves. He lifts his head, and trees swoop in and out of vision.

But there. Through the trunks. He sees it.

Orange permeates the object in a halo. Shadows flicker on the forest floor, and terror chills his skin.

He cannot speak.

Across the way, thirty yards from him, lies a large, fallen branch.

Burning.

CHAPTER 2

"Amanda, thank goodness!" The old man bustles from behind the bar and actually embraces Emily, surprising her. In spite of herself, she chuckles.

"They're on your head, Mr. Robutan." She points to his glasses. He slaps a hand over his forehead and knocks them back down. Then he shakes his head fervently.

"Not the glasses, not the glasses," he says, but suddenly Emily knows why he's so pleased to see her. The entire tavern is overcrowded with orbs of blue light, floating on every surface in the room. Her mouth falls open. "Wha—?"

"Some undisciplined gaggle of youngsters." Mr. Robutan's natural lisp becomes more severe in his exasperation. He hobbles to the bar again, leaving Emily trailing into the room, gazing around at the hundreds of blue lights upon the surfaces.

"They came in wanting water; I should have known! Produced all this light. And left!" He throws a dish towel in the air in indignation, his one lock of wispy white hair seeming ghostly in the blue glow. "Where will people eat?"

Emily sets to work extinguishing the orbs beneath her hands, but she doesn't share Mr. Robutan's fury. A prank as it may have been . . . the lights are pretty to her. She's heard of women falling in love with men over the hues of their lights alone. Several men scoff against the idea, but Emily and most women believe the specific shades of blue men produce to be unique to any other man in the world. Adam's is deep and almost purple. When she thinks of him, she thinks of his color, not his face.

She watches now the warm, soft aura of the teenager's orb shrink beneath her fingers, and wonders whether the boys who stopped for water were really trying to cause the old man trouble, or if they simply sought to brighten the room for the holiday. Mr. Robutan had made no effort.

He's under the bar now, clunking around with pewter mugs and plates and speaking to Emily far louder than necessary.

"YOU REMEMBER WHERE I'M PUTTING YOU TONIGHT? I CAN'T HAVE YOU ON THE FLOOR."

Emily sighs and makes her way across the room for more orbs. "I remember."

Mr. Robutan runs the only tavern in town and has more than enough staff. On lucky days, Emily gets to fill in a dropped shift and work the tables. On unlucky days . . .

She rubs the blisters on her hand. It would be a long night in the basement—just her and the machines.

As she walks by, his wispy head pops up from under the counter and seeks her out. Half of his tavern is already extinguished.

"Don't extinguish the light in the sconces!" he instructs unnecessarily.

"Wouldn't dream of it," says Emily. Her hands begin to sweat at the warmth of the orbs beneath her palms, and it soothes her blisters.

The last of the light is finally put out by the time the patrons should be making their way to the inn—six o'clock. Emily joins the old bartender for a moment and grabs a jug of oil.

"They're on your head," she says again as Mr. Robutan looks aghast around the counter for his spectacles. He slams them back over his eyes as if she had said nothing, and the door opens with the first pack of especially jovial customers.

○ ~ ○ ~ ○

Emily heaves her shoulder into the heavy spoke. The wooden machine turns, and inside its belly, little knobs crunch wickernut shells and reveal tiny red seeds. Mr. Robutan will malt the seeds to make wickerrye. Emily winces and pushes harder. Her muscles ache, but she will make more than thirty loops around this machine tonight, refilling it occasionally.

Footsteps clunk through the ceiling, and she can hear laughter upstairs.

The basement work is tiring, blistering. But it reminds her of what she did with her mother back home—making pies out of berries, selling them on the street. They'd have to squish the fruit, too, and that is how Emily learned almost every berry in the Empire—what is sweet, what is tart, what can heal, and what might kill you. She remembers her mother flittering a hand fan over the freshly baked pies to waft their aroma farther into passersby. Many mistook them for sisters. Both Emily and her mother have brown hair, although Emily's is longer and a shade darker. Both have brown eyes. There is a spark in Emily's though that never existed in her mother's.

Emily sighs and steps over to a small table where Mr. Robutan lit his light for her inside a lantern. She places a hand on the table's surface and drinks deeply from a cup of water. It will take years for her to be able to afford a shack at the Ford where she and her mother can open a pie shop. And it may take just as long for her to gather enough courage to tell her mother she'd rather open a schoolhouse with that real estate instead.

That secret desire relates to how Emily has tried making money in other ways. With her passion for history, for mythology, she took a few students soon after arriving at the Ford. In her classes—which Mr. Robutan let her hold on weekday mornings at the tavern—she read from history books and led a discussion for a modest fee. Some came because they couldn't read—they wanted to be taught. Others because they were curious about this lone girl's arrival—and about what knowledge she might bring from the capital, which was about as far away from Darson's Ford as the map allowed. She only remembers one student who really took an interest in the historical and mythological content. He was a young man with olive skin, curly hair, and a fashionable outline of kohl around his eyes. His voice was impatient and rude.

"What do you know of the flood?" he'd said, twiddling his thumbs and propping his feet on the round table. Emily doesn't remember his name, but she remembers the constant twiddling. The others turned to her as if eager to see if her big-city smarts would pass the test.

"The one in T.M. 121 or R.M. 0?" Emily replied. The others smiled, and she admits she was showing off a bit there in front of the arrogant young man. She's not sure all of her students even understood the year markers, though—they know they live in T.M. 823, but they may not know T.M. is from an ancient language and stands for *Tar Múch*—"After-Extinguishment." *Roh Múch,* or *R.M.* would be "Before-Extinguishment."

But the young man had not been amused. "Obviously zero."

He refers to the flooding of the Arluian Sea, a flood which was said to cover the land and destroy all remnants of fire. It likely never happened, unlike the one in T.M. 121, which very much did happen. Once a year, in summer, the snow and ice on Mt. Vestevor melt. They flood into the sea at just the same time the moons align in perigee—their closest points to the planet. That's when, with greater gravitational power than normal, they draw back the seas' salty tide and, for a short time, the sea becomes freshwater. She does not know much about the stars, but she's read that in T.M. 121, the moons' cycle was interrupted by another celestial object, and the tide was not drawn back when the ice melted, which caused the flood.

"All right." The student seems to have granted Emily his trust in her competence. "And what does history say of the Brotherhood?"

Emily purses her lips. The others tense. She knows speaking on this will frighten them—especially with the rumors that there are Brotherhood members among them. But she also can't pass up the challenge.

"You're talking about the shortened name for the Brotherhood of Rain and Cinder."

They all watch her.

"It was founded in T.M. 10 by an unknown individual, but most certainly someone from the stonecutter race, which lived here before being conquered by the first emperor." That would be Myrril Braelius. "The Brotherhood was a cult of fireworshippers who didn't believe fire should ever have been banished. Some say they knew ways of keeping fire alive, and they practiced ignition in the shadows. Most think they only tried and failed to bring back fire, however. They operated up until T.M. 225, when Emperor Euris IV had them eradicated."

"I thought that was Emperor Ilegard," said the student, twiddling his thumbs again.

"Emperor Ilegard would have been too busy building Cathair Mór."

"You mean Emperor Lurio." The student sounds frustrated.

"Lurio began Cathair Mór, Ilegard finished it. And signed the Darkwing Pact." The treaty that made Darvica a province.

"So what is the Brotherhood today?" the young student presses, shaking his head swiftly to change the topic and shifting in his seat.

Emily breathes deeply. "If it still exists, there may be some fireworshippers left. But it's more likely just a guild of criminals keeping each other protected in a network of bribes and safehouses, using the name of the old cult."

"So there's no murder required for initiation?" one of the others asks.

"I don't know," says Emily. "There might be."

That student never returned. And neither did the

others. Emily's tutoring business didn't last much longer.

The basement hatch opens, and suddenly the crowd's chatter is much louder. Emily turns to the blast of new light.

Mr. Robutan pokes his head down. "Amanda!" he says. His glasses slip off his face and somersault down three steps. "Someone is here to pick you up."

She sets down her water. *Is it time already?*

"I'm coming," she says. She grabs his glasses as she climbs the stairs.

○ ~ ○ ~ ○

"So, why are we lying here again?" Emily asks. The wet grass furrows around her. They are lying on the encircling hill above the Ford, close to the woods that surround the village. Her hands are folded across her chest, wrapped in dishcloths. There's a little less blood than usual.

Stars scatter the sky above like sawdust floating on water.

"Just look," Adam replies. His voice is gentle, low, and tonight, touched with humor. He's asked her to watch the sky for something. Emily shifts her shoulders and watches stubbornly.

In the western sky twinkle a belt of three bright stars—Dralus I, Dralus II, and Dralus III—named after three emperors. Narun, the large, pale, heavily cratered moon, shines next to its small, ruby-colored partner, a moon named Calsepheus. Sometimes, in the few days when Narun's shadow phase is ahead of Calsepheus, the moonlight looks magenta.

The houses of Darson's Ford, all on stilts within the pool, are quiet and glow through their paper-covered windows. A few silhouettes stand outside their doors on the boardwalk with their heads thrown back to the heavens.

Everyone's in on it . . . Emily thinks. She flexes her entwined, aching fingers and rustles again in the grass. Adam, lying a few feet from her, catches her excitement and smiles.

"Almost time . . ." he teases.

On the Ford, fathers lift children onto their shoulders. Whispering increases, so Adam must be right. The event must be imminent.

They wait.

And wait.

Something like fear touches Emily's stomach when Adam frowns.

The excited whispers from the Ford turn to concerned murmuring. Emily swallows and somehow knows now is not the time to tease Adam—in fact, she thinks she might never forget how his eyes look at her for a single, worried beat. His muscles tense as he keeps his elbows propped behind his shoulders in the grass.

When it becomes clear nothing will happen, Adam says, "Huh."

Back on the boardwalks, doors squawk open as spectators retreat into their homes. Emily sees their silhouettes behind the paper-covered windows—there is a lot of walking, a lot of discussion she cannot hear.

"What was . . . *supposed* to happen?" says Emily.

Adam clears his throat. "A star shower."

Emily blinks. "Okay." She cannot think of anything else. For some reason, her heart is racing.

"It's every year," says Adam. "But not always the same day. The Vicar's druids let us know."

Emily imagines someone seated in the night with a large chart in front of them, chronicling the stars and predicting the next Celestial. It seems like a lonesome and yet important job.

Soft cricket chirps compliment the calmness—the lack of event. Adam casts his eyes, long since adjusted to the darkness, around the clearing. Moonlight floods silver onto the grass. It polishes every leaf and twig. From the incline they rest upon, they can glimpse the distant, rolling lands nestled far past the forest.

Darson's Ford is a small town established literally on top of a ford. Thick poles the size of tree trunks support boardwalks that run all within the waters like a maze and serve as streets and porches to homes. Only one or two rowboats clunk against docks—most get around by walking. The water itself is deep and at one point was clean, but now it is murky in the heart of the village, refreshed only by the rain.

Deep woods completely surround the little town, and at the same time seclude it. The woods are unnamed—a fact Emily remembers pointedly. Legend says that Myrril halted his sword in midair above Gennan, the last High King of Galeduen, who issued a warning from the ground. "Raise your Empire, but name not these woods," the High King said. "The trees have names you are never to know." It always struck Emily how Myrril seemed to have heeded the warning, for none of the Empire's maps name these iconic woods. Something about Gennan's warning, complete with the threat of a curse, must have scared Myrril enough.

Only from the very high ground closest to the trees, on which Adam and Emily lay now, can one see the peaks of the Calamus Mountains and the yellow grassland before it. Adam admires those grasslands now, but the mountains are too dark to be deciphered from the sky.

"Why do the stars shoot then, Adam? What makes them fly away?" Emily feels if she keeps talking about the event, the mysterious pit in her stomach will loosen. Adam opens his mouth but struggles.

"Well, I . . . I don't think they're actually stars. Stars don't move. Shooting stars are just . . . burning rocks." He stops a moment, checking his facts mentally before continuing. "And being close to our planet is what makes them 'shoot.'"

"Burning?" says Emily. "So, there's fire out there?"

"Yes," says Adam. "The sun, the stars . . . they alone hold our fire."

"Weird world we live in," she says after a pause.

"Yeah," Adam sighs. "Weird world."

A comfortable silence hangs between them. Fireflies blaze like embers in specks around the tree line.

"So the stars aren't going to fall?" Emily's quiet voice has a tint of true concern. Adam can't help smiling gently.

"They're not going anywhere," he promises.

Adam's promises she could trust. She knew that ever

since first meeting him at the tavern.

It'd been a lucky night. Mr. Robutan's favorite employee had fallen ill, and Emily claimed her shift. In the bustle of an average business night, Adam had opened the door and simply stood there, looking around at the inn and its patrons, seeming entirely out of place. When she approached him and offered to find him a seat a little timidly, he had snapped out of his trance and studied her.

"Aren't you a little young to be working here?" His voice was not ridiculing like every other that had asked the same question. It was genuinely concerned, troubled even.

"Aren't you a little old to need help finding a seat?"

He watched her pointedly after the jab, but when Emily couldn't contain a smile, his eyes brightened tentatively, almost perplexed.

"Amanda! If you're going to sleep here, no standing!" Mr. Robutan had hollered after setting two filled mugs on the bar.

"Sleep here?" Adam spoke to her, and it was like they were already a team.

Emily pursed her lips shyly and nodded. Adam's brow furrowed.

She had departed from him, and Adam, walking

slowly, found a lone seat by the corner and slid into it. He had watched her the rest of the night as she went about her work. The further the hour, the more rowdy and drunken her tables became. Mr. Robutan seemed to pay no mind, but her step became more nervous around the strong, drunken men.

Then the door blasted open. A cloaked man with a crossbow under his arm entered. He held one gloved hand as if it were injured. "Aid," the man croaked, and then fell face-first to the floor with the boom of felled timber. He didn't move. Everyone froze. Chatter halted. Bodies melted back from the scene. Except for Emily's. She rushed forward for him.

"Idiot girl!" a drunk, stocky, smash-faced figure cried. "He could be Brotherhood! You heard the guards!"

Distrust had seeped through the small town since a few weeks after Emily arrived—when the guards started posting flyers on poles telling residents to be on alert. Now any stranger's arrival was met with hostility.

Brotherhood. Fireworshippers. Emily hesitated.

"He asked for aid . . ."

She took a step forward. And the drunkard cursed and lunged at her with a fist raised.

The drunk was knocked to the ground. His wooden

mug clattered down with him. Other thugs at his table scraped back their chairs and stood, but Adam clasped a strong hand on Emily's shoulder and yanked her back.

"Flame-rotting filth!" the stocky man howled on the floor. Adam reached down and jerked him up by the scruff of his shirt, then thrust him back towards his friends. The man stumbled and nearly fell over again. They glared at him incredulously, but Adam's returning look was unforgiving.

"That won't happen again," Adam turned and said darkly to Emily. "I promise."

And it never did.

"Get rid of him!" Mr. Robutan wagged a hand over at the possible Brotherhood member and Emily could do nothing as Adam and a few others dragged the unconscious—or even dead—man from the bar.

Adam came back the night after, when Emily was able to thank him. Slowly, they questioned one another, Adam secretly delighted by her courage and wit, and Emily unable to ward off the paternal attachment she felt towards this older man who had protected her that night. She discovered Adam to be unmarried, childless, and retired military. These days, he worked as a woodsman, making nets and arrows, chopping lumber for the craftsmen and builders. Sometimes selling his carvings. Adam discovered her to be fatherless, with a mother back home in Cathair Mór who was pregnant with Emily's half-sibling. Emily merely shrugged when she couldn't identify the father of that child.

At last, Adam offered to teach her wood carving and show her the ropes of this foreign-feeling village called Darson's Ford.

"Adam?" she says now on that hill.

There is not an ounce of sleep in his reply. "Yeah?"

Emily chuckles. "Nothing. I thought you might have fallen asleep."

"I'm going to," Adam breathes and drags himself to his feet. He groans. "I guess the show is over here. The town will talk about this."

He looks again to the sky as if giving it one more chance. "I'm sorry," he says, eyes still lingering above. "I don't know what happened."

But that is the end of it. He turns to the water. "Since when did I have knee problems?" He rubs his left knee with a half wince, half smile.

"You have a lot of problems."

"Yeah." He scratches the back of his head. "Some truth to that."

"I'll walk you down," Emily offers, joining him down the grassy slope.

The waters are black, holding only the large, glassy moon like a dinner plate on its surface. The smaller moon is too dark to see there. They shuffle down onto the first wooden planks, which clunk under their feet. The air is cool, the leaves of the surrounding woods still, watching.

They're silent.

Torches at intervals on the docks are lit in the floating blue light. Emily watches as a dark figure far down one of the boardwalks holds a hand over the top of a torch and produces the light to ignite it. It grows from a dot in the distance to a sphere of luminance blooming under the man's hand.

They reach the pub before reaching Adam's house. Mr. Robutan had prepared for the festivities to rumble into the night—instead, in disappointment, he left out a closed sign.

Adam stands by the door and turns to her, but doesn't open it yet. The inky water laps gently against the docks.

"I don't care that the event didn't happen," Emily says. "That was the best holiday I've ever celebrated."

It is hard to make out Adam's expression in the

moonlight.

"I imagine it's the only one you've celebrated." He speaks so low and bare that deciphering the emotion behind the words is difficult. He looks up suddenly to the trees beyond them and exhales deeply.

"I don't like the braziers."

Emily twirls and spots one of the blue torches nearby, thinking it was an odd comment for Adam to make.

"Why?"

"They make everything else darker."

She could see it—their blossoming glow, though warm and familiar, makes the black tree line impossible to pierce. Adam looks at it now, as though worried about something. And then he looks back to her just as suddenly.

"Let's scavenge tomorrow."

Emily smiles, but a yawn interrupts.

"I'll meet you at your place." She bravely tries to speak with firm, sleepless tones but fails.

A small, wistful smile lifts the side of Adam's mouth. His eyes are content. "Goodnight, Emily."

He steps forward. Placing a gentle hand behind her head, he kisses her forehead.

She watches as he cuts past her and walks down the dock. He throws his head and gazes at the stars but doesn't look back.

Not going anywhere, Adam, she thinks. *They're not going anywhere.*

CHAPTER 3

Adam and Emily lift a net from the forest floor. Soil showers down to the earth.

"Nothing?" Emily asks. Her hands are caked in mud. Adam drops the net.

"Not a single one," he says. They're searching for yellow tubers that grow here and taste delicious seared in oil. "Been too dry." He staggers over a crop of rocks, flicking his hand. On the other side of the rocks, he lifts another net. Only dirt rains down again.

Grabbing his sack, Adam glances up at Emily, who is prying a worm from her fingers. Adam gives her a mellow smile. "I don't think he'd be as tasty in oil. You might as well let him go."

Emily studies the worm despairingly as it swings from side to side in her fingers. She sets it on the ground and watches it curl in the mud. "Good day for him."

Adam crouches as he replaces his net into his bag and ties it. "And for us?"

"We'll survive," says Emily. She sets her own net at the base of a tree where they always leave it.

Adam stands, the pack swung over his shoulder. "Ready?"

They walk easily through the woods towards Darson's Ford, the forest green and draped in canopies of moss and ivy. Bluebells—blue, bell-shaped flowers—cover the ground. Golden light dapples the reddish bark of the trunks and Adam leads Emily with a sense of freedom she rarely sees back at the Ford. A sense of comfort she rarely sees. As usual, he's quiet until he pauses ahead of her, swinging off his pack.

"Lunch on me," says Adam. He sits on a three-foot-tall, moss-coated stone. Then he digs his hand into the bag.

"I thought we only eat if we provide?" Emily jokes. She gropes at a large leaf on a bush to wipe off the mud. Her eyes instinctively search for a berry bush, or anything to contribute to the meal. If there are any, the fruits are stripped bare.

Adam holds out a piece of grilled trout for her but wastes no time biting into his own. The skin is dressed in herbs and nearly blackened to a crisp. Her mouth floods on sight of it.

“I did provide,” he says thickly. His eyes glow with rare mischief as she takes the hunk of fish from him.

“The failure scavengers buying from someone else. It’s just sad, Adam.” But she is smiling as she takes a large bite of the flaky white meat.

“I didn’t have high expectations for us. And the widow I bought it from didn’t trust anyone but me to cook it for her.”

Emily guesses the widow must always have to trade when she needs a man’s light for cooking. It must take days of traveling to make camp at the nearest stream outside the Ford . . . only to come home and need a man to make her catches edible. It doesn’t seem fair.

“Look at all the bluebells,” says Adam.

“They’re beautiful,” says Emily. “I wish they’d stay longer.”

“Only if we carve one.”

Their blooms don’t last long—and in the woods, in the glow of dusk, the blue is almost spectral.

Emily watches Adam’s fingers reach down to brush the tiny blue flowers, and it is almost like observing a private moment.

She thinks about touching the dainty blossoms herself. But she is afraid of hurting them.

Adam stands and wipes the herbs from his hands, already chewing his last bite. Emily had just started to sit on the grass as he rose, and she nearly stumbles as she straightens herself back up, poised to follow him again.

He fights a smile. "Take your time."

Now that Adam's seat is unoccupied, she moves to the tall, elliptical standing stone. The downy moss covering it parts just enough to reveal an oddly precise indent on the rock, and she pauses. She places the last piece of fish in her mouth to free her hand and gently veils away the moss, uncovering more of the indent.

Carvings.

She swallows the trout.

"Adam?"

He turns to her. When she remains silent, he steps over.

"What is this?" she asks.

Adam studies it with a cock of his head. The shadows of leaves play on his reddish-brown hair as he dips his head lower and wipes away a curtain of moss from the stone.

The carvings are of intricate knots. Leaves dance

through them, and a precise border is chiseled around the edge of the stone's face. There are licks of flame engraved through the knots and leaves. Not blue light.

Still, Adam brushes aside the moss with growing ease and familiarity. Emily watches him, entranced. But that simultaneous fear and fierce curiosity that is instantly associated with fire impales her. She shoves the feeling away and watches Adam's hands undress the beautiful stone entirely.

"They're called Guardians."

"The stones?" says Emily. "There're more of these?"

Adam nods.

"I've seen two in these woods alone. They're ancient. No one really knows who carved them, but they were scattered everywhere. On mountains, in caves and forests. I've seen one ten feet tall on a cliff overlooking the ocean. They're not usually close to civilization. Meant to be found only by the lost wanderer or traveler. As encouragement. So they know human touch has been here. Human touch says they're not alone."

"How come I've never heard of them? If they're everywhere?" Her eyes are still locked on one of the fire depictions, flame enveloping a leaf.

"They're not everywhere anymore," Adam says with

a hint of regret. "They're getting rarer. The church pays a lot of money for them."

"The church?"

"Because of the fire images on them. They don't want that message all over the country. The stone Guardians were probably carved long before fire disappeared. Before we couldn't produce it anymore." He turns his hand towards himself and studies it. "Blue light replaced the fire long after these people were gone."

She swallows and tears her eyes from the licks of flame to the base of the rock. "If the church pays so much money for them . . . why haven't you turned them in?"

Adam shrugs and brushes a beetle off the top of it.

"I think they're prettier here."

Emily pulls a token-like square of wood from her pocket. On this piece of wood, she's been practicing whittling as Adam does. She notes the similar scrapings of knots on hers as on the stone. Adam catches her movement and smiles. "I taught you those knots." She meets his eyes distractedly, reminding herself to return his smile. Her fingers rub across the smooth wood.

"I'm—I'm still trying to get the pattern right."

"You will. I learned the knots from these stones, if you were wondering." He walks to the tree next to the

Guardian and pulls out his pocketknife. "Let's do another." He shaves a small area of the tree, hacking off shards of bark until its smooth, white undersurface is revealed. Emily pockets her token and digs out her own small knife in the same transaction.

Adam is calm and quiet as he carves a pattern of knots and leaves and blue light, not fire, into the tree. Just as he has done so many times before. She was fascinated the first time she watched him do it, and begged him to teach her. He did, and threw in a few defensive moves with the knife as well.

"For when you're not here?" Emily had joked.

But Adam's reply was soft and sincere as he lowered her knife hand with his own, relaxing her muscles. "I'm not going anywhere."

Adam steps back and allows her to chisel the border of the design.

"Why did you start this habit, Adam? Of carving the trees?" She closes off the border with the tip of her knife.

Adam gives an ironic smile, but it doesn't touch his golden-brown eyes.

"Same reason, I guess," he says. "So people know I'm here."

A deep, loud gong echoes through the trees, scaring

off birds in a flutter of wings. Both Adam and Emily jerk in its direction.

Adam glances to meet Emily's eyes, and they exchange confusion and fright.

"Follow me," he says, voice low and dark. A cold chill runs through Emily.

"What is that?" She follows Adam, ducking beneath a branch.

His step is no longer carefree but cautious and rigid. "The gong," he says. "Emperor's alarm."

CHAPTER 4

Chairs scrape aside in the dark room. The old man opens his eyes under the covers but does not stir.

He listens.

Footsteps approach his bedframe, and another closes the door to his chamber.

"Sir," a man whispers at his side. The old man turns on his pillow, and his eyes glow like lamps in the night.

"We need to evacuate you, my lord."

"What?" his deep, croaky voice is worried, and he pulls himself to sit.

"There's an emergency, my lord. We need you to come with us."

The old man hesitates. A warning breeze lifts the curtains of his open window.

"I am not going without my family," he speaks slowly, but there is no arguing his firm tone.

"They are coming, too."

Dazed, the elder swings his legs off the bed and his antique eyes lock on the adviser before him.

"Why are you taking me from my home, Cress?"

The use of his name makes the adviser hesitate. He swallows and notices how strong the old man looks, even in his nightclothes. Like an ancient eagle.

"They were wrong, sir," Cress whispers. "It's back."

The Emperor freezes.

Cress' clarifying word is barely audible. "Fire."

The elder is a statue. But his eyes are alive. A million thoughts flash through them.

"So, you are taking me, and leaving my empire to crumble?" he rumbles.

Silence.

"No . . ." the old man corrects himself, and with a musing turn of his head, he rises to his feet. "You are taking me, and leaving it to burn."

○ ~ ○ ~ ○

They hear shouting, and Adam suddenly breaks into a run. Emily follows, trees flashing by until they burst into the sun.

Adam lifts his gaze to the only path to the village—across the way to their left—and they shuffle down the grassy incline towards the ford.

Three figures stand at the banks of Darson's Ford, just feet from the dirt path. One is mounted on his horse, the shouting coming from him, and the other two are stricken as they speak back. Emily and Adam watch, slowing their pace to a brisk walk, having assured no swords were drawn.

But something is wrong.

The rider slides off his mount and falls into the water with a splash.

Adam and Emily resume their run.

The rider is dragged out of the water by the two others—Lynne, the fisherwoman Adam and Emily trade with, and a man Emily sees often but has never met. The cooper, she thinks. Orangey hair, just beginning to show flecks of grey, with a big, round nose. An image of him, looking up from his work building barrels as she passed by, flashes in her mind, but she can't place his name.

"He's delusional." Lynne has a crisp, authoritative voice, but her eyes are concerned as they rest on the rider. Her short-cut grey hair and lively blue eyes dilute the effect of her age wrinkles. The rider indeed looks like he will pass out at any moment, his clothes now sopping and his eyes twitching the water away.

"Druid," he mumbles. "I need your druid."

Adam watches but does not help. He stands still. The cooper looks up to Adam and holds his eyes for longer than a glance, as if measuring something, but Adam is stolid. Then the cooper turns his attention back to the rider, who Lynne is helping to sit. She takes a determined step back once the rider has gagged all the water from his throat, and she waits with cool expectancy.

Clunks of rushing footsteps are heard on the docks as people gather towards the scene. They too have heard the gong.

"How long have you been riding, Wes?" Lynne asks in her brisk but not unkind voice. The rider must have disclosed his name before Emily and Adam arrived.

"I haven't slept since yesterday morning." Wes shivers from the wetness weighing down his clothes. "I need to see your druid. Please, someone get him."

Lynne meets Adam's eyes as if expecting him to heed the request. Adam just clears his throat and shifts to life.

"You're not a courier," Adam says levelly, eyeing the helmet protruding from the carrying pack on the horse. The horse sneezes and shakes its mane, as if in agreement. "You're military. The Emperor's alarm—"

"The Emperor's been evacuated." Wes shakes his

head despairingly.

Fear chills through them. They are deathly silent.

Emily knows she cannot mask the terror in her eyes as she looks to Adam for his response. He is looking forward, dark and still. She thinks he's not going to acknowledge her, but then his gaze suddenly finds hers, a trace of ominous concern behind it.

"What happened?" Lynne whispers. She too cannot hide the fear in her voice.

"I can't say anything until I talk to your druid." Wes lies back and covers his face in his hands, blocking out the sun.

"I'll get him," the cooper says, but he is looking at Adam when he speaks. Again, Adam is unresponsive, but the cooper climbs onto the dock from the bank and breaks into a run for the church.

The few bystanders gathered are young, and they sit on the dock, dangling their feet in the cool water, which is clean near the bank. Their faces are tight and lined.

"Adam." Lynne is speaking, her bright, blue eyes urgent, as if hoping to find some understanding and sanity in Adam. "Perhaps the adults should speak to him." She gestures to Wes. "Perhaps Emily should—"

"Emily is staying with me." Adam speaks quietly, but

it's definitive.

A surge of pride wells inside Emily as she thinks of Lynne addressing Adam as if he were her guardian. Perhaps Adam has imitated the carved stone more than just through their designs.

Somewhere in the distance, farther than its first deep note, another gong sounds—a low, static hum that bristles through the leaves in the forest.

"It's being circulated? The alarm?" Emily is impressed that her voice doesn't crack, even if her mouth is dry. No amount of swallowing moisturizes it.

"One post hears it, and they sound their own gong a little farther," Adam explains while his eyes search the docks for the cooper's return. He drops his voice to a whisper. "All throughout Galeduen."

His gaze stays there as the returning footsteps echo down the boardwalk. But Adam's expression mingles anxiety and confusion as the footsteps transform into a sprint.

Their old druid could not run so quickly.

The cooper squeaks around the bend, and Adam and Lynne stiffen as they see him stagger, waving his arms frantically. He is yelling, but they cannot make out his words.

"Stay," Adam orders Emily, and he hops onto the dock to meet the cooper, but stops after taking only a single step.

The words can be made out now. And at the same time Emily hears them, Adam stumbles backwards, off the dock and back into the grass in shock.

"HE'S DEAD!" the cooper cries. "DRUID PARR IS DEAD!"

CHAPTER 5

The shock is broken only by Wes' confession. Lynne and Adam force the cooper to halt his whimpering so the soldier can speak.

"It's fire." Wes gulps. "Fire is back."

Lynne, already white, yelps and covers her mouth with her hand.

Vertigo tilts the ground beneath Emily's feet. She tries to catch her breath, but it's like there is only smoke in the air. Those radical prophecies on the church walls between the stained glass—prophecies of skies falling to earth—suddenly seem real.

And that reality is happening now.

The spectators sitting at the pier jump to their feet. They run down the dock to relay Wes' words, and in the next few seconds, urgent footsteps multiply as people thump down the stairs of their front porches or wrench open creaky doors, deeper in the village.

Cries echo through Darson's Ford, and Emily can focus her eyesight just long enough to lock on Adam, who is standing in front of her, head low, trying to see into her eyes. His fingertips brush her wrist, trying to clasp her hand, and there is more tension behind his fingers than she has ever felt. His lips form words she cannot hear, but she thinks she can make them out:

"My house."

Both Adam's hands guide her shoulders onto the dock and he begins to lead her down, bodies flashing by them. Adam walks with more resolve and speed than she has ever witnessed, and she tries to choke out his name—

"Adam," she gags.

"I know," he says. His voice is remarkably low and soft, but there is a fear behind it he cannot mask.

Suddenly, everywhere Emily looks—the splintered panels of wooden shacks, in the brown, churning water—her vision is spotted with orange and yellow. Like flames. She squeezes her eyes shut and tries to block them out, but still they burn through.

Finally, a door jerks open and the familiar, gentle groan of Adam's floor is under her feet. He releases her and closes his door, turning the lock with a cold click.

Adam's home is dark and sparse, wooden and small like any other. A threadbare rug centers the living room they are in, and a small hall leads to one bedroom in the back. Adam's short sword leans beside the front door. The grip on its hilt is light brown leather, and the guard before the blade begins is just a simple disc, barely wider than the grip. It is a cheap military issue—but it is Adam's, and it accompanied him on his short tour in the Sunlight Wars.

Emily stumbles over to a chair by the empty lightgrate and collapses into it.

Adam is crouching by the grate, and she watches his purplish-blue light grow from his hand like a lifeline. He hovers his hand over the grate and lowers the orb of light, which obeys and curls over the grate on its own. It gives off the gentlest of heat and a shimmer cruises across it.

Emily tries to clear her throat. She must be strong. She and Adam are in this together, not just Adam.

"What are we—?" Her voice is squeaky, but it's better than nothing.

Adam stands and moves urgently to grab the short sword at his door. "You are staying here. I need to go to the church and see what happened to Parr."

Emily stands as Adam stashes the sword in his worn,

leather sheath.

"Adam," she says in a small voice, and Adam stops and looks at her. "What's happening?"

He holds her gaze for a long moment, and the regret and sympathy in it eclipse all his fear.

"I don't know," he whispers. There is pain in every word.

Tears well in Emily's eyes and she tries to wipe them away, furious at their arrival.

"What I do know," Adam presses in his quiet voice, moving to her and lowering the hand that tries to dispel the tears, "is that you are safe here."

Emily nods.

"You're staying with me tonight. I'm going now and coming right back."

"Okay." Emily nods and swallows. "Okay."

Adam nods as well, but she catches the tiniest flash of uncertainty in his eyes. He reaches the door and turns the knob.

"Adam!" Emily cries before she can stop herself.

Adam turns to her, and there is a pause.

He rushes to kneel before her. His arms enfold her so tightly that neither speaks, and he buries his face in her shoulder.

She clutches him, and the silence is tangible.

When he stands, he seizes the doorknob once again, but Emily is sure she caught his hand wipe a tear from his eye.

After the door shuts, she can hear his footsteps walk swiftly away, towards the church.

Alone, she wanders to the lightgrate, where Adam's indigo light blazes. It is coiled around the grate like a blue coating, very much alive.

She retakes her seat next to it and buries her face in her hands. A list etches in her mind, erecting structure in the chaos.

Tonight, she will write her mother. Tonight, she and Adam will work out their plan. Tonight, she will definitely not be taking her shift at work.

And it goes on.

She lifts her head and looks out the window. Shrill voices and even the occasional splash into the waters can still be heard through the walls of Adam's home.

There's only one thing that could comfort Darson's Ford now.

A memory of Adam, sitting with her on the grassy slope above the Ford as she practiced her carvings on that little wooden token, flashes in her mind. He had watched the Ford darkly, hands resting on his knees, as if something was on his mind. He looked like this occasionally, but never disclosed why. And then, as the brooding, grey storm clouds rumbled above them, first spits, and then bullets, struck their lashes and bled through their clothes. Emily had glanced to Adam, measuring whether he would stand and make for shelter. But he didn't move. He grunted ironically and turned his head from her. "Rain," he'd said. "I wonder if it'd be enough."

He had stood, his reddish-brown hair soaked, before Emily could comment.

Now, she understands.

Rain. If it had to, would it keep flame embedded to its death, forever patting down the earth in its holy moisture?

The only thing able to comfort Darson's Ford now is rain.

And as she thinks this, a bird somewhere high above flutters over the rays of one of the strongest suns she has seen all summer.

○ ~ ○ ~ ○

When Adam's creaks on the boardwalk are long gone, Emily creeps out his front door. She has wrapped herself in one of Adam's dark cloaks, the cowl over her head. The waters of the Ford thrash with anger below the planks. There is much disturbance among it today. Emily pulls the cloak tighter and makes swiftly for the church.

She eases open the doors of the church with a mothlike hand. The hinges do not screech. She doesn't want to be seen or heard—for her safety, but also for the sake of Adam, who had trusted her to obey his wish.

But Emily wants to see for herself. She sneaks inside and crouches.

Several pews ahead of her are hushed voices. Adam is standing there, and Lynne, and Wes, and a few other townsfolk. They are surrounding something.

"It could have just been a heart attack," says one of the townspeople.

"There are no burn marks on him," another agrees.

Lynne looks doubtful.

"Can you investigate?" Adam, hands crossed in front of him, raises his eyes to Wes.

Wes frowns. "We will do what we can." He does not sound hopeful.

"Isn't it strange they left the altar intact?" someone says, turning to the brilliant blue altar made of peryx. He is right, of course—everyday robbers would have taken to the altar with a hammer, chipping off beads that would be worth hundreds of coins. Whoever murdered the druid had no interest in wealth—and this is all the more unnerving.

The people move to look at the altar as well, and now Emily can see Druid Parr's body for herself.

He is draped over the basin of holy water, head dangling over the liquid, and the tip of his nose just skimming the surface. Like one of the villagers said, his body is unmarked—no cuts and, more importantly, no burns.

"Who will help me bury him?" says Adam at last, turning back to the basin of water. And a minute later, hands have collected Druid Parr and carried him out the exit near the altar.

When she is alone in the church with the basin, Emily rises and walks slowly towards it. She stands there for a long beat, just looking at it.

A dot of color catches her eye and she looks down. On the floor is a single berry. She retrieves it, assuming it must have fallen from her pocket the last time she sat in these pews with Adam. Emotions constrict her heart.

But as she twists the berry in her fingers, she freezes. This berry was not hers. And even as a piemaker from the city, even as someone who's scavenged every corner of these woods with Adam, she does not recognize the species.

○ ~ ○ ~ ○

By night, the town takes on an eerie silence.

Emily walks to Mr. Robutan's bar to retrieve her few belongings. Adam had insisted on accompanying her there and back, but upon seeing his pasty pallor and the distant, foggy look in his eyes, Emily had assured him she would be safe to walk the short distance alone. If fire is to assault her, nothing, not even Adam's protection, will stop it.

Adam gave only shallow details about Druid Parr to Emily after his return—and Emily listened to his descriptions as if she had not seen them herself, as if she had not snuck back into Adam's house as he and a few others performed a quick burial for the cleric. Adam's hands were covered in soil and sweat.

Emily shudders at the memory of Parr draped over the basin, and only stays upright by the feeling of fresh night air on her skin. The waters under the docks are too quiet as she tentatively opens the door to the inn.

Mr. Robutan sits behind his counter, slowly rubbing a rag against an already gleaming goblet, head hung.

Three patrons linger at round wooden tables, extra mugs cluttering their surfaces.

A pang of compassion hits Emily at the sight of them. She normally has no sympathy for drunks, especially after her violent encounter with one the night she met Adam, but these men could only be here, drowning themselves in ale, for one reason. They have no family to drown in anything else with.

As she approaches the staircase to her room, and thus the counter of the bar next to it, Mr. Robutan looks up. His eyes are brimmed in red.

"Emily," he says with a harsh sniff, voice almost relieved. It is the first time Emily recalls him using her name correctly. "I didn't think you were c—coming." The wrinkly old man stands and sneezes himself free of tears. He manages a smile, and Emily pauses at the foot of the stairs.

How can she tell him she is simply coming for her things and leaving? It suddenly hits her that Mr. Robutan is just like those swaying, lonely drunks at the tables, but he has not chosen to wash away his grief in drink.

She glances at the few patrons and then swallows.

"Of course I came, Mr. Robutan," she says. "But I can only stay for an hour. I'm staying with Adam tonight."

Mr. Robutan is so grateful that he can't even speak. He smiles and sits back in his chair. He scrubs the shining goblet and nods constantly.

"Let me just grab my mom's address," she says. "I'll be right down."

She climbs the stairs, and darts to her room.

On the linen bed lay her only belongings: a sack filled with an assortment of her favorite books, a leather pouch for gathering berries, her clothes, parchment, and an envelope containing her mother's address.

She hears the tavern door open downstairs and a group of heavy footsteps enter.

Mr. Robutan will need her.

Maybe work will give a sense of normalcy. She takes a deep breath as the visual of Adam stumbling backwards at the cry of Parr's death returns to her.

She slings the pack over her shoulder and shuffles down the stairs. The room is packed with another ten mostly young patrons, male and female, filling the air with shaky voices. She supposes the younger crowd, as night wears on, seeks company to relieve tensions at home.

Mr. Robutan places three filled mugs on the bar as she hastily stores her pack under the counter.

They set to work.

"That's not my drink," a plump woman with dark skin and long, curly hair accuses Emily after nearly forty minutes on the job. They stare at one another awkwardly and Emily glances down into the frothy mug.

"Ale?" Emily asks, a little breathlessly. The woman snorts derisively, but it's shriller than sociable.

"Jaltz," the woman corrects.

Jaltz. A tangy, expensive brew of deep-red liquor from the southern, tropic islands of the Empire. This woman's mug was definitely not filled with jaltz the last time Emily served her. Emily hesitates. Tonight is not a night for arguing.

She snatches the woman's empty mug. "One second."

Clutching the tankard, Emily wrenches open the door to the basement.

Jaltz it is.

Closing out the anxious chatter is a welcome respite as she rocks down the basement stairs, the handle of the empty mug still hot from the woman's hand so often curled around it.

The damp, musty smell is powerful in her nostrils as she reaches the stone floor. The dampness, of course, is in part because of the Darson's Ford waters surrounding the other side of these cold, rock walls.

Mr. Robutan's almost colorless light nestles in the pockets of the walls and only manages dim illumination on the tall, large barrels. Emily suddenly remembers the red-haired cooper from earlier today, and that time he looked up at her from making one of his barrels. She recognizes a particularly large one in the corner and recalls when she had bought it from him for Mr. Robutan. Mr. Myer. That was the cooper's name. Dennis Myer.

Ambling deeper into the dim basement, she locates the small barrel that contains Mr. Robutan's limited supply of jaltz and sweeps off the frail, light lid. Diving her arm deep into the container, she grasps a short, dusty, brick-red bottle and pulls it up. It makes a clinking noise against the other bottles and its insides slosh hollowly.

Trying to hold the mug with her little finger at the same time, she grips the bottle in one hand and fumbles with the cap in the other.

Right when it snaps off, the fat pewter mug drops with loud clumps, clambering across the floor. It rolls away into darkness.

Emily curses under her breath and sets down the

bottle. She blindly searches the floor, keeping one hand dragging along the wall so she won't get lost in the dark.

Her foot bumps into something metal.

But before she can retrieve the object, a shock of light bursts open in front of her and she glimpses the insides of a well-lit room before a hand grabs her shirt and slams her onto the wall.

The jagged blade of a knife presses against her throat. She can feel its sharpness against her soft skin. She gurgles and shuts her eyes in fear and pain. Her feet are off the ground so only her toes touch the floor, and a strong arm holds her firm against the wall. Stone juts into her back.

And then, the tight grip loosens. The knife clatters to the floor.

Heart pounding, she is released, and her feet take her weight on the ground again as she hears the figure before her stagger backwards.

Every muscle frozen, she dares herself to open her eyes and make out the assaulter before her.

A look of stunned horror is on his face. His eyes are disbelieving and numb. And she sees, in the shadow, who it is.

Adam.

CHAPTER 6

Adam clutches his hand as if he cannot believe what it has just done.

They stare at each other, paralyzed, for an immeasurable amount of time. Emily's eyes shovel back and forth over her dearest friend, hot with alarm and confusion.

But not betrayal. No. This was some misunderstanding. A terrible mistake.

"A—Adam?" she tries.

Before any response is made, gravelly voices murmur in the hidden room, and Emily remembers they are not alone. Adam has been in there. In the concealed chamber of a dingy basement.

On a night like this.

Instead of explaining anything, or even apologizing, Adam slides to the floor and crouches on his haunches, head in his hands.

Emily watches him, and the confusion mingles with fear.

"Why are you still here?" comes his muffled voice.

Why is *she* here? Why did he just try to kill her?

"Why am *I*—?" she begins, but falters. She realizes his question isn't direct. It is asked of fate, with frustration and disbelief.

She reaches for Adam's shoulder before a voice springs her back.

"Hello . . ."

Emily spins to meet a heavily bearded man with piercing green eyes, framed at the opening of the room. He is dressed in a loose white shirt that opens in a V at the chest, and he wears a metal gauntlet on only his left hand. Emily suddenly realizes she's seen him before—he's the man who fell face-first through the door of Mr. Robutan's bar the day she and Adam met. Fear flashes through her.

"I know you." Emily's breath quickens.

"Do you?" the man is sneering.

But she decides not to say anything further.

The light from the room behind him glints in his silver whiskers and illuminates the wood-beaded cylindrical necklace around him. There is no warmth in the look he rests upon her, and he shifts his gaze to Adam. Adam is standing again and looking at this new person with intense dislike.

Emily's heart pounds. "Obviously I'm interrupting something. Adam, you're going to explain this tomorrow, and I'm going to get my mug and . . ."

"I can't do that, Emily," says Adam.

"Okay, don't explain. I'll just forget it then."

"No," Adam says, looking to the floor. Emily turns to him with an almost pleading look. "I can't let you go. Not after you've seen me."

"Seen you?"

"Seen me *here*," he amends.

The other man's platinum beard rearranges into a cruel smile at this exchange.

"Bring in your friend, Brother Adam," he says.

Emily jumps. *Brother* Adam?

Adam gives the other man a scathing look but enters the brightly-lit room and takes a seat at the edge of a long, grey table. Before Emily can react, the older man grips her shoulder and forces her inside.

The room is small, lit by a plethora of blue light in makeshift pockets along the wood-paneled walls. Around the table are three other men, varying in age, shape, and size.

The cooper grasps a mug of ale. He looks up at her the way he did as he made his barrels: his orangey, grey-flecked hair; his sheepish curiosity. Dennis Myer. He's a part of this?

Next to him is an older man in his seventies with prominent ears and almond-shaped brown eyes, touched with humor. His hair is white and he smiles at Emily, warm and welcoming. In spite of everything, Emily manages to twitch a smile back, and the man nods with a quick wink.

Lastly is a boy no more than a year older than she. His head is hung, and he watches his thumbs playing with each other, twiddling . . .

Emily's seen that twiddling before. It is the boy from her class—the one who asked about the Arluian Sea. But the tall ringleader reenters the room before she can say anything.

The door has to be shut in jerks against the floorboards, as its ends touch the wall and ground to block all light from escaping. It is well-hidden, and Emily figures there must be another secret entrance to the basement somewhere as well.

Emily steals the seat next to Adam as she feels the tall, bearded man's stride push air behind her. The chair is extremely uncomfortable. A wayward nail pierces her side. The cooper sets his mug on the table and raises his eyebrows at her when she winces.

The bearded ringleader retakes his seat with a grunt and scrapes his chair up close. Adam slumps forward on the table but doesn't meet Emily's eyes. His hand continuously rises to his face—to rub his eye, to scratch his ear—as if to conceal himself from her.

"Brother Adam," the bearded man speaks in his strong, cold voice. "Introduce us."

"This is Marcus." Adam's voice is so low Emily can barely hear him, but Marcus's face gives a twitch of distaste. Emily gets the feeling a proper title is expected for Marcus that Adam forwent. Adam straightens, but he still looks at the surface of the table.

"This is Emily." Seeing the others lean in to hear, Adam clears his throat and speaks louder. "Emily. My . . . dearest friend."

Emily's heart gives a pang. She wishes she could take his hand at these words, but she can only stare at him blankly. The others remain distant, except for the friendly-looking elder, who frowns with sympathy as he watches Adam, chin resting on his clasped hands. Marcus's gaze is frigid and evaluating, just as it was towards Emily in the hall. He seems to be measuring how well Adam will handle a painful situation, but there is nothing to suggest he cares for the result.

Marcus realizes Adam will speak no further. He turns his poison-green eyes onto Emily, speaking clearly. "So. Emily."

"Does Mr. Robutan know you're down here?" says Emily.

Those around the table chuckle darkly. Even the kind-faced elder allows a pitying smile.

"No. And he won't."

Emily swallows.

"As your friend said, girl, I'm Marcus Brawl."

"I've only seen you in Darson's Ford that one night," says Emily. She chooses not to elaborate about that event in this company—something tells her not to. But she studies Marcus hard.

"I have a shack here. Another in Southton. I get around. Keep an eye on things. What your friend forgot to add is my title. Kinfather. That's the term for 'patriarch' in the Brotherhood."

Emily's words catch in her throat. "Brotherhood.

Fireworshippers."

The following pause from Marcus, and even from Adam, causes her to shake.

"Adam," Emily croaks his name for the first time since entering, because she cannot fight back the way the room melts from the walls, and her fingernails scrape the splintered table. "Please," she says. "You didn't light it."

Adam and the fire. The picture is so unthinkable to her, she closes her eyes to drive it away.

"No," Adam whispers, and his word is so genuine and soft, she believes him. "They were just as shocked today as we were. That's why we're meeting."

"Parr?" says Emily.

"Not us."

The panic subsides in her, and things seem less dire already. And then the rest of what Marcus had said comes back to her.

"So you're the men the guards fear. You're the enemies of the church. The Brotherhood of Rain and Cinder."

For the first time since meeting him, Marcus looks human. His broad shoulders shift and his body moves closer to the table as he rests his forearms on it. The sound of his metal gauntlet thunking on the wood of the surface actually alarms him, as if he forgot he was wearing it. He glances down at it shrewdly, and then back at her.

"The what now?"

"That's the full name of the Brotherhood," says Emily.

"Fascinating," says Marcus. "Will that be on the test?"

"You don't even know your own history?" says Emily.

"Brotherhood doesn't necessarily mean fireworshippers like the olden days, pup. Some may be. And some may simply seek our networks of cover. We are almost all criminals, wanted dead by the Empire, and we know how to evade the law. Who's been bribed off. Where the safehouses are. Whether that criminality goes hand-in-hand with fire-worshipping is none of my business."

"Criminals," says Emily.

"Yes," says Marcus. "Even your dear Adam."

Emily can feel the lump in her throat. The feeling burns, which does nothing to help her already haunted thoughts.

What has Adam done to permit him in the Brotherhood? This sect of it, anyway?

What has Adam done that the Empire would kill

him for?

She thinks of all the time they've spent together. Of the pride and love she's grown for him. Of how much she trusted him.

No. How much she *trusts* him.

Right?

Emily opens her mouth to speak, but Marcus interrupts her. "Now don't be rude, girl. The others would like an introduction as well." He lifts a hand towards the elder. "This is my cousin, Brother Mason Hart."

Brother Mason mumbles something like, "Introduce myself, thanks."

"Gentlemen . . ." Marcus spreads his gaze to the others.

"Brother Myer," the cooper says without hesitation, though his voice is small.

"Brother Mason, as my cousin so aptly stated." A pause. "I was a healer for many years." He seems to throw this comment at Emily as reassurance. Marcus shoots him a glare.

Emily looks at each in turn as they introduce themselves, still dumbfounded.

"Scott Osborne," the olive-skinned young boy, her

former student, says promptly, but his voice is dull and tired and he doesn't look up from twiddling his fingers. Mason clears his throat politely before Marcus can reprimand him. "Brother Scott Osborne," the boy corrects with little care, lifting his head at last and sweeping his eyes to all of the Brothers before finally resting on Emily. He recognizes her now—leans in and stares at her so intensely that she squeezes the rim of the table. He's inspecting her like a lost traveler eyeing a lifeline compass. The black kohl around his eyes makes his gaze all the more penetrating. But he must dismiss the idea quickly, as he returns his attention back to his hands a moment later. Emily keeps her eyes on Scott even as Marcus clears his throat.

Adam had forgotten his own introduction, or perhaps pretended to forget. They all look to him now.

Adam forces his eyes closed. "Brother Adam Flanagan." He breathes deeply, and then can no longer contain himself. "End this, Marcus. She has nothing to do with this. Let her go."

"No," Marcus replies. He scratches his chin by nudging the metal fingers from his gauntlet across his beard with a scraping sound.

The others stiffen.

"What the hell do you think she's going to say? What do you *want* from her?"

"Brother Ad—"

Adam stands abruptly. "You're no brother of mine."

Marcus stands as well, but it is Mason who rises from his seat just enough to place a hand against either chest.

"Peace!" he cries. "Peace, damn you, Marcus, sit down!"

Marcus purses his lips and looks at his cousin.

"Let us finish the work we met here to finish." Mason nods at Scott now. "The boy. He has the latest safehouse map."

"Mason is right," says Scott. "We need to be leaving tonight. The Empire is absolutely coming for Darson's Ford after news of the flame."

"Get on with it," Marcus growls, but it's a concession.

Mason sighs. "Thank—"

The stone ceiling above them shudders, and they freeze. Dust floats down to the table. Their eyes are glued to the rocks above and Emily can feel her neck begin to sweat.

With a second shudder, a single tile of stone crashes to the table. And then, all is still.

Marcus looks around at his men, mystified.

"I'll go check that," says the cooper, Dennis. Marcus turns to him, surprised. The cooper stands and moves with his head down, like a frightened dog, to the door. He heaves his shoulder against the door to slam it open against the floorboards and then immediately falls to the ground.

An arrow bolts into the room and cuts right above Marcus' head, thudding into the wall. Marcus ducks.

Adam grabs Emily and forces her down with his arm. Mason and Scott flinch and scrape back their chairs, Scott drawing a knife with a metallic ring.

But as heavy boots step over the cooper on the floor and aim their crossbows at the Brothers, Marcus holds out his hand in a gesture for his men to stop.

Adam's grip is still tight around Emily as she tries to straighten and see what is going on.

A soldier reaches down and helps the cooper to his feet, placing a crossbow in his hands. The cooper turns and regards them with a non-remorseful eye, clutching his new weapon.

Wes is among the six soldiers—who don't all fit in the room—and when he spots Emily, he double-takes. There is true surprise and misunderstanding, even concern, on his face, but he doesn't speak.

The Brothers are frozen, and each of them, except Marcus, looks scared.

"Brotherhood?" the captain, the one who fired the first arrow, echoes words through a closed helmet. He is suited in full uniform armor.

"Yes," Marcus answers darkly, but his cold, green eyes are on the betraying cooper.

The captain's muffled voice continues. "We've been waiting a long time to do this . . ."

"Then do it," Marcus snarls. "Arrest us."

"Those weren't my orders, Marcus Brawl," says the captain. "You're not going to jail."

"Really?" growls Marcus. "Then where are we going?"

The captain smiles and selects another arrow from his quiver.

"You're going to extinguish a fire."

CHAPTER 7

"—and so, I say, the flame must not divide us! We must conquer it *together!*"

Choruses of agreement resound from one side of the hall. Eyes roll on the other.

The man finishing his speech is dressed in white robes with gold trim. He wears the traditional amulet of the clergy—a round, deep-blue glass marble encased in gold that hangs to his ribs—as do all seated at his side of the room. The clergyman sits with his fellow clerics in the polished wood bleachers, facing their opposing wing of Council members.

But the room is indeed divided—clergy on the right, military on the left. In the middle is smooth tiled floor for presenters to speak or evidence to be examined. At the head of the high-ceilinged room is a tall throne for the Emperor to supervise the Council, and a small row of seats along a lengthy table to accommodate his advisers.

Now, that throne is empty.

A man from the military wing, the Supreme General, as identified by the gold acorns decorating his armor, stands with great annoyance, as if they have been through this millions of times.

"But you have not the power to deal with such a *force!*" he yells this last word in frustration. It rings like a sword through the hall.

The clergy wing is silent, allowing him to continue.

"Give me bodies and I shall break them." The General looks around at his men, who nod. "Spiritual warfare is the druids' to wage." He spits something from his lips, but it's unclear if this was an intentional gesture of disrespect or a piece of his lunch. The druids holler nonetheless, and some rise. A lieutenant whispers in the General's ear, encouraging him to leave, and he seems to be considering it.

"General MacPerth," cries a young woman on the clergy side. The General, who was about to turn for the stairs to the exit, stops and looks at her.

"Sing to me forgotten words."

This is a saying common among the druids, something one might say while wiping a tear from a weeping believer and encouraging them to let flood their emotions to a safe listener.

General MacPerth inclines his chin. Her strategy touches him or intrigues him just enough to have him turn to them again. "My forgotten words are that the Empire shall not last long as the flame burns, and it is the blood of the military we shall be attempting to douse it with."

"Hear!" say the soldiers.

"Our towns are rioting—there are caravans seeking escape and gathering at the edge of Hillswallow!" He stomps his armored foot. "HILLSWALLOW!"

The last town in Galeduen before the border of Asht Vendar. Galeduen warred with Asht Vendar for forty years in the Second and Third Vendari wars, sometimes called the Sunlight Wars, and signed a treaty that prohibited either peoples from crossing the border for a hundred years save the war resume.

"You, the druids, ought thank the gods the prophecies of burning rocks hitting the land have yet to come true. But mark my words—doomsday can happen in many other ways." General MacPerth pauses, realizing he has the ear of everyone in the room. "Galeduen has trusted one religion to guide it. Never have our questions and faith summoned a rival church. It has always been you. And you have nothing to say. The cloth should be ashamed."

"General! You are in the presence of the Vicar!" the same clergywoman calls out.

"Peace, Ariana. He is protecting his men. As we are all trying to do." A new voice.

At either end of the wings, just as the Emperor's throne sits at the head, is another, smaller throne, representing the leaders of both sides. Atop the clergy wing sits a small, tan-skinned man. He holds a thick, wooden staff with both hands, so unchanged by man, it could be a branch snapped from a tree this morning. Unlike his fellow druids, the Vicar wears no shirt or shoes. His ribs are prominent. The Vicar, as a tradition of faith, eats only what the host city offers the homeless. He hangs his head. His white hair manages only a frizzy beard, and he speaks in a light accent from Fellvren, a very far corner of the Empire many forget is there.

The Vicar of Light, he is called, or simply the Vicar. Today, he looks so deepened in fear and concern that he holds the staff firmly as if to anchor himself to his seat.

Ariana sits upon his words, indignant.

"We are men of peace, General," the Vicar speaks in

his light, clipped accent, but in this room, it seems to carry no weight.

"Has peace taught you to extinguish the fire? Has it told you its secrets as to why fire is here?" says the General.

Now all eyes watch the Vicar. His head remains hung and he holds the staff in front of him. He looks like a stone gargoyle in his stillness.

"Peace has done neither."

The General's lips form a merciless line. Jeers resound from the military wing. The clergy wing is losing its ability to defend the Vicar, some even throwing concerned, skeptical glances up at him.

"Our Emperor is evacuated," the General continues to boom. "We have our hands full governing the capital. Securing the site of the fire. Fortifying Fort Rilke." The fort near Hillswallow. "If we do not quench this flame, our people's panic will lead them to flee the empire and set off the fourth Sunlight War. Is that what the druids want on their conscience?"

Murmuring.

"If any of us have a chance of extinguishing the fire," the General finishes, "it is the clergy. Not the soldiers. Or let evil overcome us all."

The General sits quickly to allow the cheers to drown

him.

"Since when has evil meant our doom?" says the Vicar. "This fire is not the first I have seen evil at work. And perhaps not the worst."

The General groans loudly. "You are minimizing it because it weakens you. It weakens all of you. When the most unholy reproach to humanity has been made, you know nothing to stop it!"

"I know nothing for sure," agrees the Vicar, nodding. "But I can guess."

"And what would your guess be?" the General presses. "To stop the flame?"

The Vicar, whose head has been hung the entire conversation, gives the merest of shrugs.

"Water."

Some laugh at this, some yell in anger. General MacPerth does neither. In fact, from dozens of feet across the hall, the Vicar looks up into his eyes, and the two share a long beat above the chaos of their followers below.

Before the General can close his open mouth, the door to the Council bursts open. All, excluding the Vicar, turn to the new arrival.

It is a dark-skinned soldier, out of breath. But he

swings up his head and looks at the Council with determination.

"My name is Maron. I'm here to give witness of the fire," he pants. "But I have news from the royal advisers. Emperor Accalon has given an order." He wipes sweat from his eye and looks up at MacPerth. "They're sending someone to the flame by force."

Both excited and worried mutterings proceed.

"Who?" thunders the General. "Who are they sending?"

"Criminals," replies Maron. "They've been watching a band of criminals. Something called the Brotherhood of Darson's Ford."

Silence. Some recognize the group, some don't. By the hard-faced frown on the General's face, he recognizes it.

"Marcus' little dictatorship?" says MacPerth.

Maron just shakes his head. "I don't know. But you're supposed to have them armed and supplied at Fort Carrick."

General MacPerth grunts, and then he turns to the rest of the Council. "They've sent someone, then," he says. "It will take them only days to reach the fire." The Council is grimly silent as he finishes.

"Which means we have only days to find their replacements."

○ ~ ○ ~ ○

"Adam!"

Emily chases after him.

He is walking furiously down the dock, both hands ripping at his short hair and not turning back to her.

"*Adam!*" she cries louder, and there is anger in her voice that he will not wait for her, will not give her the explanation she deserves.

She meets him, and when she does, his hands slide from his hair to his face. She reaches to pull down his arm and look into his eyes but he sways and falls onto the soggy wood of the dock.

Emily crouches next to him, and he pulls himself to his hands and knees. She dips her hand into the silky water of the Ford and scoops it onto his face. It splashes over his hair and drips down his lashes and nose, and she pauses as she sees his eyes are open, staring into the split boards of the dock. Just as in the church, when the holy water drizzled down him, just as in the rainfall, he doesn't move. He allows it to happen. But that is all he does.

"Get up, Adam." Emily cannot inflict the force in her voice she intends. Adam is shivering. He stands, and they hear the soft, quiet footsteps of the other Brothers disperse down the deserted docks like strangers, temporarily released to collect their belongings before departure. Heavier, booted steps clunk somewhere behind them, and the outdoor hatch into Mr. Robutan's basement squeaks closed.

Adam breathes heavily for several beats and Emily, still crouching, eyes him with true concern, afraid she is losing him in a way she cannot save. Then, as she stands slowly, he turns his eyes to her.

"Emily," he says. "You've been my reason for living here, every day."

Emily's eyebrows pinch together. Adam is not explaining anything . . . he is saying goodbye.

"I'm sorry." He shakes his head. "I'm sorry for what I've done to you." His voice cracks. "For you having

to—"

"Adam."

"—and for leaving you."

"Leaving me?" she blurts.

"You heard what the captain said," Adam says after a pause.

Emily glances over her shoulder.

"They're . . . they're letting you go for tonight. We

could . . . could . . ."

His eyes already darken as she speaks. When she trails off, he merely watches her.

"If I don't go, Marcus will turn me in for my crime."

Emily swallows. Adam had not confessed what he'd done to prompt him to join the Brotherhood and seek its protections. But he is at the mercy of Marcus now—Marcus, who probably bribed around and made things disappear for him. And for some reason, Marcus seems intent on not making a run for it himself. As Emily was leaving the hidden basement room a few minutes ago, she remembers the captain reloading an arrow into his crossbow, Wes confiscating Scott's knife, and a black-armored guard leaning in to Marcus' ear and whispering something. Marcus' expression slipped into serious concern. He glared at the black-armored guard for a moment. After a pause, Marcus looked at the Brotherhood members and said firmly, "Pack your things."

The black-armored man whispering to Marcus must have come directly from the capital. His armor was made of trithium—the only ore native to Galeduen—identifying him as a member of the Black Guard, the emperor's royal guard.

Now Adam shakes his head. "Even if I wasn't bound to Marcus, where would I run?"

Darson's Ford was given its name for a reason. The fable of the village returns to Emily at Adam's words.

Legend says that General Darson, a Galeduan general from decades ago, was wrongly accused of being a spy for Asht Vendar. When his squadron heard of the unproven accusation, they betrayed him. His second-in-command wrested authority and marched Darson to the most feared place of banishment—the tree line of an almost never-ending forest.

Since the days of the stonecarvers—the peoples who designed the stone Guardians Adam and Emily had found—this particular forest had been thought to contain spirits and stretch for infinity—the easiest place for someone to wander, lost, to their death.

Worst was that no streams of water had been found in the forest. Even scouts brave enough to search for miles returned on the brink of dehydration.

Whoever was sentenced to venture into this forest was doomed never to return.

And so they sent Darson here. He was told to walk straight and never come back lest he face a volley of arrows.

They waited at the tree line for two days to ensure he wouldn't reappear.

But he never did.

General Darson trudged on for almost twenty-four hours through the woods, straight, as he was ordered. He was steps away from collapsing and never regaining his feet when he saw, as legend describes, a break in the trees. A thinning of branches. And when he rushed to the opening, he gazed before him at a wide clearing.

It was a grassy grove. A small meadow within the trees. The ground sloped into a depression—but there, in the middle of the clearing, was a tiny flash. Darson descended the slope to find a plate-sized puddle of cool, clean water like a miracle spring.

The water touched his lips. It reconciled an innocent man. He lay in the puddle and closed his eyes. Some say the water saved his life. Others say that he perished there. But all versions of the legend agree that the next day, his body disappeared, and in its place was the Ford.

The site became a relic to some zealots: water redeeming yet again. As the fear of flame escalated under the church's sermons, areas of water became more attractive to live near. The smaller, scattered villages around this nostalgic forest gravitated to the Ford after the legend spread, and they built upon it a home on water.

General Darson's death from dehydration is probably no legend. Emily and Adam have never seen so much as a stream alive in the woods. There is only one path chiseled through the trees that leads travelers to and from the Ford now. Any other venture into the forest's depths and dehydration and disorientation would claim even a young man.

And Adam is not young.

The town guards will be watching the sole path. There is nowhere else to run.

The understanding must show on Emily's face as Adam purses his lips regretfully, but his eyes are rigid.

"Either I go, Emily," his voice is quieter than the lapping of the water, "or they take me."

She stares at one of the tall poles of the dock, numb. Silver stars pierce the curtain of the deep, purplish-blue heaven, much like the color of Adam's light. But neither seem to notice now.

"Then I'm going with you." Emily's eyes are still on the pole as she speaks. Adam lifts his head, but his expression genuinely looks like he thinks he misheard her.

Emily meets his gaze.

"I'm going with you."

Instant alarm on Adam's countenance. "You're not going with me." His voice is not level and low as she is accustomed to. It has gained luster and firmness.

"Adam, just listen to me."

"No." He shakes his head and turns away from her. "No. No."

"Adam, listen to me. How will I be any safer here?" Tears fill her eyes now. "Fire is back, and since it is, it's going to spread. At least I'd feel safe with you. Please. I can't be alone here." Her voice chokes and she glances across the water to the next row of ragged wooden houses. "I can't be here without you."

"I can't do this." Adam's voice thickens. "We're going to our *death*, Emily. Not to the fire. To our death."

"So you won't even fight it?!" she demands, but her voice is high-pitched. "You won't even try to—?!"

"*Of course* I'll *try*." Adam speaks slowly and through guttural whispers.

A pause.

"Then let me go with you." Her soft words resemble the breeze through the leaves they know so well.

Adam's bowed head is still, and then he shakes it in

sadness after another moment's silence. He turns from her.

She reaches in her pocket, takes out the token of wood she has been carving, and grabs Adam's wrist. He opens his mouth with heat to give another protest, but she places the token in his hand.

It is complete. In the time Adam had taken to come back from burying the druid, she had finished it. The designs are the most intricate yet, and several mimic Adam's own patterns and knots like on the stone Guardian. At the very top of the token are tiny carved stars.

He closes his mouth, and his expression softens into an odd mingle of pride and sorrow. His eyes are gleaming in the moonlight as they study the wooden token. She wonders if he makes the connection with the stars.

"You've given me everything, Adam." Her voice catches in her throat. "You've given me everything."

"Emily . . ." he whispers, and he's about to shake his head again when silent tears run down her face and she drops her forehead against his chest.

She cannot take anything more. Fire is back. Adam is a criminal. Adam is being sent right into the flames. And yet here he is, standing on the dock with her, and she can feel the stitching of his shirt against her forehead.

He does not move, unsure of what to do.

And then, finally, she hears him exhale. He wraps an arm around her. His hot fingers clutch the wooden token.

"Okay," he breathes. His voice returns to its quiet manner, but it shakes with pain. Emily doesn't budge, only closes her eyes tighter. His final words remind her of the day they met, and the last words he'd spoken to her before leaving the pub that night, after Emily's encounter with the thugs. *That won't happen again. I promise.*

But when he speaks, there is a heavy trace of regret in every word.

"I have a promise to keep."

○ ~ ○ ~ ○

Keeping that promise, it turns out, meant different things to each of them.

Emily wakes from the floor near Adam's lightgrate and jerks to a sitting position, throwing off her blanket.

His sword and sheath are gone. There is a note at her feet and a brass key lays over it like a paperweight. She seizes the page and the heavy key slides off, clinking to the floor.

Emily,

I had a promise to keep, that nothing would ever happen to you. I had to leave you to keep that promise. This key is for you—the house, everything I own, is yours.

- *Adam*

Even as she reads it, she stands. She grabs the sack from last night, which she'd collected from Mr. Robutan's counter before coming home, and tears open the door.

She doesn't take in the weather, doesn't know if it's cloudy or sunny, cool or scorching, she simply barrels down the dock towards the sole path of Darson's Ford at the edge of the trees. Her sack hits several people as she passes them and they step back, more concerned than irritated (most are familiar—and favorably so—with her). They turn to watch her as she reaches the end of the village, stopping herself before she can tip over the edge of the planks into the water.

They are there, at the mouth of the narrow, dark path through the trees. Guards and each member of the Brotherhood congregate, preparing to set off. Horses are being packed, and Adam ties a bag onto the saddle of a white horse.

Urgency heats her skin and she looks to her right, down the dock. The boardwalk leading to the grass, where she could run to the path, is several yards to her side. Ahead of her is brown water and Adam, who has not noticed her. She looks to her feet and shakes her head in exasperation.

Case of equipment in hand, Adam steps onto the stirrup . . .

She holds her breath and jumps.

Emily plunges in, and the world is suddenly quiet—sloshing, gurgling water filling her ears as she pumps herself to break the surface. Sun blinds her when she does, and she sucks in breath and starts swimming towards the path, as fast as she can manage with the pack on her shoulder. Though the water has the same buttery feel it did last night, she is surprised that its taste is not as murky as expected, and the coolness is refreshing.

Her splashing is heard by the others, and Adam turns before mounting the horse, as does everyone else. Some of the guards shift uncomfortably as they realize who it is. Marcus watches with the same cold amusement, and when Adam finally makes her out, he is dropping his equipment, sprinting to her.

He trudges into the water and pulls her out.

"What are you doing?!" he moans, but his hand pushes the soaking hair from her face, assessing to see if she is hurt.

"I told you," she pants, "I'm coming with you, Adam."

"Brother Adam," Marcus calls. He is stepping towards them slowly, watching his feet on the decline of the slope. Emily sees the captain of the guards behind him—short, pale blond hair and equally pale grey eyes—give a scowl towards Marcus, who has the nerve to continue using his Brotherhood terms.

Adam swallows and turns to him, his hand still on Emily's shoulder.

"I think this pup has made her point," says Marcus. He stares at Emily with a dark sort of approval.

"Marcus Brawl, you have five seconds to get back here!" bellows the captain. His crossbow is loaded and he is red with fury. Or sunburn. "And you, Flanagan. Now."

"Shut up, Marley," says Marcus, still giving a flash of teeth to Emily.

"Emily," Adam whispers. "Please. Go back, and—"

Marcus grabs the pack from Emily's shoulder and turns to the path. "I'll take this for you."

"Come on," says Emily, and Adam spins back to her,

having just jerked towards Marcus. "We're in this together now."

Adam stares at her blankly. She walks up the slope and leaves him standing in the water.

Captain Marley's pale gaze follows Emily with cynic curiosity. Brother Mason refuses to meet her eyes, but he seems disappointed at her arrival as he pats down his painted horse. Brother Scott is toweling his face dry of sweat. There is an axe lying in the grass at his feet, and she assumes he must have brought it with him, only to be unarmed by the guards.

"Are you coming along to tutor me?" Scott says to Emily. He's toweled off—accidentally, perhaps—a bit of the kohl he wears around his eyes, and it makes him look more vulnerable. She can't quite decode his tone, so she keeps hers neutral as well.

"Well, you were never my best student."

Scott looks at her, and then over her shoulder.

Marcus is the first to swing nonchalantly onto a black horse. He grips the rein with his right hand while his left, still wearing the single metal gauntlet, falls at his side. There is a tinge of a smile on his lips as he glances at Scott and Emily, as if this whole turn of events lends some entertainment.

Wes comes up to Scott and starts patting him down. Scott still looks bored and tired, as if this is below him.

"What's this?" Wes pulls a white mushroom from Scott's pocket.

"A snack," says Scott. He puts it in his mouth.

"Don't—!" Emily starts, recognizing the mushroom as toxic. But Scott swallows it. Adam walks up behind her.

"He's immune," says Adam. Emily's mouth drops. "He . . . dealt with a lot of poisons." Adam holds her gaze warily, as if to measure how she will react. "A lot."

Emily can't reply.

Wes pats Scott's shoulder, turns to Captain Marley, and says, "You can take him back. He's good."

Back?

"I'll have you do it," Marley replies impatiently.

"Take him back? Take him back where?" Emily interrupts. The captain glares at her like she's a bratty student interrupting the teacher. Wes sees her, dripping wet, and recovers his surprise just in time to clear his throat and respond.

"He's underage without a guardian. We can't send him. They're taking him back to the guardhouse here in the Ford. Try to contact his parents. Somebody."

Marcus allows himself a breathy laugh. "Good luck," he mumbles.

They ignore him, and a soldier, suited in armor like the rest of the guards, takes Brother Scott by the arm and walks him towards the boardwalk. Emily watches Scott for a second before stealing a glimpse at Marcus atop his black horse. Marcus' green eyes linger on Scott, not with resentment or jealousy this time, but with an odd touch of curiosity. She looks away from Marcus in the nick of time as he senses her gaze.

Emily thinks she can't be much older than Scott. They must have assumed Adam was her guardian.

At last, everyone seems to come to the same conclusion, mounting their horses and making the final preparations. Wes, looking uncomfortable, glances at Captain Marley, who is busy adjusting the quiver at his back. Wes moves quickly to Emily, surprising her.

"We've never really met," he says, "but I recognize you."

"You're Wes," says Emily warmly. "I know you."

Wes nods, darting his eyes to Marley again.

"You don't have to do this," says Wes. "I can take you back right now if you say Adam isn't your guardian. Don't let the other one intimidate you."

"Who's intimidating me?" she drops her voice.

"I don't want to see you go with them," says Wes, and fear flashes in his eyes, a type of fear she has not witnessed since the news of the fire reached them. "If you need anything, Maron and I—my patrol partner—we're going to be at the Council next week, to give our first-hand account of the—the fire. Come find me if anything happens. I can take you back. Back home. Okay?"

Emily nods, and Wes walks past her as if they hadn't exchanged a word.

"Come on then, girl," says the captain upon his light-brown mare. "You take the kid's horse." He throws a nod at the only unoccupied horse: a small, shaggy, colt who looks up from cropping the grass as if puzzled at having been pointed out. His muzzle is butterscotch brown and his mop of long hair covers his eyes and almost reaches the ground. His neck is shorter than all the others. He passes his large, interested eyes from one human to the next, chewing the last of his sod.

Emily nods absently and Captain Marley grunts at her hesitance.

Adam seems out of place atop his white stallion—it is too regal for him—but he watches her with concern as she is the last to approach her horse. The colt freezes at her arrival, as if alarmed in the change in masters.

The gaze of almost everyone upon her, Emily feels there is no time for greeting the horse and grips the saddle, swinging upon him. The horse picks up his head more and his ears twitch, as if slightly curious at this entire situation.

Adam pulls his stallion in her direction and she tries to balance herself, unsteady. It is the first she has ever been on a horse, and it is far more uncomfortable than she'd imagined.

"You okay?" Adam whispers as Captain Marley flicks his reins and leads them into the narrow path of the forest. Emily nods, afraid to speak for fear of falling over if she moves. Adam smiles tentatively for the first time today. "He's a good horse. You'll be all right."

"What's his name?" she asks.

"Copenhagen."

"Cope," she says, nodding. Their line of horses begins to move. "What are the other horses' names?"

"Marcus' black horse is Orien. Mason's painted mare is Precious. The pack horse is Hopskip. And my horse is Folk Tale."

"And why do we need horses again?"

She couldn't imagine why the guards would give the

convicts horses. Unless they were traveling far . . .

"These came from the ranch just at the end of the forest," Adam informs, following the others into the trees, watching Emily navigate Copenhagen at the same time. "And we need to make Fort Carrick by nightfall for the captain. We'd never get there on foot."

"Fort Carrick?"

She knows the fort, but it surprises her.

"What?" says Adam as the branches form an arch over them, blocking out the strong sun.

"That's thirty miles away."

"It's the closest fort there is," Adam replies, confused at her misunderstanding.

"But . . . aren't we going to the—the fire?"

Adam pauses.

"They need to arm us first. And we need to know what exactly is happening with the flame. They're taking us to the official at Fort Carrick and they'll send us off from there." Adam clears his throat, not meeting her eyes. "But the captain is needed there early tomorrow. So we have to make it tonight."

Just as Adam says this, Emily remembers she's forgotten to take one last look at the Ford before leaving. She twists in her saddle. Adam turns as she does, alarmed, but he sees what she is trying to glimpse and softens, looking forward again.

She is just able to make out a sparkle of the waters below the grassy slope.

And then, thumping deeper into the gnarly darkness of the forest, it's gone.

CHAPTER 8

She's never realized just how secluded in the trees they were until now. The beaten dirt path goes on for hours, and they stop just a few miles from the end to rest their horses, eat, and stretch cramped muscles. Even with the path beaten away, roots of proud, old oaks creep into the road so that by the end of the third hour, the horses' hooves are scratched, and a few bleed.

These woods are no different from the ones Emily so often ventures into with Adam. They are green and alive, though seem to be in an aggressive mood today. Squirrels chase one another contemptuously. Hoots of owls are sharper. It is as if they, too, know the world is not right.

Emily had spent the ride discussing last night with Adam, and the mystery of the cooper's involvement. Adam explained that Dennis had been a member of the Brotherhood for years, and apparently, as last night showed, undercover for the Empire. Dennis was the one who recommended Mr. Robutan's cellar for their meeting that night—intentionally so, as he knew of the ceiling's loose handiwork. The soldier's banging the floor above them so that the ceiling shook (and thus, the stone fell) was the cooper's signal to open the one-way door for the captain and his men to enter. He had been awaiting the arrival of that signal for years, as the Brotherhood turned out to be more useful to the government *active* than arrested. What better way could the Emperor keep a constant pulse on other criminal activity in the Empire?

Adam was diplomatic as he spoke of the cooper, neutral, or maybe even apathetic. Even so, the conversation had drained her, and she is grateful for the stop.

Emily dismounts Copenhagen and feels the hard earth beneath her feet. Adam follows, and the guards are quick to reach the ground, clutching their crossbows at the ready.

Brother Mason nickers sympathetically as he lifts his horse's hoof. It is muddy with blood. Captain Marley snaps his fingers at one of the three soldiers and points to Hopskip, the pack horse, who is carrying the weapons confiscated from the Brotherhood. The soldier nods and marches to stand guard next to the horse, which turns a bored, baleful eye upon him.

Emily rubs her forearm and turns to the brush of forest, leaving Adam beyond her sight—for sometimes it is hard to look at him now. She kneels near a cluster of saplings and begins to dig through the dirt in search of edible or medicinal roots. A medium-sized, pointy-leaved oak has fallen, creating patches of light for the saplings to rise towards. She claws through the earth but hardly notices her hands at work.

Adam picks up on her carelessness and allows a tentative step towards her.

"We need to talk, Adam," she says, but she doesn't turn to look at him. A worm wriggles in protest as she upturns its soil, and she is reminded of the earthworm she had freed when scavenging with Adam. It seems like years ago. "Why are you in the Brotherhood?"

Adam exhales, and she presses on when he doesn't answer immediately.

"All this time, I thought you were military." She slaps a handful of dirt over the pinkish worm so she doesn't have to look at it.

"I was."

"You retired."

A pause.

"I . . . left."

"That's not the same as retired." She stands with two roots in her fist and wipes a strand of her chestnut-brown hair from her face, forgetting how dirty her hand is. Soil crumbles into her hair and she brushes it off, stepping deeper into the thickets of woods towards a knot of young berry bushes bearing just a handful of the dark blue fruit.

She picks them with one hand, and though she doesn't raise her voice, Adam can hear her. "What's the difference?"

"Don't you need this, pup?" Marcus approaches them and holds up Emily's sack in one large, strong hand. Adam shoots Emily a look, assuring her he knows the conversation is not done, and turns back to his white stallion.

"You just show up at the perfect times, don't you, Marc?" says Emily, treading back to the path. She earns a twitchy smile from him as he thrusts the pack hard into her grasp.

"So do you."

She stuffs the berries and roots in the leather pouch next to her books.

"You don't need to hate me, pup."

Emily swings atop Copenhagen with more grace than she imagined possible since the mere sight of the stirrups makes her nervous.

"BRAWL! I want that grey beard where I can see it! Get over here! Everyone mount; tea party's over." Marley climbs his saddle with a jingling of armor and metal and his guards scurry to do the same.

"What he said," says Emily. Marcus seems even more intrigued as he walks casually towards his own steed near the captain.

They set off again, and Adam closes his eyes, pretending to doze as he bobbles atop his white horse. Emily turns her head to him. She thinks she catches his lids tighten as if in pain, and his head give the merest shadow of a shake.

Then again, it could be only a trick of the fading light.

○ ~ ○ ~ ○

"Horses in the stable."

Captain Marley seems even keener on barking orders once the soldiers at Fort Carrick greet and allow him entry into the garden of the keep. Orange rays spill over the low stone walls and into their eyes, and each is so tired that they lead their mounts to the stable at the end of the fort's wall without comment.

Copenhagen gives a self-pitying shake of his mane as he clops into the open gate, led by Emily's rein, and she ties him to a post. Even in his exhaustion, he looks to her as if saying, *You going to be okay without me?*

She smiles and rubs his nose. "Thanks for today, Cope," she whispers. "I was scared."

He stares at her blankly, his dark, scruffy ears twitching once more. *No one would have known.*

"Captain Marley?" A stable hand—a young, very plump girl—looks over to the captain, dropping a mound of hay into the trough.

The captain turns to her. "Patricia," he regards curtly, unloading the supplies on Hopskip. Patricia walks over, eyeing the large party of travelers cynically.

"You know Heckley's not going to let them all in, right?" says Patricia.

Captain Marley gives the girl a long, dumbfounded look of exasperation. He doesn't seem surprised. "What's his latest rule?" Marley yanks off a sack of bread and dried meat with more vigor than necessary.

"Entry by appointment. And he has you down for one companion."

"So he won't let anyone else in."

The plump girl shakes her head, wobbling her double chin. Her forehead is dotted with sweat, and she waits to be dismissed by the captain. A moment later Marley jerks over to her after realizing she hasn't left.

"*What?*" he snaps. "You're not my problem. Go back to work. Or whatever you want. Gentlemen!" He hails the Brotherhood and waves off the three soldiers who had ridden with them. They give a curt nod and mosey off to the guards' quarters.

The Brotherhood lift their heads to the captain. Marcus is breathing through his mouth, winded, but his muscles are still rigid and alert. Emily notices the orange sunlight baking his wood-beaded necklace and wonders if it could burst into flame.

"You get one representative. Heckley wrote a new chapter of rules to follow since the inferno's debut scared away his critics, so we're here to cater to him. Got that, Brawl?" Marley's address of Marcus is unnecessary, but he continues before Marcus can growl a response. "So, if you want armor and a blade, cough up a tribute I can present him with."

"Good. I'd throw up on sight of Heckley," says Marcus. "I vote sending the pup." He shoots her a sinister smile.

"I'll go." Adam volunteers in his soft voice, stepping forward. "Come on, Emily."

Emily is shocked at his invite but follows eagerly.

"Wait, Flanagan. I said one representative," says Marley.

"Right. And you have me. Emily is underage. And I'm her guardian."

Emily hides a feeling of pride. Captain Marley glares at Adam suspiciously, but Adam maintains an innocent expression.

"Fine, then. Get comfortable out here, Marcus. We'll be back. Let's go, Flanagan."

Marley bursts through the tall, arched doors with Adam and Emily, letting them swing closed behind him. He walks briskly and with his head held high, as if he owns the place.

Emily drifts her eyes along the foyer of the keep, resisting the temptation to rotate her head and gape at the interior. It resonates shadowed, fallen glory—ratty tapestries hanging, their red hue faded to brown. Most of the light pockets are empty, and the floor is cool, smoothed stone. Columns of dark marble block the view of most of the wings that delve deeper out of sight.

A young clerk hastens to meet the captain, clipboard

and pencil in hand, looking harassed.

"Appointment?" he asks dutifully.

"Shut it, Jerrold. We're meeting Heckley," Marley walks right past him.

Adam does not hesitate to follow, but Emily falters a step in confusion. "Keep moving," Adam whispers.

She keeps her head low and comes in step with him.

The clerk, Jerrold, scurries to keep up with Marley's crisp pace. "There were only supposed to be two guests to Lord Heckley's—"

Captain Marley laughs mirthlessly. "Is that what we're calling him now? Lord?"

Marley reaches the end of the wing to a small door and turns the knob with one hand, pressing it open with the wrist of his other. He walks in without preamble.

A light, cedar desk greets their entry, piled with documents, inkwells, and raw hunks of gold (to which Marley raises his eyebrows). A quaint lightgrate glows in the corner so that the room is brightly lit, and a man with a black mustache-and-goatee beard, perfectly parted wavy hair, and extravagantly colorful clothing sits behind the table, raising his hands at the new arrivals.

"Marley! Good of you to show. Jerrold, close the door, will you? And bring my guests some seats, hmm?"

"Of course." Jerrold bows and pulls up three chairs from the corner of the room. "Right away." He bows about three more times.

Adam glances at Captain Marley, who stands with his hands crossed in front of him, refusing to sit. Adam slides down into a chair next to Emily.

"I'm not here to play castle, Heckley." The captain speaks loudly and abrasively. Heckley feigns astonishment in his blue eyes. "These are the representatives for the Brotherhood."

"Who got off on the wrong side of the horse today, Marley? Can't we have tea first?"

Heckley selects a silver bell atop the desk and Adam and Emily watch in blank disbelief as he trills it, looking to the door.

It opens, and a young, blonde-haired girl pokes her head in. "Yes, sir?" Her voice is innocent and eager to please.

"Oh, I just *love* that." Heckley shakes his fists in jubilation at Emily, Adam, and Marley. "Five teas, darling, thank you."

Captain Marley is unwaveringly stolid-faced as he stares at Heckley.

"Charming, Heck," says Marley.

"*Lord Heckley!*" Jerrold corrects with a concerned look upon his face, as if certain Captain Marley could never have intentionally forgotten this.

Marley turns a baleful eye upon the clerk, whose expression remains the same.

"That's quite all right, Jerrold, thank you," says Heckley slowly and with a touch of cold sincerity, as if sensing Marley is truly not going to play along. "In any matter," Heckley continues, voice still a little cooler. "I thought I said only one representative." He seems to set his eyes upon the two seated before him for the first time and does a double-take upon seeing Adam, raising his eyebrows. A derisive, wistful smile curls his lip. "Adam Flanagan . . . I never thought I'd see you back here."

"I never thought you'd still be here."

A hard frown wilts Heckley's face. Marley muffles a grunt.

"And you have a daughter. Even more shocking."

Adam doesn't make the effort to correct Heckley before Marley raises his voice again. "*Heckley*. The briefing. Now."

"*Fine*, Marley. You are such a *bore!* Go on, then. You're no longer needed. Jerrold can have your tea."

Jerrold's eyes widen as if this is the greatest honor

since knighthood.

Marley scoffs. "Fine by me. I'll see them off tomorrow morning, my *lord.*" He gives a phony bow and closes the door behind him.

"There. Don't we all feel better with him gone?" Heckley claps once. "Now then. You are the Empire's front line-up, hmm? Let me take a look at you." He sighs wistfully and then whimpers. "Pretty and young. Such a waste they're making you go with them. No, not you Adam!"

But Adam has not made the tiniest gesture as to think otherwise. In fact, he has hardly done more than blink as Heckley spoke. Emily, on the other hand, cannot hold herself back.

"I wanted to go," she rectifies.

"Honey, there's more to life than bravery. A man prefers a cowardly woman over a dead one." Heckley laughs at his own joke, and Jerrold joins in, particularly loud. The servant girl returns with a knock at the door and Jerrold cuts his laugh immediately, stepping out of the room to handle the tray of hot beverages.

"Anyhow," Heckley continues. "On order of the Supreme General I'm *supposed* to provide you with weapons and armor. After that, you're off. Is the flame really such a bad thing? The smart ones like me are celebrating," he chimes. "Do you know my last name, my dear?"

Emily looks at him closer. His thin, sharp features do look familiar, perhaps from illustrations in her history books . . . "Are you . . . a Sille?" she says at length.

"How astute." He smiles. "Heckley Sille."

The Sille Family are the richest and most influential aristocrats in Galeduen. Emperor Myrril's mistress was Kyara Sille. He produced heirs both illegitimately with Kyara and legitimately with his wife. While the throne usually passed to a legitimate-line heir, now and then throughout the dynasty—when the legitimate-line rulers seemed to lose control of the Empire—the Council appointed a Sille descendant as Emperor. It's usually to smooth things out, to wipe clean a messy trail of follies. The Silles carefully carry on their direct lineage to Myrril so that they may wait in the corners of history to swoop in when the legitimate line stumbles.

"You're hoping the Council will appoint another Sille after Accalon because of all this fire business," Emily states. If so, the Sille emperor would be required to return the throne to a legitimate-line heir after his death. But this does not dampen the appeal.

Heckley taps his fingertips together. “My ambitions are not so lofty. I am not a direct-descendant Sille, but if one of my cousins took the throne after Accalon, perhaps I’d be given a nicer fiefdom than Fort Carrick.” He makes a fake gagging gesture. “Have you seen this place? Our hamlets?”

Jerrold returns and places the tea on the desk carefully.

“Very good, Jerrold, now off you go.”

“Yes, my lord.” Jerrold bows and closes the door behind him.

“Drink,” says Heckley, bringing his own cup to his lips.

Emily shifts in her seat and reaches for a cup. Before she can lift it to her mouth, she notices Adam give an almost non-existent shake of his head, his eyes to the ceiling. She lowers the cup and clutches it in her hands, savoring its warmth instead.

“Jerrold was kind enough to have the chef boil the water for me. Ah, Jerrold.” He sighs. "I just like to keep the fellow busy. He’s working for free this summer. For the *experience,* as I told his parents.”

Hearing that, Emily watches Heckley stir his tea and suspects he cannot produce light. Some men cannot. On the other hand, she has never heard of a woman producing light, but she wonders if the same exception for females might exist out there.

"What's going on with the flame, Heckley?" Adam cuts in calmly.

Heckley swallows a large gulp and sets down his cup. "I'm so sick of this topic."

The Sille goes into explanation of the flame and what happened, interjecting his own witty comments like seasoning, but Adam listens with rapt intensity, eyes darkly intent.

The news is terrifying and riveting at once.

The flame was found at Fort Myrth, a stronghold below the Empire's Fellish border, just ten miles from the capital, Cathair Mór, where Emily used to live with her mother. The flame was one long, burning branch on the ground that no one had seen lit. The soldier who discovered it was hit on the head just as he came upon it and swore no human could achieve such stealth.

But hours later, the fire did not die.

It engulfed the branch and yet continued to burn, paralyzing the wood in a black, solid state.

The gong rang at Fort Myrth, where the alarm began its journey throughout Galeduen, but by morning, the fort was burned to the ground. And as soon as it destroyed the building, it receded and died everywhere but on that one log, although not before taking two lives and injuring another three.

Fort Myrth's demolition was so abrupt and precise, it was like fire appeared for that one purpose of destroying it and left as soon as the job was done. But the fire has not spread since destroying Fort Myrth. It exists only on its branch now.

The druids have no answers. The military will not blindly send their men to extinguish it. Towns are rioting and refugees are trying to flee Galeduen.

One druid from every village in the Empire has been found dead. The manners of the killings were irregular—cut, strangled, poisoned. Emily's insides squirm at the last word, remembering Druid Parr.

The Emperor sealed the Galeduan border in an attempt to keep citizens from fleeing and to try to hide the news from the other provinces, but this seems futile.

There is no lead as to who, or what, started the fire. Or *how*.

Even with all this, the Empire firmly believes that if the fire is extinguished somehow, the killings and terror will cease. They also believe that if their people can at the very least be *told* that the Empire has sent a troop to deal with it . . . well, they'll at least have more faith in their government—enough, perhaps, to keep them from fleeing into Asht Vendar and breaking the Treaty of Hillswallow.

The Brotherhood is that troop. But as to how they might extinguish an ancient horror is solely up to them.

"That is all I know for now," says Heckley. "With the Emperor evacuated, news has been somewhat jumbled lately. I heard the Vicar won't come out of his room for anyone now. I do think we are witnessing the destruction of an empire. Which makes me so happy to send you into the midst of it! Now, the blacksmith will be around bright and early tomorrow morning. He manages all our stores. You two can sleep in the back wing for tonight, and tomorrow I'll send you to—"

The door opens, and Jerrold leans in tentatively.

"Um, Lord Heckley? There's someone here to see you."

"I said no appointments after Marley! Tell them to get—"

"It's more traders, sir."

"The Fellish?"

Jerrold clears his throat. "Vendari, sir."

Emily stops herself from jumping.

"Oooh," says Heckley, drumming his fingertips together. Emily can almost see the gold coins piling in his eyes. "How festive."

He stands, and Adam watches in mild surprise.

"Come along, you two," says Heckley. "I don't want you meddling around my office."

Adam nods to Emily and she sets down her tea cup to join him through the door. Fires and druids and poisons tangle in her mind.

CHAPTER 9

"Well, well." Heckley's echoing footsteps resound through the wide chamber as they approach the dark, closed-off wing. A collection of grubby-looking travelers is waiting in the shadows, shrugging off their walls and stepping forward. Tall, thick columns nestle the wing out of view to the floors beyond, and double doors flank the wall.

"Don't speak," Adam rumbles out of the corner of his mouth, holding his hand behind him to keep Emily back. Questions and fear race through her mind. After the Treaty of Hillswallow, she thought she'd die before setting eyes on a Vendari. These must be here illegally.

Heckley's frilly, colorful sleeves whish with his stride. He chirps an arrogant half-laugh when he makes out the features of the men and women before them. Jerrold shares Heckley's aversion with a repulsed look, clutching his clipboard to his chest and subtly over his nose.

"Over here," Adam mutters, and he leads Emily to the side of the room in the deep shadow of a column. The other two don't seem to notice their departure. Emily wonders if this is the first time Adam is setting eyes on the Vendari since he fought them during his tour in the Sunlight Wars.

The Vendari leader—a woman with ivory hoop earrings—sidles forward to meet the haughty, wry official and his clerk. The merchants have tried to disguise themselves as Fellish, wearing bone jewelry from the skeletons of extinct beasts that lay throughout Fellvren. Racially similar to the Fellish, the Vendari share their features of sharp, hooked noses, short statue, and baldness among the men. However, while the Fellish have tan skin, the Vendari have grey skin. Normally the Vendari would be seen wearing a strange type of glass armor that some say is stronger than metal. To conceal their skin tone here, however, these merchants cover themselves in light leather and hoods made of hide from the marsh rhino of Fellvren. Canteens and knife sheaths hang from their belts, and sandals cover on their bony feet. Standing out from the short group is one dark figure in the middle, almost two feet taller than the others. He is too melded in the shadows to make out, but almost certainly seems the outsider.

The one standing next to the tall figure, however, lays a hand on the hilt of his scabbard and watches with eagerness as the leader engages with Heckley.

"Jerrold, I thought the dogs were fed an hour ago? These still look hungry."

His delivery is flawless. Emily avoids a huff. Adam is quiet.

"Amazing to find you so arrogant," the grimy leader spits in disgust, her accent very foreign. "A new era, *devritch*. An era lost of hierarchy."

Adam makes a small, regarding sound, as if he agrees.

"'*Devritch*?' Who are you, exactly?" Heckley inquires distastefully.

"Her name is Rolanna, sir," provides Jerrold. "Her papers list her as Fellish. But, um, we provided those papers, my lord."

"Ah, yes. Fellish." Heckley makes air quotes.

"And . . . sorry, I don't think I should translate what she said," Jerrold adds.

Rolanna snorts. Heckley eyes her with even more disfavor, but a hint of masked curiosity glistens in his eyes.

"And what does Rolanna and her . . . gang . . . want from us?"

"Help with a little problem, *devritch*." Rolanna smiles. "My gang has a stowaway."

"Oh?" Mild alarm strips Heckley's voice of any pretense, as there doesn't seem to be anyone in restraints. He looks from one traveler to the other. Rolanna turns in the direction of the young, tall figure and smiles callously.

One of the Vendari next to the young man in the shadow gives a yank at his chainmail shoulder, but he may as well have tugged one of the columns. The dark figure turns his head at the gesture and emits a low sound—a rumble or a sigh, Emily cannot tell, but something about it makes her shiver.

He steps forward from the shadow, and they set their eyes upon him.

He cannot be older than twenty, but he is tall and broad, with short, ragged black hair, heavy eyebrows, and dark eyes. There are hairs along his arms covering his light skin and a rough line down the bridge of his nose where blood has dried. He stands with his feet spread and his hands crossed in front of him like a soldier. Chainmail and dark leather hang from his shoulders, and he shifts his surly gaze from one to the other.

"Ah. And what does the 'stowaway' have to say for himself?" Heckley recovers his airy tone and brings a hand to his chin.

"He doesn't speak," says Rolanna, that smile still on her lips. Now, however, Heckley's eyebrows pinch in disapproval.

"He crossed the borders and decided to jump our cargo carriage," says Rolanna. "Exhausted, the poor dear . . ."

Her companions snicker.

"Then he eavesdropped on our camp. Mistook us for peaceful Fellvians and thought he was safe from being turned in. But no, *malsar,*" Rolanna speaks in mock sweetness to the young man now. "I play by the rules, don't I?" She winks. "What will you give me for him?" She rears eagerly on Heckley, but the official is silent.

"How do you know all of that if he does not speak?" Heckley looks at last as though his morals are in internal warfare. "And why does he look so passive right now?"

"He doesn't understand a word you're saying," laughs one of the Vendari in the back. Emily notices, however, that at these words, the young man gives the

Vendari a dull, quizzical look before returning his eyes to Heckley.

"Was that his sword?" says Heckley. He refers to the longsword the Vendari in the back, the one who had just spoken, is holding. It is almost as long as he is tall.

"Yes. We confiscated it, but we can throw it in if you like. It's well-made."

"Hmm." Heckley pauses. "And what is his name?"

"Who knows?" Rolanna smiles. "Now . . . to business? Handsome, isn't he?"

At this, Jerrold looks hurt. He shoots a jealous glare at the tall young man.

"My good woman." Heckley leans his upper body back as if she is emitting too much heat. "I may have my preferences, but I am not a delinquent."

"A fine bodyguard he'd be then," says Rolanna.

Heckley draws his sword with a loud, resounding ring and steps forward. The others repulse back. Adam steps in front of Emily and she cranes her neck to see what Heckley is doing.

"To business—if he is worth anything," Heckley hisses, and he raises his sword at the young man despite the cries of Rolanna.

Rather than flinching, alarm sparks in the young

man's eyes. He sidesteps Heckley's blow and seizes the sword in the sheath of his captor's belt, where it scrapes out with equal volume.

The tip of Heckley's sword clangs against the floor. He lifts it and straightens himself, a crazed, satisfied smile spreading on his winded face. The others watch in intrigued, tense silence; even Rolanna is entranced, and the young, black-haired man studies his attacker with edged caution, sword raised in his left hand.

Heckley jerks forward and flicks his sword at him again.

The young man parries above their heads. The blades clang against each other.

And they spar. Heckley slashes at the young man, gripping the hilt with both hands. Each time, the tall foreigner clanks the blade away, eyes jumping in swift calculation. Sweat dampens the hair on his forehead. He grunts as the swings become swifter and then their swords lock. He pushes their locked swords at Heckley with one powerful thrust.

Heckley staggers back. He wipes his mouth and seems to think about whether or not to continue. The young man twirls his sword once in his left hand, flashing off the blue glow of the light pockets.

Heckley lunges forward again, and with another hiss backs the young man into the thick column.

The foreigner blocks one final hit, but before Heckley can pull back for one more, the foreigner darts his right hand onto Heckley's wrist and pins it there, kicking him in the gut. The official's sword clatters to the ground and he doubles over.

Heckley gasps.

And then, he is laughing.

"Yes!" he chortles, stumbling over to retrieve his sword and choking for breath. He jabs a finger at the young man. "Yes!" The young man's shoulders relax, but he looks extremely confused. "I knew it! He is a master. And left-handed at that!" Heckley praises, looking at his former opponent now as if he were a prize horse. The young man's eyebrows darken suspiciously, and he grips the hilt of his still-drawn sword in his left hand just as tightly, the veins in his wrist flexed.

Rolanna is exhilarated. "Yes, yes, a master." She plays along. "A master worth a lot of money, yes?"

"Oh, you are not going home, my friend." Heckley ignores Rolanna and continues speaking appraisingly to the young man. "In fact, you are just what I have been waiting for."

"Right. Just what you've been waiting for. Now, how about we talk mon—"

"Remove Rolanna, Jerrold."

"Remo–? What?!"

"You heard me. It's a new age, *devrock*. An age lost of hierarchy. And a poor Galeduan like me doesn't listen to bounties."

"You filth!" Rolanna cries as Jerrold and two leather-clad bodyguards (who had gathered as Heckley began sparring) seize Rolanna and her men. Rolanna is kicking and cursing in her native language. "That's my property!" she yells. "I'll kill you, boy!" She spits at the young man, who eyes her edgily, but still says nothing. "You hear me? Kill you!"

And she is dragged out of the wing. Heckley wipes the sweat off his face with his wrist and smiles toothily as they hear a large door boom closed.

"Adam, come out of hiding, will you? And meet your new companion."

Adam walks slowly out of the column's shadow, making the tiniest gesture with his head indicating Emily to follow.

When she steps tentatively out of the shadow, the young man's dark eyes meet hers. He is curious at the sight of her, but shifts his gaze to Adam, who regards him dryly. Adam slides his eyes onto Heckley with disapproval. "Why is he our new companion?"

"Because twenty minutes ago, *you* were definitely going to die as pathetic asses from Fort Carrick before even reaching the fire at Fort Myrth. With *that* kind of skill," Heckley rams a finger in the direction of the young man again, "you might actually have a chance."

"I thought you wanted the fire to get out of control?" Emily says, but there's a twinkle in her voice—she's not sure Heckley is as committed to sleaziness as he puts on.

"There's a window here for me to gain equal glory by controlling it. Jerrold?"

Jerrold jumps to attention.

"Do the paperwork on this fellow. Identify him as a Fort Carrick knight. We'll have a hand in rescuing the Empire."

"And why do you feel this young man is obligated to accompany us?" Adam clears his throat.

"I'm a Sille, Mr. Flanagan. I can have bad things done to him if he doesn't—and I'll make sure Jerrold has a translator explain this to him in the morning." Heckley pauses. "Or I could just keep him. Your call . . ."

Adam is silent as he studies the young man once

more, who is again transferring his glum gaze from one to the other, measuring.

"Is there anything else you demand of us?" Adam's voice is suddenly darker and rougher, but he keeps his gaze on the tall warrior, who, the longer he measures Adam, the more he seems to mutely be forging a comradeship.

"Just figure out his name." Heckley smiles. "And extinguish the fire."

He sheaths his sword and walks in the other direction. "You leave tomorrow." His voice echoes in the hall. "Good day, Adam."

○ ~ ○ ~ ○

Adam opens the door to their dorm at the back wing and allows both Emily and their new "companion" inside. But as soon as the door shuts, Adam rubs his hands together and sets to work, gathering things like pillows and blankets from the beds into a sack resting on the low table.

The square room is a series of several beds lining the walls, two bookshelves filled with rotting tomes, and a low, square table set in the middle of the room, supporting clutters of paper and wooden dinner plates. As always, the room is lit with pockets engraved into the wall cradling portions of the bluish, glowing light. These lights have a tint of pearly pink to them, and when the young man ducks further in, he sweeps a cynical look around them all.

Trying to seem confident and unperturbed, Emily slides around the taller boy and approaches a sack of her own belongings on one of the beds. Marley must have dropped it off for her. She pretends to check inside it, mimicking Adam.

"We're sleeping here; don't worry about that yet," Adam says, catching her activity from the corner of his eye. "I'm packing because I need to see Marcus. He's waiting in the garden, but he'll need supplies more than we will if the whole Brotherhood is sleeping in the stables."

Adam seizes the now-full sack and steps to the door, resting a hand on the knob. The young man sinks onto one of the beds, slumping forward with his elbows on his knees and looking around the room silently. Adam considers him, and then shoots a glance at Emily.

"Would you like to come with me?"

They both pause for a long beat.

"I'll be okay. You're quicker without worrying about me," she says. Adam's eyes remain dark.

"The guards are right outside. I'll be back soon." He seems to promise this to himself more so than to her, and he steps out the door, closing it behind him.

Emily's heart pounds with nerves the second he leaves. What is she thinking, letting Adam leave with only this older boy in the room? She spins around and pretends to rummage in her supply pack, which contains her clothes, container of blueberries and roots, and a few books—nothing needing to be rummaged.

He, however, remains sitting forward and staring at the floor. When she can shuffle no more without sounding artificial, she sighs and sits on her bed, rubbing her thumbs. He glances over before looking again to his feet and clearing his throat.

"Do you . . . speak Galeduan at all?"

He looks up again, but there is a curved, almost pleading look in his eyes that tells her what the answer is.

"That's okay," she says. He stares at her as if trying to decide whether she understood his incomprehension or not. She decides to take a new tactic. She shifts in her seat and pats her chest.

"Emily," she says, smiling. He watches her with cold curiosity for a second before clearing his throat once more. He does not pat his chest, but speaks his name roughly.

"Cazimir."

"Cazimir?"

He nods, still grim, and looks away. Clearly, he doesn't share her faith that this communication method will work.

She rustles in her sack and pulls out a book, walking over to him while flipping through the pages. He pulls back at her approach, almost wary. She crouches in front of him and holds out her book, which displays a map of the known world. She points at him, and then down at the map.

He eyes her quizzically for a beat and then studies the map, tapping the country east of her native Galeduen. Darvica.

So he is Darvic.

She nods and looks at the map herself, determining how far he must have had to walk before hopping the cargo carriage. Close to forty miles.

She stands and replaces the book in her sack. He rests his head down into his hands and closes his eyes.

"I like you, Cazimir," she says lightly, and he looks up at the sound of his name. "Do you want something to eat?" She pours a handful of blueberries into her hand from the container and holds it out to him. Detecting the questioning tone of her voice, he looks at the blueberries and then glances away uncomfortably.

He is definitely hungry, but too embarrassed to accept. She smiles and walks back to him, taking his rough, veined hand, which he allows her to lift, and tipping the handful of berries into his palm. He allows a small smile to crease his lips and nods at her once. His dark eyes have a surprising glow to them as they glance into hers. She blushes and takes her seat back on the bed.

He tries to shovel the tipsy mound of fruit into his mouth, but several berries roll down his arm and onto the floor. He hangs his head to muffle the embarrassed huff as he chews, shaking his head. She laughs, soft and friendly. He swallows and lifts his eyes to hers again, studying her, as if succumbing to reading her in a new light.

The silence slowly stretches, and, to avoid any awkwardness, she shifts herself to lie on the bed. They are quiet for a long while.

"I'm sorry I only speak Galeduan, Cazimir." Her voice is truly regretful.

She can't decipher whether he understands her intentions, but, catching the light tone of her voice using his name, his pursed lips soften. He runs his hand slowly forward over his hair. It seems like a nervous habit.

"Cazimir?"

He looks over.

"I could teach you Galeduan if you want. Galeduan," she repeats, patting her chest and spreading her hand toward him again. The universal word "Galeduan," and the transferring gesture she makes helps him to understand. He stares at the corner of the room and nods just slightly.

"Thank you."

He scratches the back of his neck and looks at his feet again, breathing evenly. Audibly.

"Cazimir?"

He makes the smallest sound of a rumble when he looks up to her again, like he did in the hall. That shiver comes back to her; a tingle on the back of her neck that shudders down her body. Something about the feeling frightens her. She stops, long enough so that he leans in and turns his head slightly.

"Can I . . . call you *Caz*?"

He pauses, confused. "Caz?" His voice is low and throaty.

She nods.

He thinks for a long moment, studying the floor again. And then, he smiles softly and nods.

She digs herself into the covers. He watches her curiously. Then he gives a grunt and heaves himself to lie down on his back above the blankets. Heavy chainmail still drips off of him onto the mattress, and his hands rest on his chest.

“Goodnight, Caz,” she says, patting down her pillow.

He sighs and, probably forgetting whether the word she spoke meant goodnight or something else, simply grumbles “Emily” in a very finalizing tone. She smiles and allows her eyes to close.

Perhaps she shouldn’t have trusted him so much as to fall asleep in his presence. But, in a way, she almost feels safer with him here than if she were alone.

CHAPTER 10

"Vicar . . . please . . ."

The young druid, Ariana, stands outside the door of the Vicar's chamber, holding a pitcher of water with both hands. A tray of untouched food is at her feet, and she speaks through the door, hoping to hear the Vicar's feeble voice respond.

"I have water for you. And food. Please." She sobs suddenly. "We need you with us. We need your guidance."

She turns her head down to hide her tears, and then she freezes. There's a jumbling, like several books have fallen off a table. The thump of a heavy staff accompanies the limp of an old man, and the brass doorknob shakes as if trying to be rattled open.

Ariana jumps and seizes open the door.

His head is still down, and he holds the wooden staff

with one hand high at its neck, so he appears to be a fruit dangling from it.

"Thank you," he breathes in his delicate accent. The tremor is apparent in his voice, and Ariana tries to study him, frightened.

She hands him the wooden pitcher of water, but as he takes it in his free arm, it tumbles right through him. It crashes to the ground, and water runs across the floor. Ariana's eyes fill with tears again, but she doesn't even glance at the pitcher.

"Your Grace . . ." she whispers.

The Vicar swallows, but doesn't make any regard to the pitcher either.

"I'm sorry," he croaks.

"No," says Ariana. "No, of course not." She bends to turn the sodden pitcher upright so no more water can spill and saves the tray of food from being soaked.

The Vicar takes the tray more carefully this time and backs into the room. She flinches as she catches a distortion on his cheek in the shifting light.

She cannot stop herself. She reaches her hand out to his face and lifts it.

Blisters scorch his skin. His face is wrinkled and raw, branded to almost blackness, like he is wearing an ashen mask.

Burns.

Ariana cries and covers her mouth. Tears cascade instantly.

"Druid Weymes." She gasps his old clergy name, the one she knew him by before he became the Vicar. "No." She shakes her head. "No! Someone . . . *attacked you?*"

The Vicar is still again, but then he turns his face away from her.

"Not . . . an attack . . . on me." He can barely speak. It is as if his lungs are burned, too. "An attack . . . on us all."

○ ~ ○ ~ ○

Adam rests his hand on Emily's cheek.

"Time to get up," he whispers.

She obliges, rubbing her eyes and sitting. Her stomach aches, and she is dizzy from waking so fast, but she gropes around for her pack and rummages inside for a brush and clothes. Clearing her throat, she blinks her eyes awake before looking around the room, remembering just then that she and Adam are not alone.

Cazimir is rumpled—clothes and hair both—as he sits on the bed and watches them. His eyes are red, indicating the short sleep was not enough to regenerate a body that had walked forty miles from the border. Still, he doesn't seem in complaint. He hangs his head and slowly brushes his hand forward over his black, disheveled hair, breathing patiently.

Adam makes the bed and gathers his few belongings, and Emily stands after combing her hair, realizing she won't be changing outfits anytime soon and may as well be ready.

"I'm sorry to get you up so early," Adam says. "Marcus ordered we leave first thing."

For some reason, a twinge of annoyance stabs Emily. How much longer will Marcus hold authority over a band of busted criminals? She feels his power should be curdled by now.

"So," continues Adam, "we're meeting Heckley's blacksmith, getting our weapons, and leaving."

"Where are we leaving to?" Emily asks.

A shadow falls over Adam, and his eyes harden. He hands Emily a tabletop, iron light-holder containing his purplish orb to extinguish. He must have lit it last night after he came back from his meeting with Marcus. Emily guesses he had stayed awake for a few hours afterwards, just thinking.

"Marcus and I have differing opinions as to where to

go from here," he concludes grimly. She quenches the orb in the wiry light-holder. Cazimir watches it shrink with a deep, entranced gaze that Emily pretends not to see, but she swallows, and her heart drums.

She suddenly feels a powerful urge to know what shade of blue Cazimir's light is.

Adam turns his head to Cazimir abruptly, as if just remembering him.

"His name is Cazimir," Emily informs Adam, who looks back at her. But Emily is offering Cazimir a shy, half-smile. His eyebrows furrow in attention as he catches the use of his name. He realizes he has just been added to the conversation.

"Cazimir?" Adam asks him, trying to establish a connection.

Cazimir nods slowly, but he is wary as to what they are saying of him.

Adam pauses thoughtfully.

"And you speak no Galeduan at all?" he asks.

Cazimir drops his face into his hands and rubs it abruptly. He pulls back and looks at Adam with almost stern exasperation. Emily can nearly read his thoughts. *Yes. We've established that. Now what are we going to do about it?*

"Okay." Adam nods mildly. "That may become an issue." He speaks to Emily. "It's going to be important we know each other's thoughts from now on. I don't know how patient Marcus will be with him."

"Why do we keep bringing Marc into this, again?" says Emily.

Adam sighs.

"Because he's about the only one who can bring us out of it."

Emily pauses, confused, but Adam is springing to action before she can question it. He moves to the door, says, "Cazimir," and tosses his head in the door's direction.

Cazimir stands. His dark eyes glance into Emily's, but he turns them to the floor swiftly, adjusting a leather band on his left wrist and walking to Adam.

"Emily, if you could help me," says Adam, opening the door. Cazimir ducks his head—he's taller than the doorframe—and walks out of the room, waiting for Adam to follow. "The blacksmith is on the opposite side of the keep. I'm going to get Marcus and the Brotherhood to bring our horses around. If you could go to the smith and have him prepare our armor, we can leave right from there."

"No problem," Emily says.

"I'll be right there waiting for you," he promises unnecessarily.

She smiles. "Adam. I got this."

He nods. "I know," he whispers, and he reaches for the knob behind him, Cazimir watching the floor as he waits.

When the door seals, Emily changes quickly and slings her bag over her shoulder, double-checking the room for anything they may have forgotten. She inhales a deep breath and leaves.

One of Heckley's bodyguards, somewhat surprised to see a young girl on her own, courteously directs her to the very back of the keep, where he unlocks a door and opens it to grassy ground.

"Just in there, dear," he says gruffly, pointing to a small stone hut just a few yards away. A black anvil and several pikes rest against its wall and there are slash marks on the door, as if someone had used it as a cutting board for blade-testing.

"Thank you."

She marches towards it. Adam is not around with the horses yet.

Emily can hear the metallic *ting* of a hammer at work

behind the door. It's not as harsh and clangy as she had imagined the sound of a blacksmith's hammer to be—rather, it's a precise, quick pattern of trills. She knocks tentatively on the door.

The trilling stops.

She can hear the creak of someone's feet approaching the door, and then it opens and the thin blacksmith is standing there, baffled at her appearance.

He wears a smudged apron and tools along his belt, and his skin is dark brown. His hair is short and curly and his beard is thin, just trailing the edge of his jaw and mustache. The tan nails on his calloused fingers are chipped and rough.

"You're not Jerrold," he says. His voice has a cackling manner, sharp but friendly.

"No," Emily says nervously.

"Not saying I'm dis'pointed. But I'm curious. Who are you, child?" he says softly, almost soothingly, as he rubs his hand on his apron.

"Emily," she replies. "I'm . . . with the Brotherhood of Rain and Cinder. Here to get some supplies from you. Didn't Heckley—?"

"*You're* with the Brotherhood? Now I find that hard to believe." He shakes his head but steps aside to allow her entry. "Come in, Emily. We'll just pretend I'm not here if Jerrold comes around, all right then?"

She steps inside.

The smithy is one large, round room. A long, high trough stands on the left side and holds a mixture of blue light and black coals. A longsword sits atop the mixture, and it is glowing blue with the heat of the light. Buckets of water sit at the bottom of the trough and cloths are sprawled on the floor.

Breastplates, shields, and helmets lay jumbled on the right, and across from her, displayed on pegs and shelves, are gleaming knives and arrows.

The blacksmith walks to the trough and lifts the sword from the coals, which crumble off of it. The steel blade continues to radiate blue, as if it is glowing with light. Emily sees now that this is Cazimir's sword, which Heckley must have bought back for him. The black hilt is simple. There is a dragon symbol on its silver pommel.

"A beauty, isn't it?" the blacksmith asks, taking in her interested expression.

"It is."

"It's made of strael and steel. Strael is usually dark green and reflective, but the steel gives the sword this bright, silver color. I'm tuning it up for its owner."

As the blue glow fades, Emily notices a flash of dark, teal green when the blade shifts one way.

"Is that from the heat?" she says. The blacksmith follows her gaze.

"Ooh. That'd be the strael. In certain light, it flashes off that dark green." He tilts the sword another way, and the color is totally gone—the silvery blade looks like any other.

"Wow," says Emily.

"Have you been in a smithy before?" the blacksmith asks, nestling the long, black-hilted sword back into the light and coals.

"No," she says. She gazes at horseshoes, crumpled-up armor waiting for repair, and parts of swords laying everywhere. "How come none of this is trithium?" As the only ore found in Galeduen, it's the only onc she's familiar with—but none of these armor or weapon pieces are black, the color of trithium.

The blacksmith gives her a wry look. "Trithium? You may as well wear a mud coat."

"It's soft?"

"As a lullaby."

"But the Black Guard wear it. The elite bodyguard of the emperor."

The blacksmith cackles. "All the more reason it's a miracle we still have the Braelian dynasty."

Emily smiles. Then she notices a strange pedal apparatus below the trough of coals the attractive sword is laying in. "What's that?"

"Was wondering if you'd notice." The blacksmith gestures with his head. "Come closer."

She does.

"You know men can conduct the temperature of their light a bit. Cool. Warm. Just hot enough to brown meat. But hot enough to melt metal? Well . . ."

He pumps the pedal. The blue light orbs in the trough begin spinning with the gust of a wheel-fan below them. Faster. Faster. They spin so fast they stretch and wiggle, and the air above them becomes blurry with heat.

"The spinning and the oxygen increase heat." He retrieves his hammer. "And these here coals, they maintain the heat. More so than I could ever manage. This trough's hot enough now to melt anything. Well, except a diamond maybe." He winks at her and lifts his hammer over the sword. For a moment, she is too entranced to do anything but watch.

"I'll bet you thought I'd be some hulking, muscley giant, hmm?" He cackles as he gently beats the steel blade.

"Or maybe grimy and sooty."

She shakes her head absently and steps closer to observe the trough.

"Most blacksmiths just like to show off . . ." He swings his hammer in a great arch over his shoulder as if to pound the steel with a powerful hit but halts just before touching the sword. He pauses for effect, glances at her, and then taps the blade gently again in his quick rhythm.

He laughs warmly. Emily can't help but tilt her head and smile, too.

"I have all your supplies loaded out back. And I think this is just about done," says the smith. He pulls out the sword for the last time, and the hot, blue glow fades slowly.

"Thank you," she says, for she can't think of anything else to say.

"Just a moment, now," he says softly, setting down the beautiful, double-edged sword and strolling to the back of his circular stone hut, where the wall of knives and arrows are. "I've got something for you, too."

"I thought you didn't know I was coming?" she says, recalling his surprised expression on sight of her.

"I didn't."

He studies the shelves of sharp, exquisite knives, and purses his lips disapprovingly. He crouches and rifles through a jumble of raw metals, pulling out a shoddy box, and stares at it for several long seconds. "That'll do," he says to himself. He opens it and approaches Emily.

"This was my daughter's first knife." He hands her the weapon. Its blade is nine inches long— firm and sharp, but surprisingly light. The hilt is a honey-colored wood with rich curl, and the pommel is silver. She holds it, and it feels incredibly right in her hand, like her control is absolute. It is a weapon, not like the three-inch carving knife in her pocket.

"We made it together, my daughter and I," the smith continues. "That wood came from the same tree as the Vicar's staff. At least, that's what the lady said when I bought the wood from her. The lady became my wife. So, I don't think she was lying."

Emily is about to open her mouth and politely refuse the exceptional gift when he takes her face between his hands. He looks at her with tender pride, and she is caught so off-guard that she doesn't get the words out. Instead, she looks back at him, and lifts one of her own hands to touch the loose, older skin of his forearm, holding it there.

"You take it, Emily," he says, and there is a tear in his eye. "Brave, darling girl like you. You take it." He lowers his hands and wipes the tear from his eye. "My daughter'd want it."

He gathers the large sword, hands her the knife's scabbard, and leads her out the door to the back of the smithy without another word.

○ ~ ○ ~ ○

The Brotherhood trade their casual town clothes for reinforced leather–light enough to travel in and sturdy enough to provide protection.

When Adam steps out of the smith's front door from changing and walks towards Emily and Copenhagen, she is suddenly stricken with a visual of him, years ago, as a soldier. This is what he must have looked like. The short sword at his side is the same one he served with in the Sunlight Wars. He carries himself easily in the padding, turning his head to the early sun just climbing the sky. The rays glisten golden on his reddish, mahogany hair and across the glitter of dew on the grass.

Cazimir remains in his chainmail, but he has a full sack of leather armor, casual clothes, and other belongings under his arm. They allowed him a horse from the stable—a large thoroughbred bay, whose name they probably told him, but he probably didn't understand—and he stores the items in the saddle pack, silent as always. A document, composed in rune-like letters that Emily assumes to be Darvic, is crushed in his hand and must be the charter Heckley had him sign as understanding that if he did not complete this mission with the Brotherhood, he would be imprisoned under Galeduan law as punishment for crossing the border after the Emperor had sealed it, and if he deserted, a bounty would be placed on his head. In the same breath, it declared him by his full name—Cazimir Hawcaff—a knight of Fort Carrick . . . probably the first to ever exist . . .

Just before entering their sleeping quarters last night, she'd seen Cazimir presented with the document. He'd glared at Heckley before taking the pen in his left hand and signing the page. Heckley had clapped and giggled.

"It means if you don't make me famous, you die!"

"*My lord?*" Jerrold's head shot up in alarm. Heckley waved a hand at him.

"I'm only *exaggerating*, Jerrold!" He coughed. "Sort of."

Now, they are armed. They are supplied. And Captain Marley is getting impatient.

"Remember," says the captain, "we suggest you avoid the main roads." He says it with a tight jaw. The implication is grim. They must avoid drawing attention to themselves given their mission, and the potential enemies who may want to foil it.

Not ten minutes later, the captain forces them off into the morning light. Emily watches as they pass the paved, stone road. Welcoming stone posts bearing circular dog symbols flank either side of the wide road. The symbols represent Dralus III, who, in addition to being one of "The Star Emperors," is known as "The Dog Emperor." He built roads throughout the Empire and traveled the provinces always with his pack of unruly dogs. He would have been the first emperor to make it to the isles at the tip of Fellvren had he not fallen off his horse and split his head to the howl of his dogs.

Emily longed for that safe, clean road as they headed for the grass at the tree line paralleling it.

To Emily's astonishment, Adam pulls his white stallion in to take the lead. She coaxes Copenhagen to come in line with him.

"Adam?" she questions.

Adam's smile has the smallest touch of arrogance. "Marcus and I came to an agreement. An agreement to agree with me."

"Good," says Emily dismally. And then she amends her sentence. ". . . What did you agree on, exactly?"

"Where to go. He wanted to go directly to the flame. '*Get it over with.*' I told him that's suicide and he said . . . '*What do you think we're here for?*'" Adam leans towards Emily, doing an unflattering impression of Marcus. Emily, however, doesn't find Marcus' response radical. She remains grim.

"So I told him . . ." Adam trails off as if embarrassed to continue.

"What?" says Emily.

"I told him I made a promise to someone. That I'd *try.* And suicide wasn't trying."

Emily takes in a rocky breath.

"So rather than go directly to the flame, blind and tactless . . . I told him we need a druid."

"A druid?"

Adam nods gloomily. "After the killings of the druids, there are very few who will go with us. And no *active* druid can help us without losing favor with the church."

"No 'active' druid? Then who can?"

Adam seems to contemplate someone particular, and

Emily stares at him curiously.

"An expelled one," he says. "And I know just where to find him."

CHAPTER 11

The berry bursts in her fingers and drips red juice down her wrist. It smells edible—tangy but not tart—and yet the juice looks too close to blood for her to be sure. The trail it leaves down her hand is sticky, and she shakes off the rest of the berry's flesh. She opens her pouch, then selects another stem from the wild bush, slowly stripping the bough of its clusters of grey berries.

Gather now. Decide later.

The woods have a golden quality with the afternoon light slanting through the leaves. It feels safe. For now.

Adam and the rest of the Brotherhood are making camp. She'd offered to help but found Marcus in too sour a mood to endure.

"Keep going, Brother Adam!" he'd snapped. "I'm not stopping 'til Welshire!"

That's where Adam had suggested they go—a small

village that happens to be the closest settlement to the Shrine, where the druids are trained.

"They'll be dead by morning, Marcus!" Adam had yelled back, dismounting Folk Tale. He was referring to the horses, which had traveled nonstop for nearly eight hours. Not to mention how sore everyone was from the saddle. The argument continued.

So Emily bailed to the trees. The earth is soft beneath her feet as she steps to the next bush, the berries tumbling softly into her leather pouch. The warmth of late summer greets her as a ray of sunlight catches her hand over one of the stems. She smiles and turns her palm up towards it.

Somewhere in her pocket is the tablet of wood Adam had taught her to carve, and somewhere in these trees—perhaps miles and miles away, but still in these woods—are the trunks she watched him carve upon, watched his hand brush over the ragged bark. Adam. Peaceful, quiet Adam. She always considered him gentle. Was he fierce and bloodthirsty outside of those Darson's Ford waters? How much suffering did his hands inflict on others to land himself in the Brotherhood?

And yet, she still pled to go with him. Still cringed at the thought of being left without him.

She closes her hand at the light as if to capture it.

A twig snaps in the thickets behind her and she jumps, unsheathing her knife.

Cazimir is standing there, freezing at the sight of her. His dark eyes glance at the knife and back to Emily, questioning.

She lowers the blade and slides it back into the scabbard, skin hot with embarrassment.

They're caught there in an awkward silence, both perfectly aware that neither will be able to understand the other. It is the first time she has seen Cazimir without his chainmail—he must have taken it off at camp—and somehow he doesn't look any less impenetrable. His shoulders are just as broad. That longsword she admired in the smithy drags in the brush beside him, and his feet are planted a little farther apart than average. It would take a battering ram to knock him over. Beneath all that chainmail and leather had been a simple, dark blue shirt he wears now and it brings out the onyx of his hair. His leather wristband is tight on his thick wrist.

She clears her throat and tries for a smile, still pretending to fumble with her sheath.

"Cazimir," she says.

A pause.

"Emily," he mumbles.

"What're you—?" she begins in a questioning tone. Cazimir lifts a canteen of water from his belt and turns it over. Nothing pours out. He locks her in his gaze as if to ask if she knows where to find the water.

She purses her lips regretfully. There's been no sight of any fresh streams today. She shakes her head.

He nods and looks off into the trees.

He is strong enough to overpower her. Take her to the Brotherhood by the neck and demand his freedom. Adam would give it to him. And yet he just stands there in the trees, breathing evenly and thinking to himself.

Finally, he grunts and hangs his head, turning to leave the way he came.

"Cazimir," she says, before she can stop herself.

He turns to her.

She pauses and nearly panics. She doesn't know what she was going to say.

"Emily," he murmurs again, in the low timbre of his Darvic accent. He waits for her to say or do something.

Her heart pounds, but she offers the only communication she thinks he'll understand.

She lifts the grey berries in her palm.

His look becomes cynically amused as he studies

them, and he glances into her eyes as if to assure he is making the right connection.

She smiles sheepishly.

He steps to her slowly—one deep thump at a time—but glimpses up at her occasionally as if asking permission to approach.

He lays his fingers over the berries. Shyly, he clears his throat and reaches his other hand for her leather pouch, lifting it up and guiding her hand to tip the fruit into it. It is his kind way of acknowledging their connection and yet allowing her to keep her gatherings rather than give them to him.

He is close to her now, and he must realize it because he inhales a deep breath and blinks away from her, pretending to scan the bushes.

She wishes more than anything to talk to him. To find out why he came here, where his family is . . .

Ask to see the color of his light.

"I wish I could speak to you, Caz," she whispers. It's such a soft sentence that he returns his eyes to her quickly, a hint of concern in them.

When she doesn't continue, his expression hardens as if to say *You're not going to try Galeduan again, are you?*

But she doesn't. Instead, she finds her heart in her

throat. She doesn't know why the impulse is so strong . . . but her hand moves to graze him. It is like someone else is doing it. The second her fingertips brush his warm, veined hand, she takes it.

And just as he did back in the keep, he allows her to lift it. Heat pulses through her as she draws him up to her. His flesh is strong and rough. Male.

She risks a glimpse at him. He is watching their joined hands with almost skeptic curiosity, and when his eyes meet hers, the curiosity transfers to her. For some reason, she breathes a small laugh of relief. He is not repulsed. Just curious. And at her laugh, his shoulders soften.

"I don't believe you can't understand me," she breathes.

She brings his hand to her chest, where the faintest heartbeat can be felt.

No. They are not incomprehensible. The cynic interest slips off his face and his eyes melt with comprehension.

When his gaze meets hers again, it floods out grateful understanding.

He gently pulls their hands from her chest and rests it against his own, keeping his dark eyes, heirlooms of a rough, cold, Darvic homeland on hers.

The beat is there. Just the same.

His fingers tighten their hold over her smooth hand and he swallows, letting them slide down just an inch.

He clears his throat gruffly and then lets their hands drop apart completely. He brushes his other hand forward over his black hair again. Before she can stop him, he turns, glances timidly at her once more, and walks back the way he came.

The shadows have stretched, and she can't decipher whether it is the deep-hued sunlight or the heat of their fingertips together that have made the back of his neck so red.

○ ~ ○ ~ ○

Adam and Marcus are not speaking as Emily sits on the trunk of a thick tree that Mason had rolled down the incline from the forest. Deep night blankets them in the grass. They had established a small lightpit: a circle of jumbled rocks aglow with the light—not Adam's deep, purplish orb, but someone else's powdery blue light. She tries to guess whose it was. It seems far too delicate a color to be Marcus'.

Marcus shaves the end of a branch with his knife with vigor, as if to channel his anger. He is shaping a sort of spear, but it is not nearly sharp enough to be of any use yet. Adam sits across from Emily, watching the glimmering rocks, and Brother Mason is sitting next to her on the same trunk, drinking from a canteen.

The sound of the sloshing water as he swigs reminds her of Cazimir's thirst. They had obviously not refilled his jug with the supplies from the keep. Her eyes seek him out in the night, and she finds him, standing, leaning his weight forward on his longsword, its tip in the dirt. His eyes are closed.

A glint of dark green from the strael waves over Cazimir's sword and disappears just as fast, as if in secret greeting to her.

"What's that boy's name?" Brother Mason is eyeing Cazimir with gentle interest. Emily starts, blushing after being caught watching the tall Darvican. She shifts on the rough bark of the trunk.

"Cazimir," she gets out, throat dry for some reason.

"And where is he from?" Brother Mason has a warm, friendly voice, and she relaxes.

"Darvica. He doesn't speak any Galeduan."

Mason contemplates this.

"I know some Darvic," he says politely at length. "Perhaps I could—"

"You're worried about *horses*, Adam," Marcus snarls, jerking off a large shard of wood. They tense around the lightpit. Marcus must be truly angry to have forgone his use of "Brother" before Adam's name.

"Right," Adam throws a rock into the lightpit, "because they would have—"

Marcus hurtles his pike at the incline to the trees in anger. "I'm trying to keep your head on your spine and you're *worried. about. horses*."

Emily intervenes. "What's the big deal about stopping here, Marcus?"

"You're idiots. All of you," he growls.

"Just ignore him . . ." cantors Brother Mason in a singsong voice, like he is dealing with a well-familiar tantrum.

Emily just shakes her head. "What—?"

"You want to know why we shouldn't have stopped here, pup? Why Mason shouldn't have lit this light? Because it's a *cult*. Of killers. Who don't want us threatening their flame. They're going to be after us."

"Enough, Marc," Adam warns. But Emily wants to talk to Marcus.

"You don't think there's only one flamelighter?"

"I know there isn't."

"How do you know?"

Marcus inhales but stops as if he thinks better of saying something. His next sentence is calmer. "One druid from every village was killed. Can one person do that?"

She is silent as she studies his green eyes. Even giving such terrifying news, they are like poison. Just like the poison that killed their own druid. Just like the poison that—

Poison!

Emily has to choke her breath midway to keep herself from gasping. Brother Scott picks the white mushroom and glares at her in her mind, and Adam's words come rushing back like an echo. *"He's immune. He . . . dealt with a lot of poisons. A lot."*

It takes everything she can do not to grab Adam and spill this realization. She stares determinedly ahead, although Mason seems to sense her tension with a shift of concern.

Marcus mistakes her terrified expression for an understanding of his words and smiles. "That's right, buttercup. We're not dealing with a flame. We're dealing with a cult. A *real* brotherhood. Of murderers. Just like us."

"So why don't you run?" she blurts, mostly to keep herself from sweating. Adam notices her odd behavior as well, and he shifts stealthily in the grass, piercing her with a *What's going on?* look.

Emily watches Marcus for several moments, but he doesn't answer.

"Why haven't you run, Marcus?" Emily repeats slowly.

Marcus's eyes flash dangerously. The blue light is iridescent on his platinum-grey beard.

Even Cazimir is watching the exchange with shrewd unease.

Mason sighs and stands. He moves over to Adam. "Enough of this. Let me see your knee; I might have something to ease the joint."

Adam stretches his knee out for Mason—Marcus goes back to shaving the spear. All Emily has really done was buy time to think of poison, and Druid Parr dangling dead over his basin of holy water. She must talk to Adam alone. She must tell him about Brother Scott. She must—

But whatever else she must do did not come. For Mason screams in pain and an arrow, coated in his flesh and blood, jams itself into the lightpit.

CHAPTER 12

Everyone ducks except for Marcus and Emily, who stand and draw their blades.

The second she does, she regrets it. She and Marcus stand out like beacons, but Marcus doesn't care. He is shouting to the others.

"Shields! Now!"

Another arrow whizzes by where his head was just a moment ago. He sprints for the horses carrying their plain, wooden shields. Emily's arm is suddenly seized by Adam and he tugs her to the horses, moving with his head down.

They jerk to a halt as Marcus rips two shields from the pack horse and looks over to the black tree line.

A blazing, flickering orange dot illuminates the trunks in wavering shadows. They can hear the screech of a bow being drawn.

Marcus turns and runs from the horses, whose heads are straining in each direction. He throws a shield to Adam just as a streak of yellow cuts through the night behind him. A horse neighs shrilly, rearing on its hind legs.

The flaming arrow punctures Hopskip's sack. Fire combusts over the cloth, setting his burdens alight. Whinnies and snorts deafen their ears as the horses panic. Their black eyes are bugging out with terror in the flickering fire, and they turn and flee, galloping away.

"Marcus!" Brother Mason's voice cracks. He is still over by the lightpit, holding his wound.

"Adam! Let's go!" he roars. And, harnessing the shield, he tears up the incline of the trees towards the assaulters.

"*Stay*." Adam's voice is the harshest Emily has ever heard it as he thrusts her to the ground, where she can blend into the dark grass. He draws his sword and throws down the shield for her to reach, sprinting after Marcus.

The attackers can be heard now, rustling through the trees and drawing another unlit arrow.

Emily rolls in the grass, trying to shove away the blurred streak of the flaming arrow from her vision. She looks up to the dark tree line as Adam joins Marcus, armed with only his sword.

The arrow is released, and she can hear the thud of it hitting Marcus's shield. A dark, hooded figure draws his own blade as Marcus approaches, and Marcus drops his shield, gripping the hilt of his sword with both hands and hauling a deep swing at the man.

The hooded figure jumps aside. Marcus, still doubled over from the swing, stops the incoming slash by clasping the hilt of the other man's sword, his other hand still gripping his own handle. They struggle, and just as another dark silhouette rushes through the trees, Adam rips the hooded figure away from Marcus and stabs him through the back.

The body thumps to the floor. It is that quick. Adam's sword did not hesitate.

"DARVICA!" Marcus bellows for Cazimir in the night as another attacker leaps through the trees at him. This one is wielding an axe—moonlight bleeding through the silver knots at its head. Marcus roars in rage and lifts his sword to parry the overhead swing, catching the axe head on his blade. Just as Adam rushes to help, Adam is knocked into the grass, and he rolls down the incline with another on top of him.

"NO!" Emily cries. She is on her feet, running to

them, when Cazimir is there. He snags the man's robes in both hands and hurls him off Adam. The figure falls on his back and Cazimir raises his sword, point down, to pierce him into the ground, but the hooded man kicks hard across Cazimir's feet and sweeps him to the floor.

The assaulter draws his blade as Adam comes at him again, and the two spar. Adam blocks the man's sword with skill and patience. Just as the way he lives. It is the calm control of a soldier.

Marcus is alone with the axe-wielder at the tree line, and the two of them—both fighting with heavy, double-handed weapons—exert themselves with heavy misses, reeling their great weapons back up with slow recoveries.

Emily's breath is coming in ragged gaps—she doesn't know where to turn first. She seeks out everyone, evaluating their safety and their threats. And then she remembers—Brother Mason to her right! It has been far too quiet by him. She jerks her head in his direction, jolted by some sort of instinct, and studies the darkness of their grassy incline.

Movement. She catches it in the darkness. Two figures slinking down from the trees with jagged, wavy blades glaring in the moonlight, heading for Mason.

There is no time to yell to Adam. No time for help.

Brother Mason half-lays on the ground, his hand pressed firmly over the gushing blood on his shoulder, his head low and not paying attention.

Clutching the smooth, honey-colored hilt of her own knife, she makes for them.

The first one doesn't see her by the time her knife is slashing across his back. The knife cuts through the fabric of his cloak like water and opens a long gash in his skin. He gives a gurgling cry and falls to his knees. Delving the knife into his back would demolish him for good. But she cannot drive her hands to do it, even with Mason just inches from death.

The cry of the slashed figure alarms the others. His companion jerks to him, and Mason looks up in shock.

"Emily, run!" Mason yelps. He glances down at his hand pressed over the pulsing blood.

The second robed figure lunges for Emily with his curvy knife, diving for her shoulder. She dodges and staggers up the hill, drawing him away from Mason, leaving the first assassin still swaying on his knees.

She spins to the second attacker before hitting the tree line and blocks a slash with her knife, feeling the sickly scrape of metal on metal. It is easy to deflect, as her blade snags right in a curve of the odd, wavy blade.

Sweat trickles into her eyes as she thrusts away his knife with all her strength. He stumbles, and she darts her eyes to Adam, Marcus, and Cazimir. Marcus has disarmed his axe opponent and towers over him on the ground, and she has to avert her eyes as Marcus swings down his sword for the fatal blow.

Adam and Cazimir are overwhelmed with two more hooded figures. Cazimir is closest to her, having just hacked at his opponent's wrist, causing him to drop his weapon and Cazimir to drive his sword in for the kill. Adam is at the bottom of the incline below Marcus, maintaining a clang of parries with a particularly swift swordsman. A swordsman stronger and younger than Adam. Adam's blocks are becoming slower, more tired. His short sword wobbles in his grasp . . .

Emily springs her attention back to the knifeman in front of her.

Just in time to see his blade hack into her ribs.

The pain is instant, the blood too hot. Oxygen suddenly seems like vapor in her lungs, slipping through every exit. It is a burning feeling again . . . burning through her skin . . . burning . . .

One more drive with the wavy knife will kill her, and she knows this is it. It was a stupid thing to do, she thinks, to pull her eyes away from the knifeman. But it'll all be done with now.

She hears an anguished yell from Adam.

"*CAZIMIR*!" he screams. "EMILY!"

It happens in an instant. Adam is too far as he struggles with the last, swift swordsman, terror and grief distracting him. Cazimir looks up from his deceased opponent and sees her, doubled over in pain and the hooded figure about to grab her clothes and drive the knife into her back.

Cazimir drops his sword. He tears up the incline, and just as Emily feels herself being yanked in by the assassin, a body slams into the hooded figure, dragging him to the ground.

She sways, her sight going in and out of focus. Is the moonlight fading, or is that just her eyesight getting darker?

She registers Cazimir grunting and wrestling with the knifeman on the ground before she falls and closes her eyes.

Her thoughts are not what she expects them to be. She thinks of Mr. Robutan, and how sad he must be that she had left him. She thinks of Copenhagen running away. She sees Adam's purplish-blue light growing in her mind. And she imagines the feel of a hand—younger, male, and veined—holding hers over the steady thump of his heart as she drifts to blackness in the grass.

○ ~ ○ ~ ○

Familiar arms slide under her. She is lifted into them, and she can feel the heavy breathing of an exhausted and distraught man holding her.

"The horses are gone, Adam," says the rough voice of Marcus. "We'll never carry both Mason and her to Welshire by—"

"We will." She can feel the shaky rumble of Adam's voice. He is just barely managing to keep it from breaking. His arms hold her tightly as if to clutch her to him for years. But they are tired. She can feel the strain of his muscles shaking, the heavy inhale and quick exhale of his breath.

He thumps through the grass with her.

They walk for an immeasurable amount of time. His step becomes heavier, almost a limp. When he inhales next, she can hear a sniffle that he tries to hide.

"My girl," he breathes. It is drenched in regret and shame. "I'm sorry."

Adam does not know she can hear him. But her consciousness is so dim, she cannot stir. Only breathe.

Only hear the grass flatten beneath his feet. She is slipping lower in his arms.

Another tread comes up behind them. Adam turns to it.

There is silence and a mute exchange Emily cannot see with her eyes closed.

And then Adam is stepping to someone, gently transferring her into another man's arms.

These arms are stronger. They take her with ease, but just as much comfort. Just as much warmth.

She turns her head and looks up for only a moment.

Cazimir is glancing down at her. Their eyes meet, and neither says a word.

CHAPTER 13

She is lowered to the floor. Only a blanket separates her from the hardwood beneath it, and urgent footsteps squeak in the room.

A door is closed.

It could be a dream, but she feels hot fingers ensnare her hand as her head is rested down. Feels her hand held against someone's chest and an arm slide a little too slowly from under her shoulders.

"How long has she been bleeding now?" She can hear Mason's voice of forced patience, hear him rummage in a jingling sack.

"Over three hours," Adam pants, despair in his voice. "With just your bandage."

"Then she'll have to drink two of these. And that's quelled plenty of the bleeding, Adam." Mason defends his bandage, comforting.

"Are *you* okay?" Adam asks of Mason.

"I am fine. Her wound was much deeper than mine."

The figure at Emily's side stands and steps back, allowing Mason to approach. She is too weak to open her eyes, but she can sense the wooden spoon hovering over her, feel it brush her lips. She parts them just enough to allow the liquid to trickle through them.

"There," Mason croons. "There, now."

Adam kneels next to her, and his hand is over her cheek, the last thing she feels before sinking deeper away.

"Thee," says Mason, his voice echoing. "There . . ."

The rushing sound of sand runs through her mind, shimmering in and out of focus. It's in constant movement—swirling and sinking. In the midst of the churning coast, a single, tiny flame ignites, red and alive.

Just as the alarm gongs relay throughout the Empire, so do the flames. At one's ignition, another, near it, bursts to life. And more, and more, until the golden shore is scattered with scorching fires.

Maybe they will stay here. Maybe she can lock them in this dream where they cannot hurt anyone more.

A figure blurs into focus ahead.

His reddish hair, his stitched, forest-green shirt.

Adam.

He stands upon the shore, taking in all that is around him as the sand twirls like little tornadoes around his feet.

She hears swelling, mounting seawater.

And the waves come before she can stop them. Rushing with force, the foamy ocean floods the beach, swallowing the fires with a sizzle and sweeping Adam off his feet and under the tide.

No! she screams in her mind. *Adam!*

"*Good*, Cazimir," Mason praises in a soft voice. *No*, she thinks. Is Mason here too? And Cazimir? She clutches her hand over the blanket on the floor, reeling it in and letting its fuzz tickle her nose.

Her head and limbs are anchored to gravity. She is too weak to lift them.

"You're a fast learner," Mason whispers, delighted. Emily listens. Someone clears his throat.

"Thank you for . . . teach."

She knows that low, husky voice. But did it just speak Galeduan?

"Well. I don't know much." Mason sighs. "But the languages share a similar enough root to help me elaborate for you."

Silence.

"I mean, you knew enough to—oh, I don't know what the word for 'elaborate' is in Darvic. *You knew enough*," he says this last sentence slowly, pronouncing each word. She hears Cazimir being patted on the shoulder.

"More tomorrow," Mason says, standing from his seat.

Cazimir pauses and then grunts. "More tomorrow," he echoes.

She can hear Mason move to the door. He stops, voice tentative. "Adam has stayed awake with her all day," he says. There is a heavy pause, and she can imagine Mason watching her sadly. "He's only just laid down his head. I wonder if . . . Cazimir, will you stay with her? Stay with Emily?" Mason clarifies.

Cazimir makes the connection. In the stretched silence, she imagines him nodding. "Yes," he murmurs.

"She should be waking soon. Another hour of rest."

Mason closes the door behind him.

Cazimir sighs deeply. He is motionless for several moments. And then he walks slowly to her, drawing in a chair that is only feet from her head.

He sits and leans forward, burying his face in his hands and massaging it.

The weight of her body is still too much to shift, the shaky weakness still too insurmountable. But she can feel the presence of his body next to her, can hear him breathe into his hands.

"Emily," he mumbles. It is difficult to tell through his Darvic accent, but she is almost certain it was said with worry. He exhales again and breathes words she cannot understand.

"*Ahm cara*."

○ ~ ○ ~ ○

Emily sits at the table and Adam watches her in agonized shame. He winces quietly every time she does as she pulls herself closer in the chair.

Lunch is before them—purple and red leaves drizzled in a honey-colored dressing and tossed together with crisp apples. Sun and a gentle breeze pour in from the open front door of the inn. It's been over twelve hours since Mason's stitches penetrated her skin, and her fork still shakes in her hand as she lifts it.

They are in Welshire. Mason had explained all that had happened when she woke.

The remaining assassins, including the one Emily slashed in the back with her knife, fled after Marcus and Adam ran to Cazimir's aid, who was struggling with

Emily's attacker in the grass.

Mason had passed out initially, and Marcus bandaged his cousin and Emily in a quick, messy fashion. He carried Mason on his back towards Welshire. When Mason came to, he'd murmured, "Oh, good heaven . . . get me down." Mason redid the bandages—better, tighter—on both he and Emily, and walked the rest of the two-hour journey to the small village. Adam and Cazimir took turns carrying Emily, though Cazimir ended up bringing her most of the way, as he was stronger and Adam was stumbling even when he wasn't holding her. The swordsman he had been dueling managed to scrape Adam's forearm when he was distracted, and he had pulled a muscle in his ankle when he was tackled to the ground.

Cazimir had carried her into the inn, standing there with her in his arms as Marcus slammed ten silver coins on the counter and bought a room. Mason hurried to Welshire's apothecary and purchased elixirs for both himself and Emily. One of the remedies knocks them out, which, when used on Emily, allowed Mason to stitch the wounds. The other, made of everlily—small, white flowers—restores strength. Both tempt Emily to vomit, which is why she doesn't touch the lunch in front of her.

She hasn't had a chance to speak to Adam alone. Even with the pain in her ribs after every twist or movement, even with the flashbacks of her first experience of combat, her thoughts are deafened to anything but the poison that killed their Darson's Ford druid. The poison Brother Scott is so familiar with.

They sit now at a table in the inn. Emily tries to think of a way to get Adam alone.

"You have one night to find your ex-druid, Adam," says Marcus through his mashed potatoes. He swallows and glares at the others. "We're leaving if he doesn't. That was a cult that attacked us. They know who we are and where we're going. Unless you want them to burn this village to the ground, we're leaving in the morning. If not tonight."

He reaches his gauntleted hand for the mug of water before him. Emily wonders why he still hasn't removed the metal glove.

"They had fire," Emily states.

"Wow, I didn't realize that," says Marcus.

Emily scowls. "I mean they have a way to make it. How can they do that? What could possibly give them that power?"

"I don't suppose it's rubbing two sticks together,"

Mason comments bleakly, scraping his plate with his fork.

"No," says Adam. "That's not possible. They have to have something else." He speaks meekly. Emily frowns at him. Of course, Adam would take the blame for her injury.

"Whatever," says Marcus. "I don't care how they make it. I care how to destroy it. And if you can figure that one out with your druid, Adam, I'll buy you a new sheath." He stands and makes for the counter of the inn, dropping another handful of coins in the owner's hand and wiping his mouth with the back of his wrist. Adam looks dully down at his worn leather sheath, which has become even more flimsy, revealing shine of the steel sword within.

"Mason, let's go," Marcus barks.

Mason jumps and glances at him shrewdly, patting his mouth with a cloth. "And where am I going, *Kinfather*?"

"As of today, we're out of horses, food, and supplies. Where do you think?"

Mason groans, swaying his head in exaggeration. He stands. "Little cousins," he mutters.

Marcus and Mason leave the inn, squinting as they

step into the sun. Even through her ill feelings towards Marcus, Emily can't help but notice that he has just paid for her food, medicine, and bed.

She looks back to those at the table—Adam picking at his food with his head down but bringing nothing to his mouth. Cazimir tilting his mug of water from side to side, watching the liquid jump around. This may be her best chance to talk to Adam alone. Cazimir can understand some Galeduan now, as he demonstrated with Mason, but he won't get all of this. And even if he did . . . can she not trust him to hear what she's going to say?

There may not be another chance.

"Adam," she hisses.

Adam looks up. Emily leans forward on the table.

"We need to talk about Scott."

Adam leans in as well. "Why? What's going on?"

Cazimir glances at each of them.

"I think he poisoned Druid Parr."

Adam recoils. "What?"

"I don't think it was magic. Or a heart attack." Does she admit to Adam that she snuck out against his wishes and saw the crime scene? "I think it was poison. And it had to be by someone in the Ford. You said Scott deals with poisons."

"Why do you think it was poisoning?"

Emily sighs. Time to confess. When she does, and mentions the berry, Adam is not angry—he is a statue. Cazimir senses the tension and grips the rim of the table with his hand.

"The symptoms would make sense," Adam says at last.

"And Marcus." Now Emily is on a roll. "He's hiding something, too. Why isn't he running? Do you really believe he's afraid of the law? That he really doesn't think he can outsmart them?"

Adam's head is low, eyes on the table. His face is unreadable, even in the dusty sunlight.

"I don't," he whispers at last. "I don't believe him." Adam lifts his eyes to her and they stare at each other fiercely. "Mason won't run because he's his cousin. I'm not running because of what Marcus would do to me. But something is keeping Marcus from running," Adam says slowly.

"Right," Emily says. "And what about that gauntlet he wears?" Suddenly she is feeling paranoid. About everything. "And why did he show up in Mr. Robutan's bar that one night and fall on his face?"

Adam shakes his head dismissively. "I don't know. But it's common for a warrior to wear armor like that if he cut his hand or something."

"Adam . . ." Emily's voice is scared suddenly. "What if Marc's leading us to the fire for a different reason? What if he's—"

The back door to the inn bursts open and they jump. A man with a bald, shiny head wearing an apron storms through to the front counter of the inn, throwing his arms in the air.

"I don't know where they came from!" he huffs. "They won't leave. And I'm not feeding them."

The owner, a stocky man with an orange mustache, groans and rolls his eyes.

"Can you just deal with it?" he asks the bald man.

"No. I can't. Because they won't leave. And those marks on the pack one are freaking me out."

"What's going on, here?" Adam raises his voice and turns in his seat, darkly curious about the words he's catching. The two turn to him.

"What's it to you?" says the bald one at the same time the owner vacantly says, "Horses."

"Horses?" Emily shifts in her seat. Cazimir perks up as well, turning to look over his seat at the two innkeepers.

"Yeah . . ." says the bald one slowly. "What about them?"

"They must be ours," Adam declares, disbelieving. "Ours ran off last night."

"They're yours . . .?" The bald man suddenly sounds grim.

Adam eyes him, measuring the questionable tone. "Yes," he confirms at last.

The bald man and the owner exchange gloomy looks.

"You better come outside, then," the bald one says. "There's something you might want to see."

CHAPTER 14

"Cope!"

When Emily sees the dark, scruffy colt standing outside the stable fence, she runs to him. Copenhagen turns his head to her, ears twitching forward as if surprised by her enthusiasm. She wraps her arm around his muzzle and pulls his head to her, resting her forehead against it. He is still, tolerant. But he snorts as if to say, *Good to see you, too.*

Adam and Cazimir are walking slowly behind her, a little more wary. The stern look on the bald stableman's face discourages them from mimicking Emily's warm welcome.

Emily pulls back, stroking Copenhagen's nose, but the smile slips off her face as she imagines the terror the horses had been through, the tired look in Copenhagen's eyes.

And that's when she remembers—the pack horse, Hopskip. There is no way he could have survived his saddle catching fire. She jumps her eyes over each horse, counting.

Two, four—there! He's alive! She brushes along the fence to Hopskip, confused and delighted.

"Adam, the pack horse—"

But she stops. Her heart gives a rough thump against her chest.

Hopskip holds his pale brown head high, but his eyes are stricken as if the flames are still alight. His saddle is cooked black, charred bags dangle from him, and all along his body are burn marks, deep and scathing like brandings. She studies them, feeling dizzy from something other than Mason's elixir. The black markings are grotesque, but she has to wonder . . . is it her imagination, or do they resemble the leaves on the stone Guardians? Do the spotted burns mark something legible?

And surely . . . surely the saddle and sacks should have burned through? How is he alive?

"That was *my* first reaction." The stableman approaches the fence and crosses his arms, glaring at them as if demanding an explanation.

Adam's eyes are wary as he walks slowly up to the fence. He too is considering the burns before he exchanges a dark glance with Emily, whose mouth is hanging open.

Cazimir stands back, resting a hand at his sword hilt and pursing his lips as he studies the horses.

"So," the stableman challenges. "These your horses?"

The seven horses stare at them, as if incredulous as to why the stableman won't allow them in through the gate. Emily can't imagine how famished they are.

"Yes." Adam nods slowly. He gives a low huff.

"So what happened to the pack one? What are those markings?" The stableman has obviously never seen a burn before.

Adam pauses, but Emily can see through his mind that he is deciding how much to tell the stableman.

"I don't know," Adam says at length, doing his best impression of sounding baffled.

The stableman narrows his eyes. He scoffs finally.

"Well, take them. But I'm not feeding or watering them." He yanks the strings from his apron and cuts back into the inn.

When the back door of the inn closes, Adam shakes

his head.

"What the hell happened."

"I was going to ask you the same thing," says Emily.

"That saddle was blazing, Emily," says Adam. "He shouldn't be alive."

Emily studies the scattered burn markings, trying to find the one that so resembled the stone Guardian's leaves.

Adam clenches his hands on the coarse wood fence and leans on his outstretched arms. They stand in silence for several tense moments.

Cazimir walks between them. He leans on his elbows on the fence, eyeing the roasted saddle.

"Stopped," he grunts.

Both Adam and Emily spring their heads to him at these words. Neither is accustomed to hearing him speak.

Cazimir suddenly seems embarrassed about all the attention. He watches them both, clears his throat, and shifts.

"Fire . . . stopped." He looks at them both in turn, hopeful that they understand his few words.

"It stopped," Adam echoes. He turns back to the saddle. "He's right. The fire ended before it could burn through the saddle and bags. Before it could eat up the rest of it."

"You mean it vanished?" says Emily.

"Well, I don't imagine someone put it out," Adam says.

"Why would it disappear?" Emily is mystified.

Cazimir, having given his two cents, lowers his head and slowly brushes his hand forward along his hair, the way he does.

"The fort . . ." says Emily. Adam looks over.

"The fire vanished after burning down Fort Myrth, too," Emily continues. "It didn't spread to the forest. It died somehow. Remember it—"

"WHAT?!"

Everyone jumps and turns to the voice behind the horses. The horses look over their shoulders in annoyance.

Marcus is standing there in the yellowy grass with Mason, each leading a horse, and Mason holding the reins of a pack mule in his other hand. Marcus' mouth is hanging open, and he drops the hand holding the rein at his side.

"They came *back?!*"

"Oh, dear," Mason sings, turning his head down as if already embarrassed by the tantrum coming up.

Marcus drops the rein and storms over to the horses, who are stubbornly indifferent to his complaints.

"I just spent A HUNDRED AND *FIFTY* coins for the new horses and the flaming donkey! And *they* just decide to *show up!*"

"Really, Marcus, is now the most sensitive time to curse? He's not a 'flaming' mule in my opinion," Mason chides.

"YOU don't speak!" Marcus rounds on Mason. "YOU wouldn't let the old fool sell them for fifty! YOU had to say it was *immoral* of a price."

"Well, it was! She was ninety-three, for gods' sake!"

"Unbelievable," Marcus grumbles. For a man as big and aged as he is, he impressively jumps the fence with hot anger and thumps onto his feet. He doesn't even look at Adam, Cazimir, and Emily as he marches to the back door. "Now I have to sell them for *thirty a piece.* Watch me!"

He bangs the door shut behind him.

"Oh, don't you love him?" Mason asks of the others, who are watching blankly. "Amazing we're related. I'm sorry to see these fellows go so quickly." He indicates the horses and the mule. "I was really beginning to like Patches." He pats the short, grey donkey on the head.

Patches dodders over to the fence of his own accord, nuzzling the gate to be let in. Mason follows and obliges. Just like Marcus, he doesn't notice the pack horse among their returned party.

"Cazimir," Mason says.

Cazimir looks over.

"Galeduan lesson?" asks Mason.

Cazimir nods and joins Mason. The gate has been left open, and the horses promptly line up to trod into the stable and drink.

Adam and Emily exchange one last glance, but Adam pulls it away first, as if seeing the confused fear in her eyes is too much for him.

○ ~ ○ ~ ○

Emily is sitting on the porch of the inn, wrapped in a cloak, when Mason opens the door and steps down. The Galeduan lesson must be over.

"Emily," he says, "how are you feeling?"

"I'm doing okay."

"You haven't seen any of Welshire except this inn." His voice is sympathetic and scolding all at once. Emily sighs. "Why don't you come with me? I'm making one more stop at Shinead's before we leave. The apothecary."

Emily recognizes the woman the store is named

after—Shinead is a famous stonecarver healer from centuries ago who left behind many recipes. She sometimes wrote under the name "Softshadow," which may have been a tribal honorific. Emily purses her lips and considers Mason's invitation. She is perhaps getting too used to sitting down.

"Come." It is not an option now. Mason throws his head in the direction of the village's main street, and Emily rises.

Welshire is full of druids and druids-in-training. Here, they move about like businessmen, swiftly, even coldly at times. This disturbs the vision Emily has formed of the clergy being attentive, caring, peaceful. Perhaps she's forgotten they are human, with ambitions like any other. Flower baskets with red and yellow blossoms hang from every lightpost. The streets are brick. On one corner stands a statue of Euris the Beloved, the second emperor. He is depicted embracing a decrepit woman with no shoes. Several emperors after him donned his name to try to look as compassionate as he, especially during the Southern Rebellion. The attempts failed, and eventually the Council appointed its first Sille--Brachlian—to restore order to the Empire.

Over the thatched rooftops of stores and apartments,

at almost fifty feet tall, rises the Shrine—a marble obelisk where elder clerics train and ordain the druids. Welshire is a supporting outpost of this sacred university—every druid Emily sees whisking by her with armfuls of paper, holding a page up to their eyes, is either coming from class as an initiate or getting ready to teach it as an elder. Perhaps some are moving quicker because of news of the flame. There is considerable pressure on the priest class in the Empire, Emily hears, to do something about the fire. But with all these druids, it is no wonder Adam wanted to go here to search for his ex-druid contact.

"Mason," says Emily as she walks alongside him. "Can I ask you something?"

"Hmm?"

"You're Marcus' cousin, right?"

"Unfortunately." But Mason smiles. Emily thinks he loves Marcus beneath all the exasperation.

"You're not really in the Brotherhood, are you?"

Emily has suspected it for a long time. It is just too hard to imagine Mason committing any serious crime. Then again, she never imagined Adam doing so, either, and she knows he is hiding something terrible from her.

Mason breathes deeply. "You are a smart girl. Did you know that?"

"So you're not?"

"You could call me an honorary member."

"You just stay for Marcus."

"He needs me, yes."

"What for?" Emily suddenly realizes that question may be offensive—Mason is weak and more aged compared to Marcus.

"Tell me, Emily," says Mason, pulling open the glass door to the apothecary, "have you ever seen his light?"

"No . . ." says Emily, entering the shop beneath the tinkling bell.

Mason walks in front of her, not looking back, bowls of medicinal plants on either side of him. "Neither have I."

○ ~ ○ ~ ○

"One rule, Adam." Marcus slaps the wash rag back into a metal bucket at the foot of his bed. Everyone jams into his room at the inn, tight as it is. He turns from washing his face and pins a toxic green eye upon Adam. A din of blabber, laughs, and drinking is heard outside their door. "*We don't know each other.*"

"Right," says Adam.

"Let me clarify this again," says Marcus. "I don't think this is going to work. So I'm going to bed. As is

Ma—*shut up*, Mason, you're not getting the bed! It wasn't even bleeding that much!"

"I am already in the bed," Mason pats down the pillow and climbs in. There will be no sharing. A blanket lays on the floor.

Marcus rubs his eyes and waves a hand. "And Darvica can do whatever the hell he wants." Cazimir narrows an eye, unsure of the harsh comment. "But I recommend you guys split up. *Furthermore,* you've got *one shot. One* night to find your witchdoctor druid or whatever the hell you want out there. We leave *tomorrow.*"

A loud bang is heard as something metal is knocked over outside. Raucous, drunken laughter accompanies it. Everyone pauses in distaste. And then Marcus sets his eyes upon Adam again and smiles darkly.

"Have fun."

○ ~ ○ ~ ○

"You know there's a drinking age here, right?"

The young, scanty-dressed barwoman stops at Cazimir's table, and he looks up from his wine. Men jeer for more beers, but she holds up a rude hand towards them and waits with derogative impatience for Cazimir to speak. The cool outdoor air, blue-lit torches, and star-scattered dusk are suddenly replaced by her cold, mocking stare.

"Didn't your parents teach you how to speak?" she jibes. Cazimir may not know exactly what she is saying, but he catches her tone and his brow darkens, returning the glare straight towards her.

"Go help him," Adam mutters, head down, from the table he and Emily are sitting at. Emily looks over to Adam and sees his eyes are locked to the table, gesturing just barely with his head toward their lone-seated Darvic companion. Adam then clears his throat loudly and barks, "Beer! Come on!"

His façade is kept up flawlessly.

Emily sneaks from her seat and ducks to Cazimir's table, dodging spilled alcohol along the stone-paved floor with expertise. She takes an abrupt seat next to Cazimir, looking up to the barwoman in fake inquiry.

"Something wrong?" she asks.

The barwoman seizes Cazimir's wine glass and shakes her head. "Kids." She walks off.

Cazimir repels back in his seat, his mouth dropping.

Emily mimes swigging a drink and shakes her head. He seems slightly understanding, his eyes softening, but continues to look offended.

"Hold on," she says, holding up a finger and standing

once again. She goes over to the outdoor bar where a one-armed man tends to the patrons, using pegs and knobs to stack his mugs and spin them against a cleaning rag. He stops mid-spin at her arrival, curious, but obliges when she orders two non-alcoholic knuckleberry juices.

As she takes the mugs, she risks a glance over to Adam, who is already in deep conversation with a blond, short-haired, stubbly man. Has Adam found his candidate already?

The man has a pierced ear and silver rings on each finger, and neither he nor Adam look too happy, fixing condescending looks on the other each time they stop to let the other speak.

She returns and places one of the mugs in front of Cazimir, retaking her seat. He gives it an unenthusiastic stare and then lifts it to his lips, taking a drink, dully acceptant of its virgin taste. Emily sips her own, though it tastes too tart—the berries were picked too early. She continues watching Adam across the floor. His companion suddenly straightens and his look sharpens, as if Adam had said something alarming. Adam remains dark, his head low.

Unexpectedly, Cazimir sighs and rests his head in his hand, elbow on the table. Emily tears her eyes from Adam and studies the foreigner. He suddenly seems more human and familiar than he has since adopting his surly manner as a captive of the Brotherhood. His expression is thoughtful, pained almost, his heavy eyebrows furrowed. He senses her eyes on him and glances at her fleetingly.

A wave of sympathy engulfs her. He is alone here, with no family, in a foreign-speaking country. Surely he is afraid of the fire too.

She rests a warm hand on his forearm.

"Cazimir," she says.

He watches her with his curious, lightly cynical look, but it softens almost instantly.

"Emily," he mumbles in return. They sit in silence for a long moment, but she does not remove her hand from his forearm holding the mug on the table. Instead, she mimics him and rests her own head in her other hand.

"Emily . . ." Cazimir begins uncertainly, and she turns to him, surprised. He clears his throat the way he often does. "I…learn with Galeduan. Was wondering . . . will you . . ." He looks to her vulnerably, and then gestures back and forth with the hand she is not holding, as if to illustrate conversation. "Galeduan?"

Stunned, she smiles. "I promised I would," she

whispers, more to herself than him.

She straightens in her seat, takes his mug, and says, "Mug." He actually breathes a laugh, amused at her first choice of vocabulary.

"Mug," he repeats in good humor, nodding.

They spend the rest half hour identifying any object Emily can present, as Emily does not know any Darvic to aid in the lesson the way Mason does. She thoroughly enjoys herself teaching, and Cazimir seems to come out of his shell, smiling hesitantly more often, his eyes brighter than usual in the blue light of the braziers. Emily has the idea to ask the one-armed barman (who is becoming slightly irked by her constant reappearances) for paper and something to write with, to draw out more specific words.

She sketches an unmistakably old man with a beard and a young child to demonstrate the contrast, labeling them "old" and "young." This is more difficult for Cazimir, and he furrows his eyebrows, scrutinizing the page. She writes at the top of the page, "Too young—" she points to the picture of the young child "—to drink," and, patting the word "drink," mimes swigging a mug again.

Cazimir's eyes travel from the sentence to the

diagram and back. She repeats her demonstration, this time finishing with a point in his direction. It takes him a few seconds, and then he bows his head, smiling.

"Too young to drink. I am too young to drink."

He snorts derisively and shakes his head. "Not in Darvica." There is a tint of pride in his voice.

Emily steals another glance at Adam, and a growing worry sets in as the conversation continues between the two seated at Adam's table, several mugs pushed off to the side, although Adam seems as steady and lucid as ever. Perhaps he has had less alcohol than the other is inclined to believe. Her stomach twists, however, when Adam stands and cuts to the door of the inn, leaving the other seated stonily at the table as if waiting for him to return.

Cazimir, sensing her distraction, has reverted to sipping his knuckleberry juice quietly, looking around the patio. Their smiles have already melted away, and he hunkers forward at the table, shoulders squared and muscles stiff.

It is silent for a while, save the smooth pattern of Cazimir's breathing and the rustle of warm wind in the leaves. The moons radiate dreamy cloaks over the trees in the distance, and the crystalline, glassy stars reflect the patio's glowing blue lights like a chandelier. The man

Adam was talking to seems to have fallen asleep in his chair, and the barwoman is no longer being hounded by the men with their tankards, who have drooped their heads and sway back and forth with their arms around each other in drunken humming. It is beautiful here, Emily thinks . . . but she misses the moons reflected darkly in her Darson's Ford waters . . .

Then a cheer resounds from a group of men at the patio corner, swinging up their arms. Both Cazimir and Emily look over. Three musicians stand, bowing several times—one on the mandolin, the other, guitar, and last, a hand drum. The drummer rattles his hand over the mischievous drum and they strike a deep, ancient melody.

A smirk cuts through Cazimir's expression, and there is a shine in his eyes as some get up to dance. He bumps his large hand onto his knee only once. Emily cocks her head in amusement—he is the last person she expects to enjoy music.

"Is from Darvica," he says throatily. He makes a fist and bumps his knee once more in rhythm.

The effects of her recent dosage of painkillers seem to play with her mind. Impulse throbs at Emily, very similar to the one that entranced her to take Cazimir's hand yesterday.

She stands. He looks up confusedlyBut she holds out her hand to him. "Come on." Heat wafts through her, and she tosses her head to where the others had risen to dance. He stares at her hand, frozen.

She laughs. "Caz, come on! This painkiller's not going to last forever." She grabs his arm with both of her hands, heaving him forward. He stands and shuffles after her, stumbling.

His mind seems to have washed blank. She turns to him, and his nerves look close to terror as he takes her in his arms. She can hear him swallow. This dark, foreign warrior so adept with a weapon in his hands seems uncertain what to do with a person there instead. Emily steps closer to him, and as he is easily a foot taller than her, her head is near his chest.

Inhaling shakily, he draws her in.

Then he moves.

There is so much of him, so much mass and gravity and power, but he somehow leads her gently. The pulse that is his life trembles against her skin, unsure of her wound, her comfort, the music. But as the song continues, he seems to grow more comfortable. His lips jerk into a hesitant smile as he lifts his arm and allows her to twirl before pulling her back in. She comes against his chest, and a desire hits her that feels both strange and good. She wishes light would grow from his fingers there, right then.

When his eyes find hers next, their smiles vanish. Emily is suddenly aware of how clammy her palms are. How close he is to her. She raises a hand to his face and feels his rough shadow scape down her fingers. She has never felt that on a man. Her skin flushes red; the music filling them both, and those dark eyes delving into hers.

Slowly, he leans down, eyes steady on hers, as if asking permission.

A hand clasps his shoulder and he springs back.

The blond-haired man is behind them, piercing them both with intelligent yet stolid brown eyes.

Cazimir takes a heavy, protective step in front of Emily.

"Cazimir and Emily?" says the man.

Emily nods.

"Adam's waiting for us inside. Apparently, you have a fire to put out."

He slides his eyes to Cazimir again, mildly interested, and Cazimir tries to measure him before the man turns and makes his way to the inn.

Emily, blushing, slips past Cazimir and follows him.

Cazimir stands amongst the others for a moment, his expression growing dull as he watches her go. He brushes his hand over his hair slowly and thumps after them.

CHAPTER 15

"In." Adam jerks open a door in the back of the pub. The blond-haired man slides in without question.

Adam leans back on the open door with his hands pressed to the wood behind him and waits as Emily follows with unease in her stomach. Cazimir's creaking step is behind her. They are shrouded in darkness in some backroom of the bar, where the smell of stale alcohol ferments the warped floorboards. Cazimir's eye travels down an unlit hallway full of closed bedrooms as they pass into one of the vacant rooms.

There, the blond-haired man stands at a round table and rummages in a green leather satchel with urgency. He produces small, worn boxes and foggy jars, placing them rapidly on the surface. Cazimir glides to the wall on Emily's right, his dark eyes steady onto the smudgy jars.

Their glass is too muddled to make out their contents, but whatever they are look slimy and earthy.

Adam closes the door to this room and walks with swift steps to the table the way a surgeon approaches an awaiting patient. He places his hands on the surface, watching the man unload all that is in the green satchel.

"Adam?" Emily's voice is respectful, but there is a shake of force behind it.

Adam looks up, hands still on the table, as if he's only just remembered she is there.

"This is Galen Sakole. He's the druid we need."

Sakole makes no indication at these words. He digs his hand deep in the sack to assure it's entirely unloaded and drops it carelessly on the floor, turning to seize a wooden chair and slamming it down at the table, taking a seat.

"Sit," he says, and then glances at Cazimir with a sharp eye. "You'll have to stand."

There are only three chairs. But Cazimir, even if he had understood, is not listening. His eyes are still glued to the jars sitting on the table. He remains standing as Adam takes a seat with Emily.

Sakole pierces them each with a measuring gaze. The intake of drink makes his eyes a little glassy, but he is otherwise collected.

"First, I'm not a druid," he corrects, and by Adam's unperturbed response, Emily assumes this isn't news to him. "Not anymore." Sakole's voice is harsh. "Second, never call me Galen. And third, I know about the fire. It's why I was expelled."

"Why did knowing about fire get you expelled?" Emily asks.

Sakole and Adam exchange a look. Emily swallows. She becomes quiet.

"The fire," says Sakole, "the one you're after . . ."

"Sakole, spare her it," says Adam.

"Why did you ask me to collect her if you don't want her knowing?"

"Just . . ."

Sakole speaks to Emily. "Whoever lit it was not the only one curious about it."

But Emily does not react as Sakole seems to expect her to. "You mean you tried to produce it."

"I experimented."

Now Adam rubs his face hard. "*Just tell me if you have it.*" He looks up to Sakole with intense heat.

It seems a conflict is about to explode between the two of them. Sakole pauses and sizes Adam up—perhaps deciding whether to quip back, leave, or even fight.

Emily is just about to intervene when a new voice booms out.

"The *jars*."

They all turn to Cazimir, Sakole with derogatory surprise, as if a dog had barked. But Cazimir speaks with such vigor that his words quiver. The emotion behind it is hard to place. Anger?

"What . . . what you *have* in jars?" The question sounds so much like a demand that it stuns them, and Cazimir approaches the table.

The ex-druid swallows, unnerved. Now that the Darvican is closer, Sakole is very aware of how much taller Cazimir is than he. Sakole sits farther back in his seat. Cazimir's dark stubble and the longsword on his belt betray his youth and make him look all the more imposing.

Sakole recovers before answering, but his sharp defenses are deflated.

"Let's start over, and I'll show you what I have here."

Adam purses his lips begrudgingly but nods. Cazimir breathes heavily, seeming to gather enough patience to allow the ex-druid to go on.

Sakole sighs deeply, and suddenly, he is younger, less

aggressive.

"When I joined the druids, it was nearly against my wish. Marriage didn't seem likely—there were twice as many men as women in my village in the Glens. The Calder Glens, south of here."

"I've been," Adam chips. "Go on."

"I succumbed to what my parents wanted. But I was never cut out for clergy. I was rebellious. And during my studies at the Shrine, I took an interest in the one thing we shunned. The one thing we never spoke of."

"Fire," says Emily. The word feels like spice on her lips.

Sakole nods. "My mentors tried to divert my interests. But *why*? Why do we not *study it*? Why shouldn't we be prepared for its return if the worst should happen? My goal was to find a way to fight fire if it ever came back to us."

Coldness creeps through Emily's stomach as she recalls her own intense curiosity with fire. The way this man speaks of it now . . . it suddenly seems too unspeakable and immoral a topic to engage in her quiet thoughts before sleep.

"So . . . I experimented." Sakole wriggles his silver-ringed fingers over the tops of the bottles. Cazimir watches in some sort of dark trance. Emily knows he will only be understanding half of this story. "I didn't play with fire," Sakole continues. "But I took one step closer to it. What's the natural way fire can be created, as told in stories? The way without interference from man?"

There is silence. And then Adam grunts, "Lightning."

Sakole gives him a hazy look. "Lightning. Since fire's exile from the earth centuries ago, lightning never once ignited a flame when it struck. But I thought . . . what if it could? I still remember that night like it's happening now . . ."

Sakole describes the rain. Cold, icy rain lashing the tower of the Shrine like the tail of a dragon. He looked up at the dark clouds as the water hit his face. The Galeduan flag shook furiously on the metal pole above. Its fabric roared and it resembled a fish swimming away furiously from danger. Sakole worked quickly with his hands, producing a glass orb with metal fragments inside. Lightning flashed and turned the world white.

"Are you familiar with Cathair Mór?" Sakole asks Emily.

"I was born there."

"Then you'll have seen the light of fallen Emperors

floating around the city walls."

"I used to watch them from my bedroom window."

"What you can't see from that far are the transparent cases the Shrine provides for them. Each Emperor's light is enclosed in one of these spheres to protect them from a woman's touch. They are blessed by the high druids to preserve them forever."

And that glass sphere is what Sakole tied to the flagpole in a basket, what he raised into the lightning storm. When lightning struck the metal inside the sphere, he lowered it, sealed it, and blessed it with the same words as the high druids, words he was not yet authorized to speak.

"I captured not light, but the lightning's charge. I could feel static every time I opened it and inserted my hand into the sphere. My blessing worked."

"But what did you want to do with it?" says Emily.

"Purge it. I wanted to purge the lightning's energy with holy water—the way we believed water could extinguish fire. But not all water can destroy fire anymore. The Empire wouldn't have a crisis on its hands if it could, would they? Adam told me what Heckley said about everything." Sakole nods to Adam. "But Heckley didn't tell you the whole story. Or else he didn't know."

Emily clenches her fingers together, absorbed and yet seized with a sense of dread.

"Of *course* the Vicar sent someone to try and extinguish the flame," Sakole nearly hisses. "Right after it ate up Fort Myrth. He sent *himself.* With just a jug of druid-blessed water. Poured the whole thing over it. And it did *nothing.* In fact, it rose higher and scorched his face. Those are the whispers going around Welshire."

"I hope he lives," says Emily in a small voice. "The Vicar."

The others are quiet. Sakole finishes his story. "The church discovered my meddling with the lightning. They voided my ordination but kept me employed. Shoved me under the carpet and gave me another job. A . . . lesser job."

Milk seeps into Cazimir's skin when Sakole selects one of the jars and uncorks its lid. He pours the contents into his hand and reveals dry, brown sprigs of some kind of herb. It emits a smell so strong and sweet it is almost sickening. Emily leans in.

"You . . . cook?" she says.

Sakole looks up to her, dark but pitying. She gulps and realizes her question was entirely naïve. It seems best to remain silent again.

"I prepared the bodies for burial."

"That is . . .?" Cazimir begins, his low, throaty voice catching.

"Hartwurt," says Sakole.

And Cazimir stumbles back once, reaching out behind him. He brings a hand to his mouth and nose to block out the scent and leans his head down as if to steady a rocking stomach. Adam and Sakole watch apprehensively as he slowly backs farther away from the table. Emily stands for him, but she is too late.

Cazimir wrenches open the door and disappears into the hall.

They hear the floor splatter with vomit.

Sakole, the dried herbs still springy in his hand, glances at Emily and Adam for explanation, but his eyes are actually touched with sympathy. Adam tenses, and Emily finds herself edging towards the door.

His distress seems personal.

"Leave him," Adam whispers. Hesitantly, Sakole continues, but Emily proceeds to steal glances out the door into the dark hall.

"I'm an herbalist. I can make small remedies, but mostly, I prepared bodies for the grave. Dressed them in herbs. Wrapped them in cloaks. The sort of things the families shouldn't be asked to do themselves."

He tips the handful of herbs onto the table and gentle spreads them on the surface so they are thin. Emily thinks she recognizes some from the apothecary Mason took her to. There is everlily mixed with the hartwurt.

"Do you own the shop?" she says suddenly. "In downtown Welshire?" She hadn't seem him there.

"No," says Sakole, "but I come here to restock once a month and stay for a few days. Adam timed things right."

"So you're still welcome in Welshire, then, even though it's a druid's town?"

"Yes," he says. "Like I said, I'm still employed by the church as a traveling mortician. Sometimes as a diplomat. Basically their errand boy. Just no longer ordained."

Emily nods, assuring him she has no more questions for now. He goes on.

"But there's one thing good about the job I did dressing bodies," he says. The movement of the herbs onto the table has been systematic, a pattern of his routine, his eye lingering on their crisp sprigs. "I was able to travel. To the sick. To the villages. And encounter *spring* after *spring* of water. And the church didn't know . . . that I still had it . . ."

"Still had what?" says Emily.

"The sphere of lightning. But by then I thought it was impossible. I'd poured water into the sphere from every pool I could find, and still, the lightning bit my hand each time I inserted it. I thought there was no water in existence that could do it anymore. I was exhausted, ravaged with hunger, on my way back to the Shrine from visiting several villages, from burial after burial, when I stopped a merchant in a covered wagon. I bought a bag of nuts and a canteen of water from him. I ate the nuts first. Crunched them down by the handfuls. Then I drank deeply from the canteen . . . poured some in my hand to cool off . . ." Here he stops and shakes his head. "That's when I spun around on the path and looked back. I realized I never asked where the water had come from. But the merchant was long gone. And as only irony would have it . . . when I reached my wet hand into the sphere . . . no zap. I wetted the walls of the sphere with my fingers. The energy was gone."

"It worked," says Emily, astounded.

"But the water was *gone*," says Sakole. "I'd *drunk* it all."

His voice is far too calm and vacant of anger to diminish Emily's burning hope.

"Almost all . . ."

He opens one of the battered wooden boxes, reaches in, and stops to give Adam a piercing look. Adam leans forward, and Emily can see the desperate pallor of his skin.

A tiny, crystalline glass bottle emerges in Sakole's hand and glistens off light. He keeps his eyes steady on Adam as if to not miss a second of his reaction.

Adam leans back in his chair, his mouth falling open just slightly. The smallest nod crosses Sakole's features.

"You have it," Adam whispers. He is frozen in shock.

Sakole whispers back, quieter than the breeze in the black trees Emily once lay under with Adam, far away from this room.

"I have it."

CHAPTER 16

The tiny vial sparkles as Adam sets it in the middle of the table. It catches a glisten of the pale, early sun spilling in through the open door of the inn.

Marcus leans forward, the skepticism already melting off his face, transformed into shrewd awe.

"That's it?" he says. "How did—I thought the man told you he'd drunk the canteen?"

"He scraped up the last drops in the bottle. Salvaged this much," Adam grumbles.

"Oh, good," Marcus scoffs. "Because if that thing came out yellow—"

"Oh, for heaven's sake, Marcus," says Mason, rolling up pieces of clothing on his knee in tight cylinders so they'll fit in his pack.

Emily watches them in silence, but she is

temperamental as she spears the carrot on her plate with a satisfying crunch. She and Adam had been in devout disagreement since last night.

When Sakole had briskly packed his things to leave the room and pretend their meeting never happened, Adam had grabbed his arm.

"Sakole," he had said, the doubt already written in his eyes. "When we get to the flame, if we need a druid, a druid to perform a ritual—"

But Sakole had already shaken his head and grabbed the arm Adam held him with—not abrasively, but with respect.

"I can't," he said. "I shouldn't have even given you this water. I resigned the Druidry to protect my life, and I have just endangered it again."

The cult responsible for the fire would not want the man who discovered its possible antidote alive. Sakole made for the door, then hesitated. He looked up at Adam. "Sing forgotten words, Adam." A beat. "Be brave."

Adam stood there and let Sakole slip past him, out into the hall. Sakole walked with cool resolve back out to the patio bar.

Adam had glanced at Emily, and that was when the disagreement began.

Emily believed Marcus should not be shown this ounce of water that had the possibility—not the certainty—of being the only known liquid that could extinguish the fire. They had already come to the conclusion together that Marcus may have alternate motives.

But Adam disagreed. He believed that the water would be the turning point for Marcus. If Marcus was on their side, he would lead them with faith and determination at the sight of it. If he was against them, he would try to steal it, or otherwise make his motives known another way—and that information, too, would be vital. Marcus had defended them with his life so far, had not harmed them in their sleep, Adam had argued. He deserved this much.

Adam is not the better negotiator than Emily. He is soft and often gives in. Like in the church, allowing the holy water to drizzle down him. He allows, but does not move.

It is because of this that Emily is so bitter. If Adam had won this argument with her, it wasn't because he outmatched her—it was because she must have agreed with him in some tiny way. Agreed with giving Marcus the benefit. And for that, she is morose.

Cazimir sits next to her as Marcus takes the tiny bottle in his un-gauntleted hand, twirling it between his thumb and forefinger. In a way, she feels the most allegiance to Cazimir today. She is mad at everyone else, but Cazimir is quiet and docile as he watches the sun rise over the treetops through the window.

He, too, had a lot to think about since last night. Emily never discovered why Cazimir had bolted for the door at the sight and smell of Sakole's herbs, but when she left with Adam, he had gone already.

An empty bucket had been toppled on the floor, and water washed away most of his bile. It appeared he had attempted to clean it before disappearing.

"All right, Brother Adam," Marcus says at length, as if giving into approval at Adam's decision to meet with the ex-druid. "But this will do nothing when we get to the fire. It's a mere drop. What are you proposing we do? Try and find where this came from?" He sets the vial in the center of the table again for them all to examine.

"I'm not proposing anything, Marc. I don't know where we'd even begin."

"But we know we must keep moving," Mason cuts in, as if staving off an argument. "I'll get the rest of our things from inside."

They all rise and Marcus slaps down another handful of coins for their breakfast.

"Mason, I'll get the horses. Meet me out back."

Adam, Emily, and Cazimir follow Marcus.

"I *can't* believe no one bought the burning mule." Marcus curses the donkey as he untethers his strong, black horse—Orien—from the stable. He'd yet again paid off the stableman, who begrudgingly agreed to stable their horses out back. How rich could Marcus be? Or did Captain Marley give him money also?

Emily tries to hide a small smile at Marcus' frustration—the first she's allowed all morning—as she gently secures Copenhagen's saddle. Patches the Donkey lifts his lips and shows off his teeth at Marcus, looking blissful at being housed under the luxuriously shady awning.

"I'll pick Patches up when this is all done with," says Emily. "He can work for the stableman in the meantime."

Marcus snorts. "Patches. Bet you anything Mason named him that."

Cazimir and Adam climb into their saddles, and Emily steps her foot into the stirrup. She winces from her wound. The price of that dance with Cazimir. She will need to be careful while riding to avoid damaging her stitches.

The back door of the inn bursts open.

"Our room!" Mason pants, his arms full of items that must have been spilled from their bags. Marcus turns to him, removing his foot from the stirrup. "It was ravaged, Marcus! Someone's been in our room and destroyed it."

Marcus is silent for too long. His eyes narrow. But he seems curious more than angry.

Emily's heart is pounding, and she steals a glance at Adam. The news is still too early, still registering on his face, to make out his reaction.

"Someone knows what we're doing here," Mason breathes. He looks over his shoulder. "Someone is following us."

Adam pats his pocket where the vial of water is and looks up. "This," he whispers to Emily. "They were looking for it."

"Let's go," Marcus rumbles, and he resumes his swing onto Orien.

"W—what?" says Mason, stunned.

"I said *let's go*."

Marcus pulls roughly on his rein and leads his horse out of the gate.

○ ~ ○ ~ ○

They follow Marcus out of Welshire, farther towards the edge of the Empire—farther towards the flame. He stays well ahead of the others and does not look back.

When Emily pulls Copenhagen up to Adam, he gives her a long, meaningful look. Words don't need to be spoken to convey each other's fear of being followed.

There is true unrest in Mason's almond-shaped eyes as he rides his mare, Precious, alongside them, looking straight ahead. He seems shaken up, so Emily does not ask.

Cazimir is in gloomy thought, glancing around their surroundings often.

It is only when Mason clears his throat and calls out, "Cazimir. Lesson?" that Cazimir jolts back to reality and joins Mason's side, slightly surprised, so they can embark on another Galeduan lesson. Emily guesses Mason offered the session as a distraction for himself more than anything.

So although Emily is shocked when, a half hour later, Marcus calls her to the front with him, she wonders if it is for a similar reason. Adam and she share a cynical look, but he tosses his head forward encouragingly.

"Did you need me?" Emily says.

Marcus looks ahead. "You were a history teacher,

correct?"

"Yeah." Emily is cautious. "Sort of."

"What sort of things would you ask your students?"

Emily blinks. She has no idea where Marcus is going with this. But she draws an honest answer. "I'd ask them to tell me their favorite emperor. And why."

Now Marcus barks an abrupt laugh. He twirls his rein in his metal gauntlet. "And what would they say? Accalon?"

"No," says Emily. "Most say Myrril. He's easy to remember. They like the legends surrounding him, even if they're mostly untrue. They're disappointed when I tell them the 'giants' he supposedly banished were likely Darvicans."

"Mmm." Marcus nods. Emily feels something weird—Marcus is almost bearable to talk to, really. So she keeps going.

"And they like the mystery of no one knowing what the real shade of blue his light was. Too many sources disagree. We'll never know."

Marcus is still listening and looking ahead. He chews his lip.

"So," Emily says gently. "Who is your favorite emperor?"

There is a long pause. It's clear Marcus did not expect the question to actually turn to him. He meets her eyes now and then looks ahead again. Emily thinks he will insult the Braeliuses. Make a snide remark.

"My favorite is Rhenvar."

Emily sways with Copenhagen's rhythm as she casts her mind to Rhenvar's chapters.

Rhenvar. The 25th emperor. He is the only emperor to ever stand up for the Brotherhood cult, punishing Fellvren when the Fellvians massacred a village they believed harbored Brotherhood fire-worshippers. His taking of the throne was a surprise—it should have belonged to his older brother, but Rhenvar possessed the rare Braelian "Midnight Light"—a blue light so dark it looked black, and its appearance mandated his rule.

"He was a character." Emily can think of many other stories surrounding Rhenvar.

Marcus just grunts. A beat follows.

"Go take care of Adam now," says Marcus.

"Of Adam?" says Emily.

"Good talk." He flicks his rein and rides forward, leaving Emily in his wake again.

Dusk falls quickly. The sky is periwinkle above the seemingly never-ending tree line to their left, pushing dots of stars farther into the heavens. Narun is full—a bright, orangey-yellow. Calsepheus hangs next to it.

Harvest moon. So, summer really is ending.

Marcus says nothing as he unloads Hopskip and sets to work constructing a tent.

Adam sets one up for Emily and him—a simple structure of poles to drape over with tarp. There is no door; just an opening, like a small cave.

Marcus makes his large enough for only one, forcing Mason to sigh yet again as he must erect his own.

Cazimir builds shelter farthest from them, closest to the trees. He works in silent concentration, but his hands seem experienced.

"You think this is a good idea? Spreading out like this?" Emily asks at last. She is the first to speak to Marcus since their departure. He snaps up to her from tying a knot on his shelter.

"I think it's a fantastic idea."

"What if someone gets attacked again?" She realizes this is the first night returning to the wild since their attack. The deep trees suddenly frighten her. They have never done that before.

"If they have another of those fire arrows, you can guarantee is won't spread to other tents. So yes. Fantastic idea." He throws down the rope, which would not maintain a firm knot. "And if they do come back, it'll be through the trees again."

He stops, and then smiles, looking up at her.

"You're worried about Darvica, aren't you?"

Emily glances at Cazimir, who has completed his small tent and switched to cleaning his longsword, standing with its point in the ground and running a cloth down it. Even as she does this, he looks up at them, as if surveying what they are up to now. His eyes find hers, but they look back at the sword swiftly, dully.

"Darvica can handle himself." Marcus snorts.

"What's your plan, Marc?" Adam asks abruptly.

"Stalling," Marcus replies.

Adam misses a beat. "Stalling for what?" he says.

"Stalling for me to think of a new plan. I want to incorporate that water into this plan somehow." He nods at Adam's pocket, and Adam narrows an eye, evaluating him. "So, for now, we do as we were told. Keep up the appearance of moving towards the flame. But we'll take our sweet time. Until I can think of something."

"If you have any ideas, let us know," Mason chimes in, despairing. It is the first time he has really aligned himself with Marcus.

Adam and Emily exchange a look. They agree on one thing. Marcus has won their approval.

So far.

Deep night sets in as Adam and Emily sit under the tent. Ahead, the stars and red, gold, and green planets shine steady against the purplish-blue sky. Emily gazes at them and purses her lips.

Stars. Adam. His purplish light.

Some things can stay the same, even in chaos.

Adam is entranced by a piece of wood he is whittling into his patterns and knots. It is therapeutic for him.

"Adam," she says.

He doesn't look up from carving. "Hm?"

"I'm going to check on Cazimir."

He looks up from carving.

"Check on . . . Cazimir," he repeats, dumbfounded.

"He's alone. By the trees. I just want to check on him."

Adam studies her. "Okay . . ." he says slowly and cautiously. "Don't be long, all right? I don't like you near there."

"I don't like him near there, either." Emily stands. "I'll be right back."

Adam shaves off a tiny piece of wood, but he's not

looking at it as she ducks out of the tent.

The air is cooler outside of the shelter's embrace. She tries to keep up her courage and determination as she walks carefully towards Cazimir's tent.

She is only being a good friend. Going to check on him. He saved her life, after all. He deserves to know how grateful she is.

He appears sooner than anticipated. He is standing outside his shelter, turning the sword with one hand with its point still in the grass, inspecting for any tarnish.

She stops mid-track as he raises his head to her and clamps the handle of the longsword so it stops spinning.

"Emily," he says, although he is stiff and almost wary.

"Cazimir," she replies in their usual one-word greeting. He watches her with mingled suspicion and tenderness as she approaches him.

"Are . . . do you need . . .?" Cazimir asks, stumbling through the Galeduan.

"No," she says, shaking her head. "I just wanted to . . . check on you."

He continues to watch her, not fully understanding.

"And now that I know you're okay, I'm just going to . . ." She steps back to leave.

He pauses for a moment and, just as she turns, says,

"Wait."

She looks back at him.

Standing with his feet far apart, Cazimir holds his hand out over a pit of rocks, and she stares at him now, entranced. A primitive excitement tightens her body, for she knows what he will do at last. What she has been waiting for him to do.

She had imagined, with some disappointment, that his light would be some kind of slate blue to match the cold of Darvica. And that is why, when a rich, magnificent teal—greenish blue, and unbelievably bright—grows from his hand, she is mesmerized. Her breath tumbles. Cazimir catches it, glancing at her. But is there hidden pleasure behind his eyes as well? Some sort of virile pride?

The light is brighter than any she's seen—it floods color onto the ground, onto her clothes, even yards away, and into the trees. He sends the blue orb floating down to the rocks, where it dances and slides over the lightpit, illuminating it in brilliant aquamarine.

"Stay," he says. He looks at her pointedly, as if measuring what she will do, and lowers himself to sit on the tree stump near the lightpit.

Heat flushes her body, but she can't stop herself.

She joins him, sitting across from him in the grass.

He reaches his hand into the glowing light and extracts an orb. It clings to his fingers and he plays with its orbit.

God, she loves when they do that.

She speaks softly, as if to dispel such thought.

"You don't have any family, do you?"

He closes his hands over the light and looks to her shrewdly.

"What?" she says.

"Women," he mumbles quietly. "Don't know . . . what is word . . . but always must have . . . sop story."

"Sob story?" Emily corrects.

He sighs deeply.

She twitches, taken off-guard and yet amused by the comment. "That's coming from Mr. Dark Past over here. You're alone, Caz. It's expected for me to wonder."

Cazimir swallows, and she wonders if he understood her entirely. He pauses for a moment, staring at the light in his hand, and then lifts his eyes to her. His light reflected in them overwhelms her.

"You stop asking if I tell you?"

She laughs at his ultimatum. "That seems logical."

But Cazimir doesn't smile. He continues to twirl the light that shimmers like opal and slides through his fingers, and she watches his rough hands with something more than interest.

"What you want to know?" he says.

She studies him, pulling her eyes from his hands with extreme willpower. "I want to know why you left your country. You walked forty miles. What were you running from?"

He shifts his lower jaw. The blue light is closed in his hand again and illuminates the skin between his fingers. His wrists tense up.

"Were . . .how you say . . . visit? Visiting? Friends. In Kroikcher. When we hear." He circles a finger from his ear to the horizon. He must be referring to the gongs.

"The gongs," Emily supplies.

"Then . . ." He makes an exploding gesture with his hands now. He's a good mime. "People. Fear." He smashes his hand into his palm to indicate violence. "In Darvica. We run. Think Galeduen safer."

He presses on just as Emily opens her mouth. "We were . . ." He brings his fists together and parts them again.

"Separated," Emily says softly.

"From parents." He nods. "Attacked by . . . what is word . . ."

"Bandits? Mercenaries?"

He nods. "But we agree to . . . come here. So, when . . . *separated—*" he looks at her to assure he's pronouncing the new word correctly "—I come here anyway. Walked. Hoping to meet them. At Carrick. Do not know where they are."

He pauses and looks down. The blue glow in his hand gently lights his lashes and face. "I was coward to leave them. Is that enough?" Cazimir's voice is throaty and thick.

"Cazimir . . ." Emily says, so that he has to lift his eyes to her. They are sadly defiant, as if daring her to say something against him, but she simply stares at him with sympathy. "You're not a coward."

He rumbles deeply, a growl almost.

"You're not," she repeats firmly. "Your parents were brave, too. And . . ." She is grateful for the deep night, or else he would have seen her blush. "And I'm grateful to them." She swallows. ". . . They led you to me."

He watches her for a long moment, the blue orb beginning a slow, calming rotation around his wrist now. She can't bring herself to hold his gaze, and she scratches the side of her neck and looks into the glowing rocks in the pit.

Then she hears his throaty whisper.

"I am grateful, too."

Emily shivers. A long pause follows.

"Do you want me to get rid of that for you?" says Emily at last, nodding towards the light revolving around his hand. She really doesn't want his gorgeous light to go, but she remembers how he enjoyed watching her do that . . .

He grunts and holds out his hand.

This never used to make her nervous before. It does now. She raises her own hand over it and the blue light slowly shrinks, until it is only a speck in the air, as if the atmosphere is sucking it through.

It vanishes.

Cazimir smiles smugly at her.

"I love when you do that . . ."

She actually chuckles to herself, remembering the same feeling she had towards his playing with the light. Another impulse strikes her. She sees herself slowly reaching down to grasp Cazimir's strong, veined hand.

But when she touches it, they both look down.

An odd buzz pulses between them. Cazimir glances

fleetingly at her, and neither move their hands.

The buzz continues—a prickling sensation. Cazimir clears his throat loudly, nervous, but Emily is watching with zealous interest.

"Caz . . ." she says. "Look."

She pulls back her hand by just centimeters so that it is hovering over his own upturned one.

Miniscule blue sparks burst silently between their fingertips. Cazimir inhales deep breath as if to say something, but she shakes her head, stopping him.

At the very same time he is creating the light, she is extinguishing it. The result is swift, bluish sparks between their hands. A smile flickers over his face and he watches it, bewildered.

And then he sets his eyes on her again. There is something deeper that he cannot mask as he watches her; something forceful, more primitive.

She catches it and lowers her hand, blushing deeper.

"I better go, Caz," she murmurs.

His look becomes questioning again as she stands. It is funny, she thinks, that he speaks some Galeduan now, but can still display that confused, studying look, like he is trying to understand something. Maybe she is a foreign language to him, too.

“Goodnight,” she offers shyly.

His eyes soften, and he simply looks sad to see her go.

“Goodnight,” he mumbles. It is the first time he has ever said so to her, and she can’t help but smile.

But as she leaves him behind, a pang of regret stabs her.

She had forgotten to ask him what *ahm cara* means.

CHAPTER 17

"You okay? You look kind of red."

Adam sets down the stick he was shaving. He doesn't seem to have made any progress since Emily's departure.

She hesitates at the tent's opening.

"Have you been waiting for me?"

Adam pauses.

"Yeah." He sounds as if this should be obvious.

"I'm fine." Emily ducks in and sits on the dewy grass. They'd used all their cloth for the tent coverings and blankets for draping over them, not under them. Still, it is much warmer inside the shelter. She reels in her sack and rummages for one of the books—the one she had shown to Cazimir so he could point to his country.

Adam watches her carefully. "Was Cazimir all right?" His question is innocent, genuinely interested.

"He seemed okay," she answers, turning the pages of the history book to find the map again. All that Cazimir had said—about riots in his country, the separation from his parents, and his guilt—seems like something personal to the two of them. She doesn't share this with Adam, but she does say, "How do you think the other provinces are reacting to the fire?"

Adam sighs. His eyes are serious as he studies a blade of grass.

"I've heard bad. The most civil place to be is here—and even we're starting to get unstable. I know Darvica is collapsing. Their people are so self-reliant that the Rovercaul—their chief-lord, literally 'Over-rock'—has almost no control over them. So, rioting and panic—they can't do anything to stop that."

He pauses, deep in thought. "Emperor Accalon used to be very paranoid about Darvica. The Darvicans are extremely strong people. He thought they could overthrow him. And they probably could. But he didn't realize that just because they're strong doesn't make them hostile. Darvica is tough, rugged, but not into politics. Mountains and mining. And a few local customs. That's all they care about." Adam actually laughs good-naturedly as another thought hits him. "Their Rovercaul is bathing in gold and grease, but the people don't give a damn. They're just as happy left alone in their hometowns."

As Adam says this, Emily studies the map and the Calamus Mountains, which, north of their country, arc to the east and then south, embracing Darvica. She gives a tentative smile.

"And how do you know all that?"

Adam shrugs. "The Empire trains their soldiers well."

There's an awkward pause, as they both know Adam never explained his exile from the military like he had indicated he would. He clears his throat to dispel the tension.

"As for the other province . . . Fellvren—"

Emily's eyes jump to Fellvren on the map, the province northwest of Galeduen and to the left of Asht Vendar, whose border is marked by the Misty River. Fellvren dissolves into dozens of little islands at the far edge.

"—Fellvren is proud and detached as always, as far as I know. With the Vicar coming from the top corner of the place, on one of those islands, I think they're clinging to confidence that he'll represent their 'wisdom' appropriately."

Adam leans back against the tent pole, twiddling his thumbs.

"Those merchants trying to sell Cazimir," says Emily, "they were from Asht Vendar, right?"

"Somehow. If the Emperor discovered them in our borders, we could have a third Sunlight War."

Adam stops twiddling his thumbs. The stony look he adopts reminds Emily of how terrible that would be.

"So do you think the Emperor ought to be more worried about Darvica than Asht Vendar?" asks Emily.

"I think he should be worried about Fellvren. It's ethnically tied to Asht Vendar. It has less association with us than Darvica. Its islands are more isolated from us, care less about our relationship. I could see it realizing it's got more in common with Asht Vendar and jumping ship. A secession war would be ugly." Adam sighs, contemplating. "But I think the Emperor should worry about his people and this fire most of all. Not what the provinces or the Vendari are thinking. Accalon has been better than some previous emperors, at least."

Emily was born long after the current Emperor took the throne. But she knows from history—from this book, actually— that the bloodline of emperors hasn't been broken since the dawn of the Empire's reign. And Emperor Accalon is celebrated for signing the only treaty with Asht Vendar in the Empire's history after ending the Sunlight Wars . . . which, of course, he started.

Adam chews his lip as he examines the book in her hands.

"You read about the rulers in the stonecarver days yet?"

"Not there yet," says Emily with her chin in her hand, eating up words on the page. Only the last stonecarver ruler is remembered by name: Gennan, slain by Myrril. Adam nods.

"They were called High Kings. Before the Empire, before the banishment of fire. We don't know a lot about them. Only that they left a lot of themselves behind. The roots of language. The stone Guardians."

She sets down the book. Her usual fascination is absent tonight. The true questions latching in her mind are ones she knows these pages cannot answer.

"Adam . . ." she begins, and by the tone of her voice, he tenses, knowing what's coming. "You need to tell me why we're here. Why are you in the Brotherhood?"

He looks at her for a long while, and she can see the dark memories wave through his eyes. He sighs and averts his gaze, speaking with nerves.

"After my tour in Asht Vendar, I was stationed at Fort Pull. On the Darvic border. Emperor Accalon feared Darvica would ally with the Vendari. So he fortified the fort. We were forbidden to work with Darvicans. To have anything to do with them."

A pause.

"I needed the money so badly, Emily." He suddenly drops his face into his hands and clutches it with his fingers.

She wants to feel sympathy, to feel the impulse to comfort him. But she doesn't. Instead, she watches with growing horror. What could money have driven him to do?

"Oh, this is supposed to be touching, isn't it?" Marcus appears around the curtain of the tent, looking honestly surprised at the scene he'd walked in on. But a glint of that cruel amusement is in his eyes as well.

"Get out of here, Marc!" Adam bellows, and the force behind it makes even Emily jump.

"No."

Mason follows his little cousin inside their tent. "I'm sorry, Adam," says Mason. "I told him it could wait until morning."

"Did Emily hurt your feelings or something?"

Adam leaps to his feet and punches Marcus across the jaw.

Marcus' head is thrown to the side. He retaliates instantly, seizing Adam's shoulder to pull him in for a punch of his own.

Emily is ordering them to stop as she draws her knife, but Mason steps in, pulling the two apart. They glare at each other, Adam panting heavily and Marcus' teeth tainted red with blood.

"*Barbaric!*" Mason scolds.

"Brother Adam's acting like a man," says Marcus, spitting into the grass. "Write down the date, Mason."

Adam is shaking, but he doesn't speak.

"Shut up, Marcus," Emily says, sheathing her knife.

"You even got little girls defending you now," says Marcus, his piercing green eyes impaling hers.

"And you've got little girls insulting you," says Emily.

"Enough! *All* of you," says Mason.

Adam sits, still juiced on adrenaline.

"Now that the love's flowing," Marcus begins, "we thought we'd drop by and discuss our plan. You still have that vial, *Brother*?" Marcus asks of Adam.

"I have it," Adam growls.

"Right," Mason interjects, but his voice is challenging. "Marcus, I think I'll explain this."

Marcus spreads his arm invitingly. "Cousin."

"Marcus and I *have* been thinking about this water," says Mason. "Frankly, I'm still baffled the ex-druid didn't charge you anything for it. Did he?"

"He wouldn't," says Adam. "He may be defrocked, but he's got a druid's morals. He's gotten me out of some other tangles before, too, and never sent those favors back to haunt me."

"All very well," says Mason, "But the fact is, we need to find more of this water. And Marcus and I can only think of one place it could have come from."

"Where?" says Emily, before she can stop herself.

"The sea," says Mason. "The 'holiest entity.'" He quotes a common adage of the druids—although Druid Parr used Darson's Ford water in his church's basin, most churches in Galeduen use seawater.

"No," Adam says flatly. "It's not from the sea."

"He drank it." Emily supports Adam. "It couldn't have been saltwater."

Mason and Marcus deflate. Marcus gives Mason a *Now what?* look. Mason rubs his chin. "I didn't realize he drank from it." There is silence.

"Unless . . ." says Emily. Everyone looks at her. "Unless he got the water at just the right time of year."

"What do you mean?" says Mason.

"The Arluian Sea"—and now Emily's voice gets excited, for she knows she's figuring this out before their eyes—"it's—"

"Fresh once a year," says Adam, looking up.

"Exactly!"

"You genius," Adam breathes.

She explains to them the facts she's read about—Mt. Vestevor melting, the moons pulling back the tides . . .

"She's right," says Mason, mouth ajar.

"And do you know the other name for the Arluian Sea?" says Emily. She goes on when they don't reply. "The Sea of Mercy. From the flood stories. This is it. The water *has* to be it."

"It would make sense," says Marcus. "Since the druid tried dozens of other ponds and lakes, the reason the water he found worked was because it came from the sea."

"So, you think being from a *sea* and not an inland body of water has something to do with it," Adam clarifies.

"Inland doesn't matter," says Emily. "We can get the water from the Calder Glens—the sea floods the rivers there. It's inland—closer than us having to go all the way to the shore—but it'll be the same water."

"So just as long as it's *from* the sea," Adam amends.

"You know what the church always says," Marcus cuts in gruffly. "The seas and oceans are the holiest entities."

No, Emily thinks, as the dream of Adam being swept off his feet by the rushing wave returns to her. *How can it be?*

But still . . . hadn't the seawater fizzled out the flames in her dreams as well?

"And *you* believe that?" Emily asks, probing Marcus the way that only she can.

Marcus scoffs. "I don't know if I believe in any of it. I doubt there's even a god to spin these stories together. But I don't got a damn thing better to try."

She stares at him. But Mason interjects before she can pursue it. "The sea is so far from the flame—no one's had a chance to test seawater on the fire. But obviously, someone's tested it on *lightning*. And it worked."

"This is our only shot," says Emily.

"Okay," says Adam. He is weary, as if wanting

nothing more than to put this discussion to an end.

"So, it's settled." Marcus stands. "We're heading for the sea now. Not the flame."

"What about Captain Marley? What if he finds out we're taking a detour?" asks Emily.

"Then you sweet talk that other guard, Wes, for us. Didn't he tell you to find him if you needed anything? Back at the Ford?"

Emily didn't think Marcus saw that. She reddens.

"Wes was escorting Scott to his parents."

"Scott." Marcus laughs. He and Mason make to leave, both with tired, sagging shoulders.

"What about Scott?" Emily blurts at the last second.

Marcus stops, his back to her. "Scott is either a coward running for his life, or he's with the cult that started this whole thing." He doesn't move though, because he knows Emily will ask him more.

"Which do you believe?" she finally says, her voice weaker than she'd hoped.

Marcus smiles. But she, of course, doesn't catch it.

"Actually," he says, "both."

○ ~ ○ ~ ○

Emily lies in the grass, on her side, hours later, still unable to sleep. A blanket has been laid over her, and she can hear Adam scrape away at that piece of wood. He will not sleep either.

"Adam," she sighs, although she is certain he could not have heard it. Her eyes are not even open, and the grass had brushed her lips as she mumbled it.

But he does hear. He is by her side instantly. He lays the stick on the ground, just inches from her, as he kneels to see if she is okay.

"What's wrong?" he whispers back, worried, gentle.

The thoughts that had kept her awake—they were not of flames and tidal waves. But of a simple comment. One she is sure no one else had given a second thought to.

"Marcus said something," she mumbles, for sleep is still tugging desperately at her.

"What is it?" says Adam, stroking her hair.

The strong scent of the grass sends a chill through her.

"There's no god."

His hand stops its stroke, surprised and thoughtful at the same time.

The hesitance is longer than she'd hoped for, but she can't tell whether it is doubt or tender curiosity that keeps him silent.

And then he whispers to her, leaning down to kiss the top of her head.

"There's a god," he says. "Somewhere. I promise."

Adam's promises she can trust.

CHAPTER 18

Emily approaches Cazimir's tent, but she doesn't pay it much mind because she is sure he must be asleep. Grey creeps through the black branches of the trees, and dawn hasn't broken. No one is awake yet. This far west, she should find suckleberry—a white berry that grows in clusters similar to grapes, shaped like elongated ovals. The way they resemble miniature udders earned it its name. Emily has never seen one in person. Her hand is on the honey-wooded hilt of her knife, her thumb rubbing over the ripples on the wood.

Could this wood really have been the same tree as the Vicar's staff?

Her history book says little about the Vicar and even littler of his staff. But she does know from class and private reading that the sacred stick has been passed from

Vicar to Vicar for centuries. It is said to be a branch taken from the very first tree ever to adopt the blue light as it would fire—allowing the blue orb to cling to it as a torch.

How or where such a tree could be found, she hasn't a clue. Which is why she doubts the knife's authenticity. But still . . . it is a nice thought. And a nice gesture of the blacksmith.

She halts when she hears rustling in the brush.

Cazimir emerges from the woods ahead of her. He is dressed in his dark blue shirt that is loose enough to reveal a scar on his collarbone. That same leather band is around his left wrist, and he does his habitual, slow brushing of his hair once before catching her appearance.

He stops. It is clear he is surprised to see her, both of them up so early. She must be wearing the same gentle, surprised expression because he softens into a small smile.

Emily can see rather than hear him clear his throat as he hangs his head and walks to her.

"You are . . . up," he says.

"So are you," she says.

"Could not sleep." He grumbles and shoots a glance at his tent. "Am . . ." He hesitates for a long while, the muscles of his face giving tiny movements of frustration. Then he gives a huff and just jerks his head in its direction. "Come."

The knife gives a sharp ring as she sheathes it and follows him to his shelter. The crisp early-autumn air is what's responsible for her chill. Nothing else.

There is a bucket of water at his camp, and she is alarmed at his teal light still reflecting on the surface. She looks at the lightpit still aglow.

"I should have taken care of that for you last night."

He looks over questioningly and she indicates the lightpit. He grunts and nods.

"You left," he says.

She approaches the lightpit, kneels, and extinguishes the light for him as he ducks into his open tent. Disappointment sinks through Emily as she straightens. Usually, Cazimir is enthralled with her hands when she does that.

When he returns, he places a wooden bowl in her hand as she rises.

He does not speak, but reaches into his pocket and produces a handful of suckleberries. She gasps. His dark eyes glance into hers, and he tips the berries into the bowl. They roll off his palm.

She can feel herself blush, looking into the bowl.

Cazimir turns away before she can say anything. He

dips his hands into the bucket of water and bows his head, splashing his hair and running his hands down his face.

She eats one berry at a time as he dries himself with a rag and musses his black hair. This is her first time tasting them. They have less flavor than she expected—a gentle burst of juice, warm from Cazimir's hand, and a hint of milky richness. She can't quite call it sweet. They would not make good pies, but maybe mixed into a bread . . .

A line of gold shimmers on the horizon, brightening the grey.

"Cazimir," Emily says softly, swallowing the last bit of fruit.

"Emily."

Her heart swells when he does that.

"Where did you find these?" She lifts the bowl. "The berries?"

"In woods."

"Can you take me?"

Her heart pounds as she says this, and she feels a rush of guilt for not admitting to herself that it is him she wants, not the berries. She wants to preserve this time when it is just them, and with the pink and canary streaks in the east, retreating into the woods will be the only way that is possible.

He understands. She can see something blend in his eyes, something of mingled hope and restraint. His voice is husky. "You want . . .?"

She nods, setting down the bowl. "Take me. Just for a little. Maybe we can bring back some for the others to eat."

He watches her for a beat. Then a smile tugs at the corner of his lips.

○ ~ ○ ~ ○

"Your time . . ."

"Turn," chuckles Emily.

"Your turn," Cazimir amends. His voice is hoarse and soft as he kneels at the trunk of the tree-sized berry vine, doing something between spotting her and admiring her. She is in the vine's branches, balancing herself to reach a cluster as Cazimir looks up at her steadily.

They had begun a game of questions, at Emily's request. Cazimir had given her that cynical look of his when she promised it would be a good idea. The two had begun with simple questions, such as what certain words meant in Darvic, and what the name of her horse was.

She struggles to dangle from the branch and then drops to her feet on the forest floor. He raises his eyebrows, standing.

Emily holds up a full cluster.

Cazimir stares at her, but there is a gentle touch of humor in his eyes.

She tucks the cluster into her pouch—now filled with nuts, roots, and the leaves of a few plants she recognized as pain-soothers. She turns back the way they came. He follows.

Cazimir sighs, realizing their morning is coming to an end. They are silent as they slowly brush through the trees. Cazimir seems to indifferently accept that she has discarded the question game.

But she hasn't. She has been saving this question for after he'd been warmed up, and when they had nothing else to distract them.

"What does *ahm cara* mean?" she asks.

Cazimir snaps his head to her. Quickly he recovers, looking forward into the trees.

"I do not . . . It . . ." He sputters.

She is silent. He gives a loud grunt.

"That is not Darvic," he says firmly.

Awkward silence stretches.

"My turn," Cazimir says roughly. When he speaks next, his voice softens.

"Your father . . ." Cazimir begins. "He is not . . . Adam?"

Emily hesitates. ". . .No," she agrees. "He's not."

Cazimir looks at her pointedly.

The Darvican is not the first to ask what Adam and her relationship really is. Adam is old enough to be her father, but only just. If he were younger, and she were older, things may be different.

But he is not. And she is not.

"Adam is . . . my best friend. He's like . . . my guardian. At least, I want him to be."

Although she is certain Cazimir doesn't know what a "guardian" is, he continues to watch her raptly.

"My real father . . . I don't know who he is."

"He . . . he would . . ." Cazimir attempts to weave the sentence he wants to say—it is some intricate thought, she can tell, but he fails. He sighs and settles on, "He would like you."

Emily blushes.

"Yeah . . ." she says. "Maybe."

Cazimir can sense the discomfort. He trudges on.

"But Adam . . . Adam is . . . *sovcaul.*" He smiles at his indulgence in a Darvic word.

"*Sovcaul*?" Emily smiles tentatively as well.

"Soft stone," Cazimir translates. "Is . . . good thing in Darvica. Like . . . soft heart."

"He is." Emily nods, loving the enthusiasm in Cazimir's Darvic accent. "He is *sovcaul.*"

Cazimir snorts at her pronunciation, giving her another of his looks. But again, the warmth behind his eyes transfers to pure heat in her body.

They break the tree line. The sun climbs the sky, new and warm, scaring off the chill of fall.

The shelters of the Brothers are already torn down and being packed away on the horses.

Marcus' hulking form swings a large sack onto Hopskip, and Mason approaches behind him, offering his cousin a drink of water. Adam is saddling Copenhagen.

And then Emily realizes there is no one at her side. She turns to empty air and then catches Cazimir, head low, thumping up the slight slope to his shelter.

○ ~ ○ ~ ○

They ride.

Adam is grateful for the gatherings Emily brought from the woods and takes his time gnawing on a root.

There's no flavor to it, but it gives him something to do. Particularly, something to keep Emily from inquiring about what he was going to confess to last night.

The root would not stop Emily from inquiring. But she doesn't want to now. She has better sense than to have this conversation with Adam in broad company. Especially near Marcus, who seems only inches away from lunging off his saddle every time he and Adam make eye contact.

Instead, she watches Mason and Cazimir.

Mason has kindly included Cazimir on the Brotherhood's new plan for seawater, and by Cazimir's reactions, Emily can almost guess exactly what parts of the plan Mason is disclosing.

Cazimir nods at first, recognizing the vial of water given to them and the small backstory on what the water can supposedly do. And then he gives Mason the same skeptical look he has given Emily. Mason obviously just proposed that the vial contained seawater.

The following reactions are confusion, deep thought, and finally a dull acceptance, lingering on doubt. Cazimir does not fully believe in this plan. But he knows he will have no say.

They conclude and commence their Galeduan

lesson.

The next hour passes with Emily studying the eerie burns on Hopskip in a daze. Her eyes are so strained from staring at it for so long that she can't be certain that what she catches in her periphery is real:

A flash up ahead. A glint of sun like off a brand-new coin. Emily squints and tries to make it out. It looks golden or bronze, something large. It blinks in the sun again as they near it.

"Adam, what's—?"

"Dismount," Marcus orders. "Now."

Her heart races, and she reaches for her knife hilt as she slides off Copenhagen. Copenhagen raspberries indignantly.

They walk their horses closer, and she can now make out what it is.

A giant disc of hammered copper glimmers in the sunlight. It is a massive, suspended gong.

An Emperor's alarm.

There are two soldiers standing guard near it, one male, one female. A small, circular stone tower—not large enough to be considered a fort—stands behind the gong. The soldiers have their arms crossed and they watch the nearing party apprehensively but calmly.

"Name," the female guard calls, relaxed but authoritative.

"Marcus Brawl with the Brotherhood," Marcus bellows back, leading his horse closer still.

At those words, the guards draw their swords.

"*Re*-lax." Marcus rolls his eyes.

They meet the soldiers at the gong.

"Come no farther," the woman orders.

"Give us a second, huh?" says Marcus in his regular volume now that they are face-to-face with the soldiers.

"Captain Marley told us to arrest you if found off-course. Drop your weapons."

"Marley makes everyone feel special," says Marcus. "Look, we've had a change of plans."

The two soldiers' expressions darken, and the woman raises her sword tip at Marcus.

"That wasn't on the agenda, Brawl. What's going on?"

"We need to cross the tree line here. Going south." Marcus nods just past the tall, gigantic gong, at the path cutting south through the endless tree line towards the Calder Glens and the Arluian Sea.

"Oh, really? And why's that?"

"Tell you what. You worry about this masterpiece,"

Marcus gestures to the gong, "and I'll worry about that. We're helping Marley. You can tell him it's either my plan or a century of wildfires. I'm fine with either."

There is something both dark and intimidating but also genuine and believable about Marcus' words. The two soldiers study him. Then the one holding out her sword lowers it.

"Approach and explain."

As Marcus begins negotiating, Emily looks away and gazes at the gong.

Emperor Polontius installed these beauties nearly three hundred years ago. He considered himself a prophet and claimed to foresee grave danger for the Empire, particularly involving fire. That is why he commissioned these gongs.

Cazimir is next to it, and he actually lays a careful hand over one of the poles suspending the gong. Emily glances at Adam for permission, but Adam and Mason are listening carefully to Marcus explaining. She sneaks off to join Cazimir.

Cazimir lets his hand slide down the pole. It is almost as if he recognizes it.

"You have these in Darvica, don't you?" Emily asks.

Cazimir purses his lips. "Not where I am from. Do

not . . . go in that far."

"Where are you from? Your town?"

"Skevholm." He answers automatically, eyes still glued to the gong.

"That's—?"

"In mountains. Far . . . east. We do not see . . . these." He motions to the gong. "But we mine metal to make them. In Skevholm."

"This isn't copper?" Emily asks, surprised. The deep, reddish-gold color had immediately brought copper to mind.

"Is mixed copper and strael. We mine strael."

Strael is a dark green, flashy ore found in Darvica. Its most famous quality is its flexibility. She is thankful for having read that only weeks ago, or else she would have sounded naïve to Cazimir's homeland.

"Strael give this," Cazimir gestures the gong again, "very . . . deep sound. Loud. More than bronze. So it can reach farther." Cazimir speaks often with his hands, and he illustrates "farther" by sweeping his hand over the horizon. He obviously knows his metal.

"We only have trithium here," says Emily, "in Galeduen."

At the word "trithium" Cazimir gives her a look

similar to the one the blacksmith had given her. But Cazimir adds a superior-sounding huff. "Is weak," he says. "Paper. Not like . . ." He moves a hand towards the copper and strael gong again.

"Hey! Don't touch that!" one of the soldiers yells. Cazimir and Emily both whip towards the guards. "Who is that guy?" the other demands of Marcus.

"He's Darvic," Marcus drawls, as if that should explain the offense. "Darvica! Get over here!"

Cazimir obeys. Emily follows him, and she catches Adam's eye, which is concerned and beckoning her to join him. She does.

Marcus turns to them all.

"All right, listen up. I've worked a deal with the guards. They'll allow us to stay in the guardhouse tonight while they seek approval from Marley to let us go. I know it's only the afternoon, but the Glens are one *hell* of a trip tomorrow. So rest up. Horses next to the guardhouse." He waves a hand. "Let's go, Adam."

He singles out Adam in his orders yet again. Adam gives Emily a long look, as they both have caught it.

"Let's go, Adam," Emily echoes Marcus. Adam looks at her with tentative amusement, just the way he did when she made her first joke to him in Mr. Robutan's bar.

Some things, she thinks again, can stay the same.

They thump up the narrow, circular staircase, panting.

"We're old," Marcus groans. "Adam and Emily get the top floor. Mason and I take the first. Darvica...wherever."

The stone steps are barely enough for their feet to purchase, and Marcus gropes a hand along the rough rock wall as he ascends. He heaves a great sigh of relief and sidesteps into the first door, Mason hobbling in after him. They hear Marcus' satchel drop to the floor and a mattress creak as he collapses into it.

"The drama . . ." Mason mutters under his breath, closing the door.

Cazimir, Adam, and Emily continue their climb. Adam is panting and shaking his head. Cazimir huffs occasionally, but is not complaining.

Adam bypasses the next door, and Cazimir stops at it, confused. Emily glances back as she senses the hesitation. His lips are parted slightly, breathing hard, but his eyes question her innocently. "You can take it." Emily nods him into the doorway, giving permission, as Adam is already invisible around the curve of the stairs.

Cazimir purses his lips disapprovingly, but steps into the room, his hand on the knob.

The top room has a musty smell, but its wooden, reddish flooring looks rich and almost regal. The bed across from them is not. It is small with olive-green coverings and a brown sack pillow. Beneath it is a circular white rug with diamond patterns.

"Great," Adam sighs. She honestly cannot tell if he is being sarcastic or not. He unslings their two sacks and lets them fall to the floor, wiping sweat from his temple.

A small desk is off to the side with parchment and ink and an iron ladder is built directly into the stone wall on their left. Above it, on the ceiling, is a hatch.

"Guess this is a watchtower, too?" Emily comments, closing the door and gazing at the hatch. Adam, still catching his breath, nods when he sees it.

"Yeah," he breathes. "Sounding the gong never means anything good, does it? Watchtower would be good."

He kicks his sack to the edge of the bed and then unpacks two blankets and a pillow, laying the blankets on the floor.

"I'm sleeping on the floor, Adam," Emily declares, unpacking a few books from her own pack, setting them on the desk.

"No," says Adam. "The mattress hurts my back."

He hasn't even lain laid on the mattress yet. Emily opens her mouth to argue this point when she remembers something.

"Shoot," she says.

"What?"

"I never wrote my mother." She stares into oblivion, measuring the consequences of this.

Adam tries to give a casual, regarding grunt, but the contempt is evident. The mere mention of her mother turns him sour, but he has always tried to stay neutral in front of Emily.

"I'm going to write something now. I wonder how she felt about everything."

"Maybe you'll see her. If we make it to the city sometime."

Emily wistfully appreciates Adam's effort.

"I don't think you two meeting each other is the best idea." Emily already pens the header of her missive.

Adam pauses, trying to imagine the scenario.

"No," he agrees at last.

She gives a small chuckle.

The letter doesn't take too long to write. She begins

with assuring her safety after the news of the flame. About Adam, she simply writes, *Adam is taking care of me through all this. We've left the Ford and have resolved to do what we can to help figure out this fire.*

Vague, but not untrue.

I have not saved up enough to buy the shack for the pie shop yet. I still think you'd do good business here, though. Just know that since I left, I won't have any money to send from Mr. Robutan for a while.

She ends the letter, as always, with,

I hope you're okay. Take care of your newborn, Mom.

Love,

Emily

Writing the parting word "love" is not as difficult as she always predicted it would be. At this point, maintaining such space from her mother, she views her as an aunt or some other noncommittal relative. That doesn't mean she doesn't love her. Her mother has never been cold or heartless. Just irresponsible.

She seals the letter and turns to Adam.

"You think if I give this to one of the guards, they'll have a courier deliver it for me?"

Adam lies on the blankets on the floor with his hands behind his neck.

"I'm sure they would. Just be careful around that big one," he says of the female guard. "She scares me."

"She scares Marcus, too," says Emily.

"Okay, never mind, then. I like her."

Emily laughs and opens the door. "Be right back."

Downstairs, the female guard is sitting at a desk and writing feverishly—presumably to Captain Marley. Emily holds out the letter, and the guard gives it a long look. Then the woman makes up her mind. "Fine," she says lightly, taking the envelope addressed to Dawn Byrnes, Emily's mother.

"Thank you." Emily raises her eyebrows, stunned there wasn't a bigger ordeal.

"Hey," the woman says as Emily turns back to the staircase. Emily faces her, cringing. "Is that bearish Darvican who talks funny with you?"

"I'm sorry?" Emily's voice squeaks.

"That good-looking foreigner. Is he with you?"

This woman is in her forties, perhaps twice Cazimir's age. Why is Emily feeling uneasy about her interest in him?

"Oh," says Emily. "No. I mean, he's with us, but we're not . . ."

The woman's smile is sisterly. "Well . . . even though

I'm familiar with the rumors about the men from the mountains . . . I've never met a Darvican like him." It is blatant what the woman is implying. She's never met one as striking as him.

Emily can't bring herself to comment. She just nods again, feeling the room get hotter.

"He left this." The woman holds up Cazimir's beautiful, long, black-hilted sword.

Emily steps forward immediately.

"Where'd you—?" she begins.

"We had to inspect all your weapons for burn markings. We've been told to keep an eye out for blackened metal that could've involved flame. He forgot to get it back after being pulled aside for questioning."

"You never checked me."

"You're armed?" The woman is genuinely surprised.

Emily unsheathes her knife, dumbfounded, as if this should have been obvious.

"Well, are there burn marks on it?"

"No," says Emily, replacing the knife.

"Then take this to your Darvican." The sisterly smile returns and she hands Emily the blade.

Emily takes it with both hands. She winces. It is heavy. But the sword is so familiar to her ever since she witnessed its forging in the smithy. Every time the blade flashes in the blue light of the tower's light-pockets, it is as if in warm recognition.

She holds the sword vertical against herself, point down. Climbing the stairs again, she passes the first door, where snores rumble the hinges.

"Oh, Marcus," she hears Mason grumble and sigh. She can imagine him pressing a pillow against his ears. It seems like something Mason would do.

When she reaches the second door, she knocks gently.

Someone rises from the mattress in the room, and she can hear heavy footsteps approach the door.

It opens. Cazimir is alarmed but pleased to see her. Before he can speak, she holds up his sword.

"You left this."

He takes it off her hands instantly, a perplexed look on his face, as if he can't imagine how he could have forgotten it.

Then he steps back and looks at it in his left hand. He spins the blade forward once. It makes a whooshing sound and pushes the air. "Thank you." He's still looking it up and down.

Emily swallows. The way he handles the weapon that

is nearly as tall as she is amazing. She's seen Adam defend himself competently with his short sword. Seen Marcus hurl around axes with bedlam. Cazimir, though, expertly manipulates the sword with absentmindedness, the way he plays with his light.

Emily turns to climb the next stair. Why are her nerves fleeting away these days? She used to be so outgoing.

"Emily," he says.

When she turns to him, his head is turned away, his eyes tightly shut, as if it had taken him every bit of courage to say her name. She smiles in spite of herself.

He sighs and his expression softens. "Your turn."

Emily moves into the room as if someone else is doing it. She closes the door behind them both.

There is a pause. They look at each other, and suddenly the space between them feels very stiff. He is almost too handsome for her to take it. Her hand even reaches behind her for the doorknob again.

And then, almost mercifully, Cazimir steps back with one foot and turns to the side to open the room to her. She sighs in relief before she can muffle it. She walks in, and the line of his lips forms a tight smile as his eyes follow her. She surveys the room, which is almost identical to her own, except a painting of Emperor Accalon is on the wall. He wears a long purple robe with black and white fur trim, and the expression in his green eyes is both powerful and stricken—an almost frightened appearance—something the artist probably hoped he would not notice.

"It is your turn," Cazimir says again.

Emily turns to him. She does have a question, but she's not sure he'll like it. Her voice is very soft.

"Why did you run when you saw the herbs, Caz?"

He is dark and unreadable. His hands still grasp the sword, turning it over slowly. She watches his knuckles at work, the veins that trail up his strong wrists. That dark blue shirt is smudged with dirt from the saddle but perfectly contrasts his black hair and light skin. Closer to him, she can make out that darkness that mottles his face. Scars and bruises that came from either mining or battle–a line down the bridge of his nose. A ragged nick at his left ear. The scar on his collarbone.

Then his eyes flicker down and around the floor.

"Okay," he croaks at last.

Emily sits on Cazimir's bed. He sheaths his sword and lifts the chair at his desk with one hand, setting it down to face her. He sits and then simply looks at her, a despair and vulnerability in his eyes that she's never seen before, as if he needs to measure her before working out what he will say. He leans forward and wipes his hands down his mouth.

"Caz," she croons. "You don't need to—"

He gives a loud clearing of his throat as if denying her offer of retreat.

"Those herbs . . ." he says, and he looks up at her. His expression is almost pleading, begging her to understand. "Those herbs," he repeats.

She nods.

"I had to put . . . on brother." His eyes are brimmed in red.

Emily frowns. She considers touching him but decides to keep listening.

Cazimir hangs his head. Something new waves over him. Something darker. Angrier. He is still for a long moment, brooding in some grim memory.

Unease trickles through her.

"Was eight," Cazimir chokes. "Little brother."

Emily's throat tightens.

"My father . . . when we are eight . . . he take us on trip. To outside. Just him and us, for night. My father took brother on trip, four years ago . . . Just them. Was cold—winter . . ."

His Galeduan is fractured, but it doesn't prevent the image from being painted in her mind.

After the second day, when Cazimir's father and little brother, Milo, didn't return from the pre-light rite of passage—a Darvic tradition marking the final months before the boy would begin producing light—Cazimir's mother worried. She sent Cazimir into the wild to find them. It was midwinter in Darvica—one of the coldest places one can be. But Milo had turned eight then, and his father insisted they make the excursion anyway.

Cazimir's father, in his family's opinion, was a perfect outdoorsman, erasing any concern that he and Milo wouldn't be okay. But the doubts started to creep as Cazimir, sixteen at the time, set out in the biting wind in search of them.

Darkness fell by the time he caught a shine of his father's blue light amidst whipping snowflakes and grey trunks with peeling bark.

He ran to it, and undoubtedly, it was their camp.

His father was gone. The snow had already piled three feet high, and Cazimir fell to his knees in search of Milo.

He found him—weak, small Milo—shivering

underneath the snow. He had been unconscious somehow, and now juddered with chills.

It seems very important to Cazimir to explain his actions in great detail from here.

"I took him," he breathes to Emily. And then he moves his arms in front of him, as if embracing air. "I lay on floor with him, and held him like this." He shakes his hands to emphasize the action. He is swallowing a lot, but will not make eye contact with her.

"I took off shirt," he pats his own shirt, "and held him against me. Wrapped him in shirt."

He shakes his head again, hanging it, but this time, he does not stop shaking. He covers his eyes with his hand.

Cazimir had produced his light for Milo. It warmed him, but was not enough.

At this point, Emily's own tears sparkle on her cheek. And suddenly, she can feel it. The freezing snow on Cazimir's bare back, laying in it, clutching his little brother, and pleading with him to stay alive. But the hypothermia was too far.

Milo died in his arms.

And later, Cazimir had to wrap him in the very herbs Sakole had stored in the jars. The leather band Cazimir wears on his left wrist belonged to his little brother.

"What happened to your dad?" Emily whispers.

The red around Cazimir's eyes is suddenly bitter with ancient fury. "Someone thought he was . . . spy, my father. Took and beat him. Leave Milo . . . in snow."

"Was your father—?" Emily remembers Cazimir explaining the separation from his parents the other night but wonders now if his mother was widowed and remarried.

"Was okay." Cazimir chokes down another swallow. "Whoever it was . . . let him go. After . . ."

"After they realized they were wrong," Emily says gravely.

Cazimir nods, and he meets her gaze for the first time since the start of his story.

Emily shakes her head in despair and disbelief. "Caz," she sighs, her own throat burning. "I'm so—"

They hear the wood panels above them groan as Adam must have moved to the door. He is probably concerned about her delayed return.

She purses her lips, not appreciating Adam's fatherly motives right now.

But then, the footsteps clump down the stone stairs and pass Cazimir's door completely, only to knock hastily on the door below them—Marcus' room.

They hear someone underneath rise to meet the door, and then Adam's rushed voice talks with Marcus.

"What?" They can hear Marcus' dark tone rumble even through the floor.

Cazimir, despite his grief, gives Emily a speculating look.

Then, two footsteps pound their way up the stairs.

Emily stands.

"Stay here . . ." She moves to the door, waiting until the two heavy footsteps pass upward.

Cazimir watches suspiciously as she leaves and closes the door behind her.

She follows the other two into her and Adam's room. Adam is about to climb the iron ladder up through the hatch. Half of Marcus is already through it. She catches only his legs climbing up.

Adam is mute, but he sees her and waves her over, more out of convenience than true invitation.

He climbs the ladder and Emily, her mind racing, follows only a prong behind.

The night is clear, and an autumn chill makes the air brisk and clean.

Marcus is standing at the bulwark of the tower as

Adam joins him. Their backs are to her, but she sneaks around the side to glimpse what they are looking at, hoping not to alert Marcus to her presence.

"I don't believe this," Marcus seethes.

Emily searches the patches of moonlit grass for what they are seeing, but cannot—

There! A lone, mounted traveler. *Okay*, she thinks. *That's not too uncommon . . .*

She cranes her neck farther to study the figure, and then she can't contain a small gasp.

Even from this distance, she can see him, his horse lazily approaching.

The boy is young, olive-skinned, and wiry.

An image flashes through her mind—that intense look he had given her on the night when she first met the Brotherhood. Something bleak and desperate, as if she might be of use to him. And then he'd returned to playing with his thumbs.

"Brother Scott," she whispers.

"What the hell is he doing here, Marc?" Adam asks. His expression is stone.

Marcus is molded to the bulwark. His platinum-grey beard glows in the moonlight. But Emily can see the strain in his finger muscles as they clench the stone of the tower. The fingertips of his gauntlet scrape and leave white scars on the grit.

"Following us."

CHAPTER 19

The knock is at the door at the same time Marcus shuffles down the spiral staircase, Adam and Emily close behind.

Adam nearly crashes into Marcus as he suddenly stops and wrenches open the door to his and Mason's room.

"Get in," Marcus hisses.

They obey and Marcus goes in as well and closes the door almost all the way, leaving a seam open to hear through. They hear the large female guard walk to answer the knock, and Marcus leans in his ear.

The hinges squeak on the guardhouse door, and heavy footsteps—the other soldier from outside—march to join the female guard. The soldier's voice is awkward and reluctant.

A low, friendly chuckle is heard in response, and Marcus winces into a scowl.

"What—what's going on?" says a voice behind them.

Emily spins and sees Mason sitting up from the bed, rubbing one eye. His white hair stands up on its end, but when he lowers his hand, his bleary eyes are just as concerned and alert as ever.

"*Shh*," Marcus hisses.

Mason ruffles and scrunches his face, agitated.

Marcus' ear is completely to the door now, and his eyes are locked on a wad of grey dust at his shoe.

And then it is unmistakable—the soldiers allow someone inside, and the door is closed.

Marcus actually gives a snarl of frustration and jerks open the door. He doesn't seem to care who stays or who follows him, so Emily jumps along.

They storm down the steps.

And there he is—Brother Scott, looking tired and worse for the wear. His curly, plum-black hair is longer, he sports a puffy lip, and his countenance is as foggy and indifferent as ever. The black kohl eyeliner he usually wears is faded to an almost imperceptible grey. But nonetheless, he is standing in the middle of the small, circular room, nodding his apparent thanks at the soldiers, who look exasperated. They aren't used to this many guests at once.

When the small, olive-skinned Brother hears the heavy step on the stairs, however, he looks up to see Marcus descending towards him.

Marcus has managed to arrange his face into his classic sneering, unbreakable amusement. The look is so familiar to Brother Scott that he shrinks on sight of it.

Marcus' cold, trademark smile lifts at the sight of Scott's fear.

"Brother Scott. Did Marley let you come play with the big boys again?"

"Wait a minute. You know him?" the woman demands of Marcus.

"Of course. My youngest little cub. Well . . . maybe not my youngest anymore," Marcus purrs, giving the quickest of nods at Emily behind his shoulder. For some reason, Emily doesn't feel that twinge of hot anger towards Marcus this time. She has the feeling that Marcus is forcing his behavior. The jabs seem false.

"Kinfather. I had no idea you'd be here," says Scott. He choreographs his face into mixed confusion and relief, but again, it seems like theater.

"Likewise," says Marcus. His green eyes are trained

on the boy before him as he, Marcus, takes the final step onto the ground floor. Scott watches the others descend with him, lingering on Adam in long-term recognition, but Adam's expression is guarded.

When Scott sees Emily, however, a small, haughty smile touches his lips. He looks at her as if they are in on this together—as if they are sharing some joke at the others around them. Emily lowers her brow.

Marcus catches this transaction.

"Don't worry, Brother Scott. She's not your replacement. I don't think anyone could replace you . . ."

Marcus takes another long step towards the boy—his sneering act is slipping, and Scott inches back.

Marcus stops just a few paces before Scott.

"What are you doing here, Scott Osborne?" he whispers.

Adam takes a small, precautionary step in front of Emily. One hand is on the hilt of his short sword, the other extended behind him, making the slightest contact with Emily's wrist.

Every guard grabs their sword hilts as well. The tension in the room is tangible.

"I was sent by Captain Marley," Scott replies. His eyes still preserve the indifferent, cocky attitude, but his neck is bent upwards to examine the grey-bearded man before him.

"He said he needed boarding," the male guard interjects. "Is there a problem here?"

"No problem," Marcus assures, but he does not remove his eyes from Scott. "Marley sent you?" he repeats, just a tad too much sweetness behind it.

A wave of pain crosses Scott's face at some distant thought, but he recovers.

"My parents wouldn't take me," Scott confesses. "I was supposed to go to them. But they wouldn't come. So I was going to be put in jail. I begged Marley to let me join you instead."

"And he knew where we would be, did he?" Marcus challenges.

"He said you'd be heading west. To the flame. I didn't think you'd wander from the forest. These trees go all the way to the western border, don't they?" Scott looks around for confirmation.

"They do," Adam says from the wall, level and cautious. "But I don't see why Marley would trust you to stay on course."

Scott turns to him, his mouth falling open. He has the expression of one being bullied upon, as if the whole situation were preposterously unfair.

"Can we wrap this up?" the female guard pipes.

Marcus gives a start. He eyes her, but seems to buckle.

"Fine," he says. "The kid is back with us. Hope you know what you're in for, Scott."

Marcus turns for the staircase.

"Where is he sleeping?" Adam cuts in, calm but calculating.

"Introduce Osborne to Darvica," Marcus answers, although he has already begun his climb upstairs.

"Darvica?" Scott scoffs, his eyes defiant again.

"Yes," says Marcus. "Darvica."

○ ~ ○ ~ ○

Cazimir had opened the door immediately when Adam knocked.

It was an awkward first meeting. Scott gave a derisive snicker at the sight of Cazimir.

"This is what he meant by 'Darvica?'" Scott had said. Adam fidgeted, eyeing both young men before him.

"Cazimir," Adam had said. "This is Scott. One of the Brothers. He's coming with us now."

Emily was watching the whole time as Cazimir and Scott shared a look of mutual dislike. Cazimir had lifted his surly gaze to Adam as if condemningly, and then stepped back to allow Scott entry.

Scott had shouldered by him into the room.

That's when Emily decided she had to get out of that tower.

Copenhagen judders a raspberry at her. He turns his shaggy head away, ignoring the feed in her hand, and she tilts her palm and lets the feed rain to the ground. "Antisocial much, Cope?" she says. He doesn't reply. She sighs and sits on the ground just outside the guardhouse, twisting grass in her hand. Copenhagen folds his legs beneath him and lays down as well. She loops an arm over his neck. Then she looks at the stars.

The memory of Adam lying in the grass next to her on the night of the Celestial comes back. She pictures his gentle happiness, watching her excitement. She smiles.

They're not going anywhere, she thinks about the stars, about his words. She closes her eyes.

And suddenly she knows how Adam feels when he smiles but there is sadness behind it. That is how this smile feels. How can Celestial have been only a week ago? How can quiet Adam be affiliated with a band of criminals? That short sword of his had slid so easily into the back of that assassin the other night.

And how, most of all, can fire be back? What created it? Will it spread? Will she see orange and red glimmer on the horizon and come for her?

A silent tear rolls down her face, the grass still knotted in her hand. It can't all be real.

She wipes her nose and stands. Silly to mope, she thinks. But she doesn't want to go inside yet, and return to all those people.

Not thinking of any cult or flame, she leaves Copenhagen behind and walks into the forest, crickets chirping and pouch on hand.

The trees here, close to the southward path that cuts through the woods towards the Glens, are less dense. Less brush and with greyer, thinner trunks that are smooth and make it easier to walk through. The moons, high at midnight, are both full and bright. The pale one's light mixes with the maroon one's and creates a mosaic for her to see by. It makes the twigs on the floor look like silver bones. But she isn't really looking for anything. They could use some food, and they could definitely use some medicinal plants for the days ahead, but her eyes give up almost as soon as they start.

It is just comforting, being protected by the trees. By the same forest, somewhere far, far, away, that encloses

Darson's Ford. So instead of gathering, she draws not her weapon knife, but her pocket knife that Adam gave her.

She chooses a young tree and digs the point of the blade into its soft bark—much easier to carve than the reddish, rough trunks of the Ford.

She carves one of Adam's patterns into the bark, like creating her own Guardian. She doesn't notice the moisture running down her cheek, or the fact that it dried quicker in the cool night air.

A branch shudders behind her. She jumps and turns, squeezing the small pocket knife in her hand.

The tree trunks are radiated in a bluish-green. The grasp on the knife loosens when the step comes closer and she can see the teal orb in his hand, his black hair reflecting the moonlight.

"Caz?" she says, stepping forward.

He sees her, and relief is instant in his eyes.

"Emily," he sighs. He lets the blue orb stray away from his wrist, floating like a companion in the air near him, and he steps towards her. It illuminates the dark forest, the trickle of ants over antique leaves. "They asked me to . . ." He clears his throat. "What were you . . .?"

Emily blushes. "I'm sorry," she says. "We're just going a long way from these woods tomorrow. I was saying goodbye."

Cazimir is silent, watching her.

She stuffs the knife slowly into her pocket and breathes evenly.

"Cazimir . . ." she begins.

He continues to gaze at her. It is not his cynical look, but that look from the other night—the night their hands produced the sparks. Something deeper. Something male.

She wants to use this time—just the two of them—to say how sorry she is about Milo. To thank him for saving her life. But her throat clogs up and the blue-green light hypnotizes her. She wants to be closer to it.

Emily shakes her head, hoping against hope he cannot see her distress.

The body of the assassin Adam killed thudding to the floor—the streak of a yellow flame firing from an arrow. It all blocks her thoughts. Her voice is like a croak. She tries again.

"Cazimir—"

And it happens.

He steps towards her and takes her face in his hands. His lips are against hers, and she can feel how badly he has wanted to do this. Weakness drains her body as heat courses through her. She is certain he must be holding her up entirely, or else she'd have fallen to the floor by now, but he is so tall that he is nearly stooping to reach her.

She brings her hands to his face, feels his soft black hair and runs her hand down his rough shadow.

He pulls back first, swiftly, and meets her eyes. He is breathing hard, but the light of his orb glints in his Darvic eyes, showing something she doesn't expect—disbelief. It is like he cannot believe what he has just done.

It feels like there is too much blood in her body, and she cannot speak although she desperately wants to.

He blushes deep red, holding her gaze, and then clears his throat. He drops his hands slowly and steps past her, through the trees towards the guardhouse, taking his light with him and twirling it in his hand.

CHAPTER 20

Emily raises a hand against the rays as her breath is stolen by what's before her. They squint and rein their horses. Copenhagen snorts.

Miles of open field sprawl ahead. It is an ocean of grass as far as they can see. Soft wind waves over the plains, twirling up butterflies in the distance. The land slopes downward from the trees behind them until becoming level. She is sure the land will go on forever.

Adam pulls up to her and inhales a deep breath. "You're looking at the gateway to the Calder Glens," he says.

Emily drags her eyes from the serene valley to rest on Adam. He squints. "We should reach them in a day or so. But until Endraft"—the town on the Arluian Sea—"there's nothing but this."

"I wouldn't be so sure," says Marcus gravely. He has walked his black horse up to them and begun his way down the slight decline onto the flat ground. Adam remains silent.

That morning, Scott presented his orders from Captain Marley to the female guard. Whether or not they were forged—Emily has her doubts—the female guard was convinced. But the fact that their party now outnumbered the soldiers at her post may have also had something to do with it. She allowed them to leave the guardhouse and divert south.

Cazimir makes an effort to stay close to Mason during this trip. Emily even notices him trying to make small conversation with Mason, who seems delightfully surprised at the Darvican's effort. She can't help but remind herself that Mason has no idea *why* Cazimir is being so talkative to him . . .

Emily hasn't spoken to Cazimir since last night. She'd let him go after their first kiss, simply standing where she was, filtering air in and out. She wasn't sure if it was nerves or happiness filling her body that kept her rooted to the spot like another sapling among the trees. But when she finally followed him back to the tower, he had retreated into his and Scott's room.

He was wide awake, already mounted on his horse and listening to something Mason was saying, by the time she stepped into the morning light in the groggy, early hours, ready to saddle Copenhagen.

It was hard not to look at Cazimir in a new way then. He wore his leather and chainmail again, and today the metal of his sword looked green. He had turned to listen more attentively to Mason, but she couldn't help but watch the sun glistening off his hair, the way he squinted as the rays shone over him. He looked so strong and alive, as fresh as the morning light. And of course, that hand, holding his horse's rein, that had been holding her last night . . .

Was he simply embarrassed by his boldness, or did he regret doing it?

The knot of emotions is impossible to shake off, she realizes, as Cazimir continues to stick near Mason even after they have walked through the path of the trees and reached the southern side, facing the Glens.

Tonight, she thinks. *I'll have time with him tonight.*

In the meantime, however, she'll just have to focus on avoiding Scott's curious eye for the rest of the trip.

"No lightpits. No tents. No loud talking. And we're taking shifts."

Marcus thumps to the ground off his horse hours later and begins setting out a bedroll. The others, rolling out stiff necks, follow his lead.

They have ridden all day and are nearly halfway there, but the journey was a long, dull blur. The land stretches on so far that the tree line from whence they'd come is invisible now. The Calamus Mountains are the only feature to be viewed on their left, and even they are so distant they merely resemble grey rumples on the horizon.

Marcus has been more paranoid than normal. He prodded Brother Scott to walk ahead of him as if mistrustful of riding with his back to the boy. "Young eyes up front . . ." he'd said.

Emily's neck is so sore she can barely keep it up without craning it from side to side, but she unpacks Copenhagen mechanically.

"Long day, Cope," she breathes. Copenhagen studies her for a moment, and then tips his shaggy head to the side in exhaustion.

The sun is dipping low, blood-red on the horizon. She steals a glimpse at the sky and sees rows of clouds breaking over the hues of yellow light, illuminated like meat roasting over a grill.

"Might be some rain coming our way," Mason comments to her side. She was so distracted, she didn't realize he was there.

"Mason," she says brightly.

Mason gives a welcoming smile. "Hello, Emily." He slips the saddle off his painted horse and rubs him down. The horse gives a mighty shake, relieved.

"Hey . . . Mason . . ." Emily chooses her words carefully. Mason looks at her keenly, warmly. "Thank you for . . . for teaching Cazimir."

Mason shrugs. "Oh. Well, that is my pleasure. Cazimir is a brilliant young man."

Emily nods, knowing she hasn't pinned the question she really wanted yet.

"Can I . . . ask you something?" she says.

Mason pauses and gives a surprised, wistful smile as if complimented by her interest. "Hmm?"

"What does . . . what does *ahm cara* mean in Darvic?"

He searches his thoughts, lowering his brow and staring into oblivion.

"*Ahm cara?*" he repeats slowly, sizing the words. He thinks for a long moment. "Actually . . ." He straightens and meets her eyes. "I don't think that's Darvic." He looks at her inquiringly.

So Cazimir wasn't lying? Had she misheard the words that night in Welshire?

"Did he say that or something?" Mason asks in a hushed voice, in case Cazimir were to wander over.

Emily shakes her head absently.

Mason holds up a finger and wags it as if a thought is coming to him.

"You know what that sounds like to me? That sounds like the stonecutter's language. Doesn't it to you? Ancient-like?"

"*Mason!* Things are going to get really awkward if you don't stop pampering that horse," Marcus barks. "What are you going to do next, let him ride on your back?"

From where the others are, it does look as if Mason has been patting and tending to Precious for a long time, but he huffs at the sound of his little cousin's voice.

"I swear to the Vicar, Grandfather dropped an *anvil* on you as a child," Mason retorts, abandoning Emily and going to set his own bedroll.

Emily stands there for another moment. If Mason is right, Cazimir spoke in the language of aboriginals who used fire almost a millennium ago. She swallows.

By the time night falls, the clouds have moved in so

that the stars are hidden and the area is gloomy and foreboding.

"Some rain will feel good," Adam remarks, trying to set a positive tone to the menacing calm of the air.

No one says anything, but Emily is sure she catches Adam glance at her fleetingly and look away just as fast. Perhaps he does remember being rained on with her in Darson's Ford.

"We need two lookouts," Marcus says. The usual firm gusto behind his voice has wilted, tired. "I'll be one of them."

There is a long silence. Adam just opens his mouth when Emily says, "I'll be the other."

Her words stun even herself.

They sit on the ground, legs outstretched, with their backs to one another, and Emily can already sense this will be some of the strangest few hours she's ever experienced. She tries to pretend like there is no one behind her and wishes she could mimic Adam's habit of whittling random pieces of wood. But of course, there is no wood to be found here.

Instead, she plucks the long grass from the ground and uses her pocket knife to slice them in halves, then quarters, and so on until they sprinkle through her fingers and back to the earth.

The others are already snoring. Marcus is silent behind her, but definitely awake. He watches one side as she watches the other.

"You awake, pumpkin?"

She gives a start.

"*Yeah*," she responds hotly. "Why?"

She can feel Marcus' shoulders shrug. "Thought you might've drifted off. Dreaming about you-know-who or something."

"Excuse me?"

They speak in hushed voices so as not to disturb the others, but she can almost swear she hears Marcus smile.

"Who's it going to be, sweetheart? Darvica or the kid?"

Emily snorts. "Are you scared of the dark and need someone to talk to?"

Marcus' body rumbles a silent laugh. "No," he says. "I just can't help but be amused by you."

Emily pauses. She can either let it go or pursue it, right now . . .

"I want to figure you out, Marcus," she says.

"What's that, buttercup?" he goads back.

"What is it with you and me?"

There is a silence before he answers. But something shifts. Emily can sense something drain out of Marcus. The arrogance, hopefully.

"You want to know what it is . . ." Marcus ponders, as if curious about the question itself. "Hmm. Maybe it's because you're a lot like me, Emily."

That's a shock.

"H—How so?" Emily manages.

Marcus pauses thoughtfully.

"That first night we were attacked—when the arrow jammed into our lightpit. Two people stood and drew their swords. The others flinched."

The memory seeps through her, but he goes on before she can speak.

"Two people were needed for a watch tonight. No one volunteered. Except for two."

Something about this frustrates her. She feels the need to deflect it, but Marcus goes on.

"Adam told you to stay in the Ford. You didn't listen."

"That was for love," Emily snaps.

"And you believe I am a stranger to such?"

Emily shifts her thumb over her knuckles at that, silent.

"Only two people," continues Marcus, "aren't on this mission because they were forced to be."

Emily freezes. Is he referring to herself and . . . himself? Is that why he hasn't run? He wants to be doing this? "What are you saying?"

Marcus breathes out. She can feel his back muscles move as he lays his head back. There is a pause as if he's deciding how much to admit.

"I was promised something if I succeeded," he says at last. Emily remembers the guard whispering in his ear.

"A reward?" says Emily.

Another pause. "You could call it that."

Emily blinks. What is it that Marcus wants? What could the Empire have promised him to make him do this? She waits for him to say more, but it becomes clear he will not.

"So, you're like me. In some ways," she admits. "Why is that amusing?"

"Let me ask *you* something now," says Marcus.

She waits apprehensively.

"What are you most afraid of?" he whispers.

She stiffens. For some preposterous reason, her heart wants to answer this question. Marcus did not ask with spite and slickness the way he usually does. His voice was low, genuine.

She thinks of her answer for a long time, watching bugs jump from the tall grass ahead of her.

"Losing him," she whispers.

Marcus is still, waiting for her to clarify.

"Losing Adam."

"That is the most amusing of all," he breathes back.

Emily is instantly offended, but Marcus continues before she can stop him.

"The fact that you choose him," says Marcus.

"Choose him?" says Emily.

"The fact that Adam . . . the most uneventful, modest, ordinary person in the world could win you over. That you could find him so captivating. That is where we differ."

"You don't know Adam then, Marcus."

"I do know Adam, Emily. I've known him longer than you."

"That doesn't mean you know him better."

Marcus is quiet, considering.

"If the tables were ever turned, Emily . . ." he says. "If for some twist of fate . . . I was the one you latched onto as a father figure, a year ago . . ."

Emily is so shocked she cannot speak. Rather, she lets

him finish.

"Well," Marcus chuckles, "we would have been an unstoppable team, is all."

The moment stretches into the night.

"Can I ask you something else?" Emily says.

His silence is permission.

"Can you produce light?" She knows some men cannot—she thinks of Heckley at Fort Carrick, and what Mason said in Welshire . . .

Marcus scoffs. "Is that a real question? Of course I can." There is the same hint of pride in his voice that she's observed in Cazimir surrounding this topic. She believes him.

"Then why don't you?"

Now his silence sounds different.

"Let's keep our watch," he says at last.

Emily purses her lips. Ten minutes turn to fifteen. Finally, she speaks one last time.

"Marcus?"

"Hm."

"What are *you* afraid of? Is it the fire?"

"No," says Marcus.

A small breeze rushes through the grass, akin to the deep breath Marcus inhales.

"What I'm afraid of . . ." he says, "has already happened."

○ ~ ○ ~ ○

Mason and Scott wake to take their watch. Adam and Cazimir will be last.

Emily is so grateful for sleep that she falls into a black, dreamless rest, sure she will doze through until morning.

That is why she is so startled to be shaken awake by someone.

"Emily?"

It is an unfamiliar voice, but she brings herself up on her elbows. Her eyes focus on darker skin, curly hair.

"Scott?" she says. Her eyes search for Mason and find him, asleep, where he should be watching.

Scott sniggers, following her gaze.

"He didn't last thirty minutes."

"What—what are you doing?" she whispers, blinking herself awake.

"Trying to save you." He shakes his head, as if exasperated, but doesn't comment further.

"Look, Scott, I don't know what—"

"I'll explain later," he says. "I just want to show you something now. So you'll trust me."

Unable to push back her interest, Emily stands slowly.

"What's going on?" she says.

"Do you trust Marcus?" he asks abruptly.

"What?"

"Do. You. Trust. Marcus."

A pause.

"That's what I thought," says Scott. "Look, Emily . . . Marley sent me on purpose to find you. He released me because I gave him information."

Can Adam wake up? Can Cazimir show up behind Scott? Can Mason not act like a senile old man and stay up through his watch?

"What kind of information?" She plays along.

Scott scoffs darkly. "Who the flamelighter is."

"You think you know?" Emily can't hide her interest, keeping her voice low.

"Emily," says Scott. "Have you ever seen what's under Marcus' gauntlet? The one he wears all the time?"

Emily shakes her head slowly, though a trickle of suspicion enters her eyes.

"I have," Scott whispers. "When he wasn't looking. I knew he'd kill me if he knew. But I had to tell Marley . . ."

Scott sneaks over to where Marcus is sleeping and

Emily follows. When he reaches Marcus, asleep on his side facing them, Scott turns to flash Emily an anticipatory look.

"You have to see this, Emily," he whispers. "Then you'll trust me . . ."

"*Scott, don't—*" Emily warns, as soon as she realizes what he is about to do.

But Scott leans down. His fingers are gentler than a snowflake, prying the metal gauntlet off Marcus' hand.

Emily holds her breath, sure Marcus will wake.

But he doesn't wake. The metal gauntlet slides off his hand.

And even in the darkness of night, she can see it. It is all she can do not to give a cry of shock.

Marcus' hand is scorched black.

CHAPTER 21

"Why can't he feel that?" Emily manages to choke as Scott gently pushes the metal gauntlet back on.

She is horrified. Marcus' hand is charred—blackened on some fingers and deep red on others. Disbelief and confusion pound over her, but she must stay calm. Nothing is right about what she is seeing. This cloudy night, the impeding storm, is playing tricks on her.

"Same reason he wears it," Scott replies. "His skin can barely feel there anymore."

Emily shakes her head and presses a hand to her forehead.

"Scott, I—"

"Do you trust me now?" he says, forcing her away from Marcus and back to her bedroll.

The real answer is that no, she doesn't trust him

because of this. But it changes things.

"Why didn't you tell the guards about this? Back at the tower?" she says instead.

"Shh," he scolds, looking over his shoulder. "Because I needed to get you guys on my side first. Marcus would have killed me in there—and Adam, and the oafish foreigner—they outnumbered the guards."

"If you're talking about Caz—"

"Marcus probably killed Druid Parr, too, you know," Scott sighs.

No, Emily thinks. *I think you did.* But in this moment, alone with Scott, she fears for her life. So she keeps the thought inside. "That makes no sense, Scott. Why would—?"

Marcus grumbles and turns in his sleep behind them. Both Scott and Emily freeze. When it is clear he's asleep again, Scott continues. "I just needed you to trust me. When the time comes that we do something about him, you'll know who the enemy is."

Scott forces a hand on Emily's shoulder to push her down on her bedroll.

"Scott, wait," Emily protests, sitting but not lying down. "Humans can't make fire. Just because his hand is burned doesn't mean *he's* the one who—"

"Humans can't make it. Are you sure about that?"

Emily opens her mouth, but Mason rustles behind them, finally waking.

"Brother Scott?" he squeaks, giving a cough.

Scott gives Emily one last, meaningful look before turning and joining Mason.

She pretends to sleep for the rest of the night, allowing hundreds of thoughts to stew in her mind. Humans *can't* make fire. The Vicar was burned, too—but Sakole said that was because the Vicar tried to *extinguish* the fire . . . Maybe Marcus had the fire *inflicted* upon him. Maybe he tried to extinguish it, too. She remembers the night he burst into Mr. Robutan's bar and fell—he'd been clutching a gloved hand then, too.

But no. That was before the flame returned. And on the evening it did—how could Marcus have tried to extinguish the flame, on the opposite end of Galeduen, when he was in Darson's Ford the night after it was lit?

Under different circumstances, Emily would have shaken Adam awake and dragged him into the trees to talk about this in private. But with an expanse of featureless valley, secretive discussion will be hard to have.

So when she hears Mason and Scott wake Adam and

Cazimir for their shift, she remains lying with her eyes closed, listening.

Thirty minutes is the longest she can wait for Scott to fall asleep. Quietly, she rises, seeking out the silhouettes of Adam and Cazimir.

Adam is sitting on the ground with his face buried in his hands as if this hour of the morning is ungodly. Cazimir stands with his back to her—his head hung and arms crossed—but he sways slightly, making her wonder if he dozed off on his feet. Neither speaks to the other, far too tired.

Emily stumbles towards them, and both are so spaced out that they don't notice her approach. *Some watchmen they are,* she has time to think.

She gives Adam a shake on the shoulder and he jumps.

Cazimir turns to them, alarmed. His arms are still crossed and there is a bleary look in his eye. Emily's gaze lingers on Cazimir for a moment before turning to Adam.

"What's wr—?" Adam starts.

"Can I talk to you? Alone?"

Adam shares a mystified look with Cazimir before standing slowly. Cazimir looks on as Emily leads Adam behind the horses.

"Is everything okay?" Adam asks, his voice still thick with sleep.

"No," says Emily. "Listen, Scott woke me up during his shift—" Adam's look immediately darkens "—and he showed me what's under Marcus' gauntlet."

"*What?*"

"Marcus wears the gauntlet because his hand is burned, Adam. Marley sent Scott because they think Marcus is the flamelighter."

Adam gives her a long, gloomy stare.

"Emily," he says at last, "I agree with you that Marcus has other reasons for going after this flame and not making a run for it. But I don't think he—"

"I *saw* Marcus' hand with my own eyes. It's worse than what's on the pack horse."

Adam purses his lips.

"Okay," he says. Emily thinks he is agreeing with her, but he goes on. "Okay, Emily, I'm going to tell you what Marcus *and* Mason told me when we met in private last night."

Emily musters her patience.

"Marcus thinks Scott's been following us. This entire time. That means he's probably the one who broke into our rooms in Welshire."

Emily furrows her brow in confusion.

"Why would Scott just show up at the guard tower if he were following us? He would have stayed back so we didn't know."

"Because Scott would never have thought we were there, at the guardhouse. The guards stopped us extremely early that day. We could have made it well towards the Glens if they hadn't. Marc thinks we gave Scott a good surprise by walking down those stairs to meet him. And I'm inclined to agree with him."

"So why's Scott following us, then?"

Adam is silent.

"We don't know," he says. "And I don't know about Marcus' hand."

He does not mean he doesn't believe her—he is saying he doesn't know what to think of it, and Emily can hear so in his voice.

"Should we just confront him about it?" says Emily.

Adam inhales a great breath and looks away. A humid, ominous wind weaves through the grass as the dark clouds brew above them.

"I don't know that, either. Let's wait until we reach the Glens. Anything could happen out here . . ."

She nods. A gentle patter of raindrops hits the grass around them.

"One thing is certain, Emily" says Adam, looking back at her. "It's only a matter of time before Marcus and Scott turn on each other. Either could have a lot more strength behind them than we know."

Emily swallows.

"And before that happens," Adam finishes, the rain intensifying and seething onto the grass blades around him, "we need to know whose side we're on."

Thunder rolls on the horizon. Emily and the other sleepers pull their blankets over their heads. The steady precipitation is not enough to rouse them after the exhausting journey of yesterday, but it takes some time for their fidgeting to cease.

Adam had forced Emily to return to her bedroll—a place she's found absolutely zero rest in tonight. She settles in for the third time this evening by Adam's demand.

"You okay?" she hears Adam ask Cazimir softly, the pat of raindrops hushing his words.

Cazimir must have nodded, for he doesn't respond.

"Sorry," Adam sighs. "I just had to talk with . . ." He trails off awkwardly.

Adam has never been the most adept in social situations. Instead, he clears his throat and allows the rain the fall.

"I feel so bad sometimes," Adam whispers at length.

It feels wrong to eavesdrop now. What will Adam say to Cazimir that he hasn't already said to her? She wonders if Adam, like she, feels more comfortable speaking to Cazimir than to the others. Is it the Darvican's minimal understanding of Galeduan that makes him so easy to talk to? The way one could tell their secrets to a beloved dog? It seems like a rude analogy, but there really is something to say about a listener who won't repeat what he hears. And Adam hasn't spent the time with Cazimir, like Emily has, to fully realize just how insightful he is despite his language barrier.

"I brought her into all of this," Adam continues. "I brought her into everything. She's already been so hurt by me."

Emily listens to their silent breathing.

"She love you," says Cazimir at length.

Emily can hear Adam shift towards Cazimir, as if he wasn't expecting a response.

"I . . . I know," Adam replies, a hint of surprise in his voice. He swallows. "She's . . . she's the world to me."

Thunder rumbles in the distance again, but the rain keeps its steady pace.

"She likes you a lot, too, Cazimir," Adam offers in a whisper, as if in return of a compliment.

Now, it is Cazimir's turn to shift towards Adam. "I . . ." He clears his throat and stutters, slow and careful. "She would not . . . she would never . . . with . . ." He stops talking, and, after a beat, he grunts.

A pulse of realization surges through Emily. Was Cazimir about to say *with someone like me*? Had that been why he's been hiding from her? Because he believes she'd never take him? A Darvican, a sold man?

The fatherly response from Adam to what Cazimir had just implied—that Emily couldn't like him in *that* way—would be gruff silence. As if in approval of Cazimir's accepted defeat. But Adam surprises her. He sighs deeply.

"If she can love someone like me, Cazimir," says Adam, "she can love anybody."

○ ~ ○ ~ ○

Copenhagen plods through the grass, which has puddled in the rain. He looks just as miserable as everyone else with his head hung low and his shaggy hair covering his eyes. But Emily can't help but admire his endurance.

After the first lightning flash, Marcus had thrown off his blanket and cursed loudly, yelling at the others to rise. He mustn't have been the only one who could no longer sleep through the weather, since the others rose swiftly and without objection.

Now, having ridden for an hour in the early morning, the rain is finally coming to a respite. Marcus squints to the east, where the storm clouds are swelling away, making room for the glow of sun between their haze.

There has been nothing in the land. A simple gravesite appears to their left now—an unmarked stone hoop, like a round window, and a mound of dirt. They each look at it.

"We must be nearly there," says Marcus.

"Why? What is that?" Emily says.

"The grave of Larede Sille," Adam replies. A shiver runs through Emily. Known as Larede the Farmer, Larede Sille was the 26th emperor who ruled about a hundred years ago. He shied away from stately duties and lived and worked in the farms of the Calder Glens nine months out of the year, returning to the capital only in the winter months. His wishes were to be buried simply, in the Glens. Still, Emily never thought his gravesite would be that unremarkable.

"Adam," says Marcus.

Scott, riding the farthest from Emily, watches Marcus speak with anticipation, as if Marcus' next move will be violent.

"You make the same of this puddling as I do?" Marcus continues, peering around his horse to look at the ground.

Adam hums. "Looks like we've just enjoyed the first rain this place has seen in a long time."

Emily looks down and sees the thin layer of water squishing through the grass at each step of Copenhagen's. She knows when there's a drought, the earth becomes hard and the water doesn't seep through.

Cazimir follows the gaze of the others but seems unsure of what he is looking at.

A twinge of regret stabs Emily as she watches him. He is just as magnetic in rain as he is in sunlight—water wetting his hair, rain dripping down it as he dips his head to study the ground. Why couldn't she have said something after he kissed her? Why did she have to leave him wordless, making him mistake her silence for rejection? She wants more than anything to steal him alone now.

Which is absurd, she thinks. How do these thoughts have any place in her mind with Marcus' hand, a cult's attacks, and a returned fire demanding her attention?

The rain ceases entirely within the next ten minutes. Sunlight shines through, breaking over the storm clouds, and during the following four hours that they ride, it is stronger than ever, burning up the glistening raindrops in the grass. Emily catches Marcus visor his eyes with his hand in the glare. The renewed brightness is anything but cheerful to him.

That is why, when they reach a crest in the valley leading to a downward slope, he halts upon sight of the Calder Glens below them.

The streams of the Glens stand out immediately, just as the books have described them. They are charcoal lines against a canvas of green glen, resembling growing roots stretching throughout the meadow. The dark contrast of the steams is due to the excess of smooth, black stones mounding in the river, although such finer details cannot be determined from here.

Small homes—earth mounds with stone framing and grass or straw coverings—nestle throughout the stream tendrils, accompanied by humble farms. Since most of the province's food comes from here, Emily is surprised not to find fields and fields of crops rather than these small, individual gardens.

They look on for a moment, and once again, Emily steals a glimpse at Marcus in an attempt to measure his expression.

"Not good, Adam," Marcus says.

Adam looks over.

Emily expects Adam to question Marcus, or else restrain his frustration at constantly being called out upon.

But, for the second time today, Adam's response surprises her.

"I know," he replies almost immediately, his voice low and menacing. He stares at the Glens with the same stern concern that Marcus does.

"What?" says Emily.

"The rivers," Adam answers. "You should hear them from here."

And it hits her why they are so forbidding. She finally registers what she is hearing from the streams.

Silence.

CHAPTER 22

The black stones glare like scales in the sunlight. Moss creeps between their crevices.

Marcus looks up and down the stream as if in search of where the water could be held back. Mason kneels at the riverbed, retrieving a stone and rubbing it in his hand while Adam walks the bank, kicking in rocks and shaking his head.

The horses crop the grass. Scott pretends to chip something off his horse's hoof, but he watches Marcus warily, shifting his gaze from him to Cazimir.

Cazimir stands a little away, hands resting on either side of his belt and gazing downstream to where one of the small, earth-mound houses is. Emily watches him bring a hand to his hair and brush it forward as he often does. He takes a step towards the house and drops his hand back to his belt, exhaling. She can almost see the clockwork thought of his mind. He is so much smarter than the others grant him.

"Unbelievable," says Marcus at last, though he still doesn't bring his eyes to anyone.

"This is peculiar, Marcus," Mason agrees diplomatically. "But there must be an explanation."

"These rivers should be flooded by the tides," snaps Marcus. "Something is trying to keep us from getting this water."

"Or there's a dam," says Mason. "There are many natural possibilities."

Emily jumps into the riverbed with Mason and Adam, inspecting things for herself. It is a wobbly walk among the stones, and even more so with their slippery, wet sheen. She makes her way to Adam and he catches her arm in precaution.

"Careful," he says.

"How many rocks are under here?" she asks breathlessly.

"About a few feet's worth." Adam smiles, trying to hide his amusement at her tipsiness.

"So the seawater runs through here when it floods?"

Adam chuckles. "Floods is a strong word. Even when

the stream is at normal height, the water only rises a few inches above this top layer of stones." He sweeps his hand horizontally over them. "The rest surges through the rocks underneath. It makes the seawater more nutrient-rich. They say that's why these farmers can support the entire province."

Emily reaches down and selects a palm-sized stone, turning it in her hand. It seems like the strangest thing in the world that the river would be filled with so many–

She throws the stone onto the ground and jumps back.

"What?!" says Adam.

"There was something on that stone," she says shrilly. Adam gives the stone she discarded an edgy look and bends to pick it up.

There are carvings. Just like on the stone Guardian. Knots and leaves and tiny licks of fire.

Adam blinks. "What is this?"

"What's what?" Mason approaches them, noticing their interest.

"This stone. It has . . . carvings on it. Like the stonecutters.'"

Mason takes the stone and studies it.

"Oh," he says at once, casual. "Well, who do you

think put all these rocks here, hmm?" he chimes.

"They filled the rivers in the Glens with rocks?" asks Adam, incredulous.

"So the story goes," sighs Mason, stumbling back to the bank and onto solid ground. "Don't ask me why. Some people think they were aware of the agricultural benefits. My guess is that they threw a stone into the river for every member of their tribe who died. All of these rocks were carved at one time, ceremoniously. Most of the indents on them are just washed away by now." He turns to Marcus, already retiring the conversation. "Marcus, I'm ready to go. You've had enough time moping about this sit—"

"*Goddammit*, Mason. The Glens are *dry*. This hasn't happened in centuries. And it's happening now. We needed *this* water for that flame." Marcus gestures heatedly with his hands. Mason stops in his tracks, watching his little cousin in mingled disbelief and curiosity, like he can't imagine why this is causing such a tantrum.

Emily is only half paying attention to Mason and Marcus, still lingering on the legend of the stones being thrown into the river by the stonecarvers. If one stone was tossed for every loved one who died . . . she is standing on thousands and thousands of departed. It should feel eerie, but she scans the ones at her feet now and swallows. It is like anchors for the souls, the rocks. Tokens for the people to live on through.

"Can ask them."

A new voice speaks, and everyone looks at Cazimir.

He wears the same alarmed expression he does when receiving a shock of attention. He swallows and continues nervously. "House down there . . ." He gestures to the house along the bank downstream.

Marcus doesn't even acknowledge the validity of Cazimir's suggestion before he adheres to it. He swings atop his horse with such swiftness that the black steed cranes her head to give him an anxious look.

The others hasten to follow.

When Marcus storms up the small front garden of the farmhouse, he curses and tears draping, delicate-leaved vines from his way. "Disgusting farmers neglecting their jobs," he snarls when another vine dangling from a tall lamppost snags him. He swats it away with both hands.

"I think they're supposed to be like that," Emily says. Their overgrowth seems to be an ordered chaos, tangling up the earthen house. On closer look, their leaves protect hard, tiny, maroon-colored pods, and the source of the vines is a jungle of leaves and greenery to the left.

"Dirty, all of it," says Marcus. "An earth house, too. How sanitary for those who make our food."

"Now *you* are just in an *exceptionally* bad mood, Marcus," Mason chides, walking up alongside him.

"I have a right to be."

"And where would these people find enough wood to build their homes with otherwise, hmm?"

Cazimir has to duck under the vines as he follows Emily, and he seems almost regretful of having made this suggestion. Marcus marches to the front door and raises his fist to knock.

"Marcus," Mason calls patiently. "Perhaps I . . .?"

Marcus glares at Mason for a moment, and then huffs and exhales, dropping his fist. He steps back, allowing Mason to approach the door.

Mason clears his throat and brushes off his clothes from the murk of the riverbed. He inhales and knocks politely on the door.

When it opens instantly, he jumps and exclaims, "Oh, dear. Hello."

A woman is standing at the doorway, opening it just halfway and inspecting the assorted party before her. She is older, with long, auburn hair that falls past her shoulders and garden gloves that go up to her elbows.

"Who are you?" she demands, shifting her eyes to everyone in turn, slow but not frightened. "I've been listening to you walk up."

"Oh, dear," Mason repeats. He recovers and bristles, clapping his hands together. "Yes. Forgive the . . . platoon behind me. My name is Mason Hart. We—"

"Hands off your weapons, please," the woman interrupts. Mason spins to see who the offender is, and Adam coughs uncomfortably, removing his hand from the hilt of his short sword, which he had rested there unconsciously.

"Right," Mason sighs, realizing his diplomatic skills won't be able to avoid the tension here. "We're working to rid of this flame," he admits.

She shifts and opens to door a little more.

"And we needed water from the streams."

"Well, there's none, as you can see," she says.

Mason pauses and nods. "Yes." His voice is sad and empathetic. Emily admires his emotional intelligence—he has a sympathetic effect in the farmer's doorway, just standing there and giving space to her struggle. She would have slammed the door on Marcus by now.

"Come with me to the garden," the woman says at last. "Around back."

She closes the door and locks it.

"Well." Mason sighs.

"Let's go," Marcus groans, but he turns to leave the farmhouse entirely.

"No," Emily speaks up. "I'm going around back, Marcus."

"This is a waste of time, Emily. She's got nothing to say to us."

Emily ignores him. She cuts around the house to the back.

Cazimir is the first to follow.

"My husband and a few of the others went south to see where the water got clogged. They suspected a dam. There's no other way the Glens would become dry. It's our entire life that relies on those tides." The gardener sighs despairingly. "The rain is not enough."

She turns out to be extremely hospitable. Her garden in the back is a small, stone-paved patio surrounded by the snaking vines they saw in the front and the occasional flower. She seats the Brotherhood party at the outdoor table and provides them with some kind of roast bird—a poultry Emily is unfamiliar with. But it's juicy and tastes miraculous after the berries, dried beef, and bread from the guardhouse she's been living off of.

"Something must be stopping the tides from funneling in," the woman sighs.

Marcus seems highly interested in her commentary, listening darkly as he lifts his portion of meat with his fingers.

"Sorry about the plates and utensils," the woman adds. The lack thereof. "Wood is expensive out here, as you can guess."

"Where did your husband go, ma'am?" Brother Scott inquires, not even touching his meal. Marcus looks over at Scott with narrowed eyes. "South where?"

"Towards the shore, of course. Our economy—the food supply of the entire province—is going to take a big hit if they don't reconcile the clog, or whatever is stopping the flow."

"I think the economy isn't the biggest concern," Adam comments mildly. "And perhaps neither even is the risk of famine. I'm worried about this in light of the fire." He doesn't look up from his food.

The woman pauses, collecting her thoughts. "About that," she says. "I think it's your turn to give me a little information. Why do you need water from here so badly? And what's this pretty young lady doing in line with you rugged lot?" she adds on a lighter note.

"We needed water from the Glens because it was closer than water from the sea—pretty much the same thing." Marcus grunts. "And we're not going back without this water." He looks around at them all, as if making sure his decision was relayed.

"I see," the woman answers, placing her elbows on the table and resting her chin on her clasped, garden-gloved hands. She seems to accept this is the most information she'll be given from the gruff, grey-bearded Marcus. Her gloves remind Emily of Marcus' gauntlet—which of course he still wears—and her stomach flips.

"And you?" The farmer turns to Emily.

Emily swallows the last morsel of her portion.

"Someone had to keep an eye on them," she says.

The woman returns a smile. "What's your name?"

"Emily Byrnes. Thanks so much for having us . . ." She hesitates, realizing she's never caught the woman's name.

"Leonie," the woman provides.

Emily smiles and nods, as if in renewed greeting.

The men watch in stunned silence. The women seem

to interact so seamlessly.

"What do you grow here?" Emily turns in her seat towards all the vines and plants. She studies the maroon pods clustering under the leaves and a thought strikes her. "Is that wickernut?"

Leonie follows her gaze and raises her eyebrows. "It is. I'm surprised you knew that. It's not a very popular crop to grow, and not just because of the cuts the thorny parts can give you." She laughs and lifts her forearms, shaking them to show off the thick gloves. "But my husband and I actually pick them to brew—"

"Wickerrye," Emily finishes.

Leonie straightens. She smiles widely, surprised and delighted. "How did you know that?"

Emily shakes her head, realizing the humor in an innocent-looking girl being so familiar with liquor. "I used to work at a bar," she clarifies. "Back in Darson's Ford."

The woman shifts, suddenly intently curious about something.

"You wouldn't happen to . . . you didn't work at Nestor Robutan's bar, did you?"

Adam cocks his head at the connection. Marcus cracks his knuckles impatiently with this exchange and

Mason and Cazimir, sitting at the far end of the table, had decided to break off into a small Galeduan lesson as they finish their food. Brother Scott still has not touched the bird.

"Yeah," Emily replies, dumbfounded. "How did you—?"

"We trade wickerrye with him for wood and chairs and such. I see him every few months when he makes rounds to markets. He was one of the first to move to the Ford when it was built thirty-some years ago. I think he had *just* hired you when I met with him many moons ago. You should have seen how happy he was. You would have thought he had a granddaughter just born."

Emily is at a loss. She never imagined she could have meant so much to the old man.

"Except . . ." Leonie adds, "I thought he said your name was Amanda?"

Emily laughs.

"Did you quit, then?" Leonie asks with a hint of concern.

An uncomfortable expression crosses Emily's face. "I . . . I had to go without telling him." She gestures to Adam. "So I could go with . . ."

The woman nods slowly, understanding. She pauses

and says, "I think you brought much more joy to Nestor than you know," in a would-be comforting voice.

Emily's expression stays down, though. A wave of guilt pours over her as she imagines how sad Mr. Robutan must be to think she had just abandoned him.

"Can you do me a favor?" Emily asks suddenly. "Next time you see him . . . can you tell him I'm okay? And that I *had* to go, but I promise I'll be back. Please?"

The woman watches her kindly for a moment. She is about to nod when Emily adds,

"Tell him I love him, too."

"I'll tell him. I don't think he needs his children or a granddaughter when he has you. You're certainly better to him than they were."

So Mr. Robutan does have kids. Estranged, by the sound of it. Emily doesn't say anything.

There is little more after this conversation, and the others finish their birds and push the bones to the center of the table. They thank Leonie, and she refuses the coins Marcus offers.

The horses are waiting dutifully for their return. Emily mounts Copenhagen without direction from Marcus, who imitates her almost immediately.

"That was worth the lunch," says Adam, "but we're

not going to find anything else here, Marcus."

"I know," Marcus rumbles.

"So, let's not delay," says Emily, her voice more authoritative than she anticipated. "I guess there's only one place to get what we need now. We'll get there before midnight if we leave now."

"I'm sorry," Marcus scoffs, "are you in the lead?"

Emily smiles. Mason, atop his horse, smiles too. "Maybe."

"And where would you lead us?" Adam plays along warmly.

But that warmth is stolen from inside her as she follows with her eyes a dry river tendril down to the southern horizon. So much uncertainty lies ahead. And somewhere in that direction is something big enough to dry the Calder Glens. Still she knows where they must go.

"The sea."

CHAPTER 23

When they reached a signpost, Emily had stopped. The sign spelled ENDRAFT and pointed right with the path. To the left, the dry riverbed diverged. The others halted with Emily, their horses snorting. To her surprise, Marcus looked at her. And instead of declaring a next move, he continued to look at her. It was not with cruel amusement; rather, for this moment anyway, he almost seemed to buy in to letting her lead.

"Which way?" Adam had asked, but it was almost of no one in particular. He'd glanced at the moons, perhaps judging the time.

The choice was difficult. Pursue the riverbed—for however long it would wind—and find the source of the clogging, or pursue the path to Endraft and reach the seawater quicker. Emily felt Scott's stare on the back of her neck more than any of the others.

She thought. And without a word, she led Copenhagen towards Endraft.

Now, a taste of salt tingles her tongue.

Rhythmic sounds play in the back of her mind; distant, unfamiliar. She cannot place it, but the only connotation she can apply to it is motion.

The sound becomes louder, more present. Like constant, deep sighs.

A flash of blue light ahead distracts her. It glows atop a tall stone tower in the distance, encased like an oversized lantern.

The others lift their heads to it as well, with the exception of Marcus, who looks determinedly ahead.

The light blinks atop the tower, long enough that she barely notices how much closer they are to it—how much more she is raising her eyes to it.

And that is why, when Copenhagen stops and gives a small toss of his head, she nearly falls off him in astonishment at what she is seeing.

The silver moon and its ruby companion drape over the ebony sea spreading wide before them. It stretches to the corners of the horizon, as if it will spill over the earth's edge. In the midground, a strip of sea in front of it, rises

Mt. Vestover. It is farther than it appears. No snow reflects on its surface—its melt has already happened.

Dots of blue light illuminate the line of wooden buildings along the shore. The light hangs from ropes and clings to the railing of decks.

The whole atmosphere has a breath to it—the constant exhale of the sea, the seethe of foam on the sand. Other than this, the town is quiet.

Emily is startled to find Adam, to her left, watching her.

There is a gentle light behind Adam's eyes. A tender, meek smile on his lips. It is the same way he had watched her on the night of the Celestial, when she was exhilarated with anticipation.

"Amazing, isn't it?" he says, low enough so the others won't hear.

The light atop the stone tower, standing on the shore, blinks again.

Emily shakes her head in marvel. "Is that a lighthouse?" She indicates the tower.

"Yeah," Adam answers. "We're in Endraft."

"Let's find an inn, guys," says Marcus to their left. His voice is tired, worn. "Careful down this sand."

○ ~ ○ ~ ○

"They have vacancy," says Marcus, shuffling down the stairs of the restaurant's back door. White sand dusts the grey driftwood steps.

Emily stands at Marcus' arrival. She had been sitting in the soft, cool sand, digging her fingers through it and watching the horses twitch their ears and survey the unusual texture of the ground beneath them. Her other companions are either too sleepy—like Mason and Scott—or too enamored with the surroundings—like Cazimir and Adam—to speak.

"I bought three rooms," says Marcus. He hands Adam a key and reaches over to drop another in Scott's hand as well. Emily notices an odd change in Marcus. He is weary for once. Docile. "Same boarding partners. Me and Mason. Adam and Emily . . ." He trails off.

Emily is amazed Marcus hasn't depleted a year's worth of savings yet, purchasing all of their facilities. Food. The new horses. Where did such wealth originate?

"Let's rest a bit." Adam comes up next to Emily and speaks in her ear. "Then you can check out the sea."

A childish flutter of excitement wells in her stomach. It is a weird sensation having her feet sink in the sand as she walks, but she catches the railing of the stairway and climbs it after Marcus, towards the inn's backdoor.

Heavy, tired footsteps clunk up behind her.

The inn is more restaurant than anything else. Large and long, it is constructed with the characteristic, greyish worn wood and decorated with fishing nets and enormous crab shells hung on the wall.

Adam and Emily both eye a particularly big and well-woven net similar to those they use to harvest tubers.

"That'd be a good one, wouldn't it?" says Adam in his gentle voice.

Emily can only shake her head in playful envy and rub her fingers.

He unlocks the door to their room and they step in gratefully.

It is small but quaint. There is only one bed, but a chest at its end provides extra, fluffy blankets. The bed itself looks the cleanest and most comfortable they've slept in yet—even better than Emily's back at Mr. Robutan's bar, which he had always prepared especially nicely for her.

A small residue of sand gathers in the corners of the room, accompanied by two or three tiny brown shells.

Adam pauses upon sight of it. "You think that's there on purpose? Decoration?"

"It's supposed to be subtlety, Adam," Emily responds

in mock chide. "Something you wouldn't understand."

Adam unpacks his things in silence and then does the same for hers, folding her clothes neatly on the red covers of the bed. He swallows. "I don't really need to use the room." He watches his hands stack her books over the chest delicately. "I'll leave you to change or whatever you need."

Emily lets him work for a moment, wondering if Adam is distracting himself by so compulsively attending to their things. Something seems different about him. He won't meet her eyes. It is as if seeing her belongings occupying the room has upset him.

"You okay, Adam?"

His hands stop their work.

"I'm so sorry, Emily," he says unexpectedly.

"What? Why?" Emily takes a sympathetic step towards him.

"That I brought you into this. That you're here because of me." He studies her clothes and books for a long time, as if thinking again and again that they shouldn't be here. They should be back in Darson's Ford. "The damage I've done to you . . . it's irreparable."

It is true that she is scared of going to the flame. She is afraid of Marcus' burn. She is afraid of what Adam could have done to land him in the Brotherhood—what secret Marcus is keeping for him. But her heart breaks when she hears his voice speak these words. She cannot say anything that will justify what she feels.

So she doesn't. She steps to him and drops her forehead onto his arm, taking his hand at the same time. He turns his head from her immediately, pinching his eyes with his other hand.

"No, Adam," Emily murmurs against him. "*I'd* be irreparable if I never met you."

He places his hand behind her head. Leaning down, he kisses the top of it. She can hear him sniffle.

Then he shifts and she pulls back. He slides to kneel before her and makes gruff, throaty noises to compose himself as he fishes in his pocket. He brings out a small carving affixed to a needle—it is the carving he's been working on in their tent at night. His knife intricately chiseled a miniscule bough of dainty, bell-shaped blue flowers. It rests now in his palm—next to the small carved token Emily had attempted to make for him. She'd been proud of it at the time. But her work looks like a cutting board compared to his.

She recognizes the flower instantly. Bluebells.

"I thought you'd miss our trees," he says thickly,

giving another rough clearing of this throat. She watches as he pinches the needle and pins the tiny bough to her shirt, over her heart. "Now you always know where they are."

He stands and squeezes her wooden token in his hand before replacing it in his pocket.

○ ~ ○ ~ ○

An older man behind the bar scrubs a rag over the surface, looking up at Emily's arrival. His hair and beard are salt-and-pepper, his skin a tough sun-tanned, and his nails are yellow on the hand that washes the counter.

"Dinner's closed, dear," he says. "I can throw some clams on for you if you're hungry, though."

She smiles, endeared. "I'm okay," she says. "Thank you. I actually just wanted to see the sea . . ."

The man stops and leans on the counter with both hands, studying her warmly. "Where you from?"

"Darson's Ford."

"Well, Darson's Ford, the deck's open out front. Best view in Endraft."

"Can't pass that up," she says.

He winks at her and resumes wiping off remains of shellfish. She opens the front door quietly.

The verandah wraps almost entirely around the bar.

Ropes tied with lamps of blue light drape along its wooden awning.

Past the deck is pearly, moonlit sand. Inky, purplish waves crash over the shore, rushing to caress the beach. Its foam seethes as the tide pulls it back.

The rhythm continues.

She is so entranced by it that she hadn't noticed him a little to her left. Her heart thuds.

He leans deeply on the rail of the deck, hands clasped in front of him, watching the sea.

Her body is frozen for a moment on sight of Cazimir, the backdrop of the water, and the ease of his posture. They seem in harmony—him and the waves. And it hits her that the two are much alike. Cazimir, the most out of place among the Brotherhood, conducts his own rhythm. His own way of motion. Just like the sea before them.

Cazimir doesn't hear her come up to him until the last second. He sees her from the corner of his eye and turns, surprised. He is about to speak when she throws her arms around his neck and kisses him.

The reaction is instant. He melts in her, plunging deeper into the kiss. Gentle warmth caresses her back as light accumulates over his fingers—an unconscious response. He makes the smallest sound of exasperation before pulling back, meeting her eyes cautiously.

She is blushing, but still able to mumble his name. "Caz . . ."

This confirms something for him. His eyes light gently, a blissful smile tugging at his lips. "Emily," he breathes, bringing his hands to her face and dropping his forehead over hers.

He closes his eyes and breathes deeply, just holding her, and she registers the waves tumbling over the shore. Her heart pounds the whole time, but the warmth of his strong hands brings a feeling of safety she cannot comprehend.

At last, he shakes his head slowly and pulls back. "I thought . . ." he croaks.

"You didn't think right."

Cazimir sighs in happiness and retakes his place at the rail. He swallows and looks at her as she joins him and leans the way he does. The Darvican's mesmerizing teal light floats at his wrist. Emily is sure other men would be embarrassed by its sudden, kiss-induced appearance. Cazimir is not. He is proud of his light. Comfortable with it. He lets it glow on his skin.

"It's beautiful here," she says.

Cazimir nods, but his eyes linger on her. He looks at

the water as soon as she catches it.

“I’ve never seen . . .” He shakes his head, indicating the Arluian Sea.

“Me neither.”

“I’ll have to . . . go in.” He rolls a hand in its direction.

“Go in the water?” Emily asks, surprised.

“Only chance probably. I live in mountains.”

Emily gives an amused laugh. “Alright, Caz. Do it. It’s probably freezing, but have fun.”

“I don’t mind cold.”

“Go on, then,” she taunts, nodding at the waves.

He straightens from the rail, determined. She follows him with her eyes until he walks behind her and appears on her other side, next to the verandah’s stairs. There is a mischievous look on his face and he just stands there.

“What?” she says. “Come on, tough guy.”

“You are coming.” He takes her shoulder, waiting for her to follow.

“What? Absolutely not.” She stiffens and grips the rail.

“Yes. You made me dance. Now you come.”

“I’m not going in there, Caz,” she says, and there is a resolute note in her voice, still clutching the rail.

Cazimir gives a sigh of mock impatience and takes her shoulders in either hand. "Let go," he says in false strictness.

"No," she says.

"Yes. Let go."

"Caz, I'm *not* going—"

He leans down and scoops her off her feet.

"Caz! What the h—!"

Emily is forced to release the rail, tipping into his arms completely. He ignores her protests, and even risks meeting her eyes with humor as if to see if she *completely* hates him.

She is suddenly reminded of the night he carried her to Welshire with Adam. The way he glanced sheepishly down at her, the concern written in his eyes, and the stars alight above him. Now, he looks down at her again, but there is no concern, despite the thrashing, cold water she is now doomed to plunge into. Instead, there is tender playfulness.

The stars, however, are in the same place. Twinkling above him.

"Fine," she says. "Onward!" She clutches his neck in terror—and excitement—as he walks her down the stairs and into the fine sand.

He stalls letting her down, walking a few more paces to where the sand is firmer with wetness.

She is set back on the sand just as the sea's froth rushes over their feet. Cazimir doesn't even bother to remove his shirt. He detaches the sheath of his sword and throws it into the sand. Then he gives her his amused, cynical look, as if seeing if she will go through on her promise.

"Yeah, one second," Emily deflects, watching the force of the waves rise under the moonlight.

Cazimir walks slowly backwards into the uprush, and Emily follows with tiny steps.

He endures the waves over his back, still facing her, and then he is waist deep in the water, already past the breakers, maintaining his bearings in the current. He tries to contain his entertainment as Emily walks ankle-deep into the water as if it is liquid acid.

Finally, he gives a dramatic roll of his eyes and, making sure she can see, deliberately falls into the water.

It is so smooth that one second she sees him, and the next he has submerged, only to reappear a moment later, hair soaked, and spitting from his mouth. His eyes are tightly shut and then he blinks them clear.

Thinking he'd hurt himself, Emily forces herself in,

inhaling sharply as the cold water rushes over her. She plows through the tide and bubbles until she reaches him. "Are you—?" she begins, but stops. Although his eyes are red from the sting of salt, he smiles and shakes his head. And that is when she realizes she's been hoodwinked.

The sea thrashes over her, and she shudders. They are not quite chest-deep in the water. Adam's tiny flower is still safely pinned to her shirt. She can just feel the seafloor at her feet, but still the waves lift them up and down, and Cazimir rests a steadying arm around her shoulders, as if to make up for his trickery.

"That w—wasn't fair," she shivers, but she can't help but feel a rush of exhilaration in the sea. Its motion and rhythm—just like Cazimir's—is hard to deny.

"Ah, Emily . . ." he sighs.

"Emily nothing." She splashes him, aiming to make his stinging eyes a little redder. He ducks and blocks it with his hand, smiling again.

From the water he lifts his wrist, where the blue light clings to him the way his soaked hairs cling to his forearm.

"Remove for me." His voice is hushed, even a little eager.

"No," she says, lifting a hand to feel its aura but not willing it to shrink. He bobs closer to her, and she is not certain how much of the waves that was. He rumbles a long, playfully annoyed rumble.

"I don't want to remove it," she whispers.

And at that, he makes a sound she's never heard before—a groan mixing frustration and pleasure. He reels her in.

"What am I doing here?" Emily closes her eyes and laughs against his chest.

"I said let go . . ." he murmurs once more.

"I did," she says. "You caught me."

Cazimir hums in agreement. He presses his wet lips to her forehead. His words are barely audible.

"*Ahm cara.*"

CHAPTER 24

Day shines down on Endraft, and Emily sits on the verandah of the inn. The sun has just climbed the sky in early morning, and diamonds sparkle in the water.

Though she should be hungry, she hadn't wanted breakfast this early, politely turning down the eggs and ham the innkeeper had offered her.

"Fine, but if you don't eat, you drink," the man had said, turning behind the bar and grabbing a pitcher. He had poured her a thick drink of juice, which he boasted was a blend of the tropic fruit grown off the islands beyond their sight. He handed it to her with his yellow-nailed hand and smiled beneath his beard, eyes a foamy hazel.

She takes a sip now and savors its sweet, tangy chill.

In the light of day, Endraft takes on a new character.

Seagulls glide along the air, cawing in harmony with the crashing waves. Fishermen can be heard calling to one another, or else laughing as they climb the docks to their boats.

Which is another thing the night had disguised from her. Small, shabby boats are anchored in the water, hosting lone, standing figures and their rods, or else several people, hauling in nets from the sea. Two long docks, one on either end of Endraft's street of sea-facing buildings, harbor unoccupied boats bobbing in the swells. Larger traveling ships are anchored there as well—cargo vessels, most likely, to relay imports to Endraft from the islands offshore.

Or maybe farther.

Emily's books never showed maps spanning farther than the Empire's provinces and the continent's lone adversary, Asht Vendar. But looking now to the apparently endless sea, there is sure to be more beyond this. More that they don't know about.

Emily sighs and sits back in the chair. No one else, as far as she knows, is awake.

Cazimir and she had only waded in the sea for a few moments before returning to shore last night. She'd asked him again, now that he'd repeated it, what that insolvable *ahm cara* meant. Rather than being embarrassed and evasive on the subject, as he was when she last asked him, he simply smiled and shook his head, water dripping down his clothes as they plodded up the beach.

When she had returned to her and Adam's room, she found Adam fast asleep on the floor, leaving the bed for her use yet again. She changed into dry clothes and left the bed untouched. Instead, to make a point, she had lain on the floor next to him, wrapped herself in a blanket, and fallen asleep.

A harbor bell dings lazily somewhere down the beach, and she inhales a deep breath of fresh, salty air. Today will most likely be the last she sees of the shore, if Marcus jumps out of bed within the hour, fills a jug with saltwater, and herds them off to Fort Myrth as she expects. She will miss it here.

She stands and shuffles down the stairs of the deck, reaching warm, smooth sand. Endraft is no tourist hotspot for Glens people, weary of their plains. It is a productive fishing village, which is why the empty beach doesn't surprise her. She takes a few steps towards the water and then stops when she sees him from the corner of her eye.

Adam walks along the shore in the distance, watching the waves roll in. He holds his shoes under his arm and wears his favorite, forest-green shirt with brown trim.

She is frozen. It is a vision precisely from her dream. A wave sweeps up the shore, surging across his feet. She expects him to fall—to collapse under its power, as he had in the dream.

But he doesn't. He continues walking, calm, relaxed, watching the sea as the undertow sucks the water back in.

She jogs over to him.

"Hey," he says, lighting up with surprise on sight of her.

She comes up beside him and wraps her arms around one of his, walking in step with him. He cocks his head in befuddlement. "What's that for?"

"Nothing," she says sincerely, still walking with her arms wrapped in his one. "I'm just happy to see you."

"I'm happy to see you, too, squirt." He chuckles.

Water churns over their feet again from another wave as they continue walking down the beach. It is an amazing feeling, being able to talk with Adam here as if nothing has happened. There is no fire at Fort Myrth. There is no Brotherhood. The Emperor is still on the throne. All seems okay, walking with him.

"Did you go in the water last night?" he asks.

"I did, but . . . I was scared. I'm not gonna lie."

He laughs. "So you'll pounce on an assassin with your knife drawn, but you're afraid of the sea."

"I can control what I do with my knife," Emily defends. "I can't control the sea. I can't fight the waves."

Adam is silent for a second.

"So don't fight the waves."

Emily blinks. "Then how am I supposed to swim?"

"You don't fight the waves to swim. You let them lift you."

She remembers Cazimir and herself being lifted up and down as the surf rolled in last night.

"My mother told me the same thing," Adam elaborates. "I was afraid of it, too. But she said, 'Adam Lawrence, if you can't swim in the sea, you sure as hell can't swim in the Ford.' I knew she meant business if she used my middle name. And she always thought the Ford was the foulest water in the Empire."

"And yet she stayed there," says Emily. "You've lived in Darson's Ford as long as it's existed, haven't you?"

Adam nods and smiles shallowly, looking to the sand.

That would be about thirty years—just after General Darson's sacrifice turned him into a folk hero, when pilgrims built the town on top of it.

They reach the steps of the porch and turn for it. Emily notices a jug that is slung over Adam's shoulder, hanging at his other side.

"What's that?" she asks.

"The seawater," he says, hopping up the stairs with her. "I got it for Marcus. We're leaving."

○ ~ ○ ~ ○

"What do you mean we're *not allowed to leave?!*"

Marcus is at the bar, clenching his fists upon the surface threateningly.

The innkeeper raises his arms. "I don't call the shots, buddy!"

Mason, Cazimir, and Scott are with them, but they are all seated at a table as Marcus argues with the innkeeper. Mason rests his chin in his hand. It seems as if this has gone on for some time.

"What's going on?" Adam closes the door behind him and Emily, eyebrows knit together.

"We're on lockdown, that's what," Marcus snarls.

"It's like I told your friend here." The innkeeper raises his voice to Adam. "I don't call the shots. No one is allowed to enter or leave Endraft today."

A dark look crosses Adam's features.

Emily catches eye with Scott. He gives her a grave, knowing look, and she knows exactly what he means by it.

Scott thinks the town is on lockdown so that Marcus cannot leave.

"Why's that?" Emily says, lingering her eyes on Scott for just a moment before turning them to the innkeeper.

"I don't know the details, but I think we're exporting some classified cargo today. They must be worried about thieves. It doesn't happen often, but it does happen. Like when we brought in the pearls for the Vicar to bless. The ones decorating the empress' crown when Accalon got married."

Marcus gives a roar of anger and hurls over a chair. The innkeeper raises his palms.

"Hey, *hey!*" spurts the innkeeper. Marcus clutches his face in renewed emotion. "Something wrong with the Emperor now?"

"*Damn* the Emperor!" yells Marcus.

Emily looks at Mason, expecting to find him rubbing his eyes or making some other embarrassed gesture. Instead, he watches his cousin with a serious look, almost one of solidarity.

"There's nothing you lot can do about it," says the innkeeper. "Try and run towards the Glens, if you want. If you can get past the guards, I'll keep my mouth shut. But good luck, because Endraft's crawling with them today."

And he leaves into the kitchen behind the bar, abandoning the fight.

"We'll wait one day, Marcus," Mason reasons. "What can happen in one day?"

"Anything," says Marcus. "We need to get out of here. And I mean today. Not tomorrow."

A trickle of suspicion seeps through Emily. The town is on lockdown . . . guards are barring the exits . . . and Marcus is going crazy. What if he *is* afraid of being caught for something? What if Captain Marley, or even MacPerth—the Supreme General—gave the order to arrest him, and he knows it?

"They usually try to get their shipments out by early afternoon," says Adam in a placating tone. "Let's wait until then and I'll go down to the harbor and ask if all is clear. Maybe they'll make an exception for us to leave before nightfall."

Marcus doesn't answer. He collapses into a chair and

stares at the wall, his face pale.

And that is where it seems he will stay for the next few hours.

Mason nods at the others to leave him alone with Marcus, quiet and cautious as if there were a death in the family. Adam obeys and steps outside to identify the luxury cargo boat that must have arrived. He intends to visit it later that afternoon to ask permission to depart Endraft.

The second Emily enters the hallway to reach her and Adam's room, Scott grabs her and leads her into his own, snapping the door shut.

"They're going to arrest him tonight," says Scott immediately.

"Marcus?"

"Of course, Marcus. Why do you think this is going on? Did you see the guards out back?"

She had only been out front today, on the shore. She shakes her head.

"They're everywhere. Must have been called in from other towns. Emily, Marcus may put up a fight. The cult might come in and make things bloody before they can arrest him."

"Scott, his hand is burned. The *Vicar's* entire face is

burned! That doesn't mean he's on the bad side! Where are you getting these crazy ideas that Marcus *lit the flame?!*"

"Because he's *playing* you, Emily! Why wouldn't he have run by now? Why is he not fleeing right now, but doing *everything* the government tells him to? Because he was playing them to make him seem less suspicious. To rule himself out to them. Who are you going to trust? Me and Captain Marley, or him?"

Emily hesitates.

"I risked my life coming here to save you guys from him. You're not the guilty ones. I've been in the Brotherhood, Emily. We've done *bad things.* Mason, Adam, and I. Bad. But nothing compared to what Marcus is doing."

"No, Scott," says Emily, shaking her head. "Marcus runs the Brotherhood to protect you guys from getting arrested. Not to *keep doing* bad—"

"You think Marcus runs the Brotherhood?"

Emily pauses, seriously confused. Scott gives a dark smile and shakes his head slowly.

"The Brotherhood's outlived Marcus by about eight hundred years. He runs nothing."

"It was a cult of firelighters," says Emily, drawing on

her history knowledge to make sense of this. "But it must have different sects now. Real fire-worshippers in one small sect and petty criminals in the other. Marcus runs the latter." It was a wild guess, but she tried to make it sound confident.

"Are you sure about that?"

Her efforts clearly failed.

"Adam's not a part of this," Emily declares suddenly, almost desperately. Scott stops, surprised and uncomfortable.

"No," he agrees slowly, "he's not. Neither am I, or Mason—Marcus' own cousin. Like I said, Marcus brought the Brotherhood back. And its new generation members aren't evil like before. We were all just criminals who needed protection by him. Needed to know where we were safe and undercover from the guards."

"How did he protect you?"

"He paid off people. Worked the system behind the scenes. Haven't you seen he's loaded?"

Yes, she's seen his unexplainably endless supply of money.

"So, what do you want to do, Scott?"

Scott inhales a deep breath. "Leave. You and I could

sneak past the guards."

"What about Adam? And Cazimir? And Mason?"

"We can't all leave. Marcus would know. That would set him off."

"Then I'm not going."

"Adam can take care of himself, I know he can. Just leave him tonight and we can meet up with him at the gong outpost."

"Scott, no!"

The door opens behind them, and Emily jumps.

Cazimir steps in without preamble, his eyes dark and suspicious. He closes the door behind him.

"We're busy, Darvica. You can sleep later," says Scott. "Get out."

"What is happening?" Cazimir demands. There is a dangerous timbre in his Darvic accent.

"None of your business, miner. I said leave."

Emily would scold Scott, stand up for Cazimir, if she wasn't so intimidated herself by the tension in the Darvican's body as he watches the other.

"I heard her." Cazimir gestures to Emily with his head but keeps his eyes steady on Scott.

"And what? Afraid I'm hurting your little girlfriend?" Scott reaches out and takes Emily's forearm in his hand.

Cazimir reacts so quickly she barely sees. He disarms Scott's wrist with such force that the other staggers.

"Filthy coal miner!" Scott seethes, and he steps forward to retaliate. He pushes Emily aside by the shoulder, but the second he touches her, Cazimir is set off again.

He grabs the scruff of Scott's shirt with both hands and rams him against the wall. As soon as Cazimir pulls back his fist, Scott whacks a punch across Cazimir's face and blood sprays off his nose and onto the wall.

Cazimir struggles to hold onto Scott with one hand while using the other to grope for Scott's fist, catching the next punch.

Emily draws her knife, having no idea what she is going to do with it, and rushes to separate them when a loud voice booms from behind.

"WHAT THE DEVIL IS GOING ON BACK HERE!"

The innkeeper storms into the room, wielding a club and looking furious, a vein throbbing at this temple. He seizes Cazimir and pulls him off Scott with all his might.

Cazimir stumbles backwards and wipes blood off his mouth with the back of his hand.

"Both of you! If I hear *one* more sound from this damn party, you're out for good and can sleep in the sand! *Understand*?"

Scott and Cazimir are both panting, but the innkeeper accepts their silence as confirmation. Still fuming, he turns, but manages to give Emily a sympathetic look before leaving, as if excusing her from his harsh words.

Emily leaves, her mind too filled to say anything, too shaken even to check on Cazimir. But she can feel the dark, resentful glare of Scott following her from the room.

○ ~ ○ ~ ○

"Not just you, Adam," says Marcus. "We're all going to the port. Pretend we're leaving. Everyone get your things. If they let us go, we leave from there."

Dusk has set in, and Marcus jumps down the steps of the porch into the sand. Everyone hoists their respective bags and follows him.

The innkeeper was not lying about the town crawling with soldiers, but most pay them no mind, occupied in conversation with other guards or trying to placate villagers upset by their presence.

"Ignore them," Marcus rumbles.

Among silhouettes of dark, shabby boats floats a long, walnut-colored vessel. It is slender and its bow is elegantly curved into a swirl. A small, roofed cabin is built near the stern, and there is a border of intricate bronze along the bulwark. The vessel seems to be made of uvarde wood—an expensive lumber that is buoyant and heavy at the same time, said to produce stable watercraft that minimize rocking. Uvarde is found only in Fellvren.

This is the boat Adam identified as new to the port and wealthy-looking enough to carry cargo precious enough to induce a lockdown.

Black waves lap against the posts as they climb onto the dock; the purple dusk falls deeper into night. The seagulls have stopped their squawking, and it is eerily silent besides the creak of the wood beneath their feet or the groan of tight ropes holding onto bobbing fishing boats. The sea air is cool against their faces.

"Can I help you, sir?" A guard approaches Marcus, stopping them.

"We need to see who's in charge of the lockdown," Marcus replies, as calmly as he can. "It's critical that my party and I leave tonight."

"What's your name?" the guard asks. His tone is a little too light.

Marcus stares him down before answering.

"I'll tell that to whoever's in charge."

The soldier narrows his eyes. "Fine, then. If it's that much of an emergency that you leave tonight, I'll ask if he'll see you."

"He will see me," Marcus presses.

"I'm afraid that's—" the soldier begins, but he cuts off. Emily sees his eyes flutter on Marcus' gauntlet and then back away swiftly. "Fine," he says. "Follow me."

Did Marcus see the movement? He follows the guard in grim silence.

They are brought to the plank leading over the water onto the slender vessel. The guard nods them down and Marcus doesn't miss a beat.

But something feels wrong to Emily as the soldier stays back and watches them cross. When Mason, the last person, boards the ship, she hears a sound that makes her heart jump.

There is a clatter and then a splash.

Marcus spins to the soldier.

The plank has been kicked off the ledge and into the water, trapping them on board.

"*What the hell are you doing!*" Marcus roars, running over to the rail of the ship.

"Your man is right inside the cabin, Marcus Brawl,"

calls the guard. “We’ll be waiting.”

Marcus is breathless, nearly choking for air as he searches in panic for an escape. He is sweating, and it is the closest look to terror Emily has ever seen in him. Her heart pounds.

Scott was right. Marcus has just been caught.

“Adam—” she whispers, terrified.

“Shh,” says Adam, but his voice is just as shaky and frightened.

“Marcus!” Mason steps forward and grabs Marcus.

“Get off me! I need to get off!” Marcus is trying to climb the bulwark.

It can’t be true. Marcus isn’t the flamelighter. No. But why else is he panicking like this?

“Let’s go in, Marcus,” says Mason.

Marcus swats Mason’s hand away, but he does not search for an exit anymore. His distress molds into resolute fury.

He storms to the cabin door.

As if in a daze, Emily and the others follow. She notices Cazimir has a tight grip on his sword hilt. And Scott . . . Scott is as passive as ever.

“Let’s go!” Marcus barks at the others. He tears open the door to the cabin and dives inside without hesitation.

Adam has a firm hand on Emily's shoulder, but she is the first to follow Marcus into the well-lit cabin.

The second she enters, she gasps.

There is a table in the center of the room. And across from her, at its end, is Emperor Accalon.

CHAPTER 25

"Have a seat, Marcus."

The door is sealed behind them by one of the guards on the ship. The Emperor's royal guards—the Black Guard—stand at each corner of the room. They wear black trithium armor rather than silvery steel.

Marcus nearly dives for the circular table, fists clenched. He offers no formality to the ruler of the Empire, who watches the party now with steady green eyes. He is a big man with a curtain of shoulder-length grey hair. He wears a coat of deep red accented in arctic fox fur. He resembles an ancient eagle, and something about his size and strength seem familiar to Emily.

It is surreal. The room spins despite her standing firmly in place. She is immobilized, which seems to intrigue Accalon, who is watching her above any of the others. And yet she tries to avoid his gaze.

Cazimir is standing to her left, his mouth hung open and eyes glazed in disbelief. Mason wears a peculiar expression: restraint. He is not shocked by the Emperor's presence. There is something he is exerting great effort to hold back, and his amicable demeanor is very forced as he sits next to Marcus.

Emily cannot see Adam's expression, for he still stands behind her, holding her shoulder steadily.

But Scott . . .

Scott is not disoriented in the least. He creeps around the table and sits to the left of Accalon, unfazed.

"You brought a young girl with you, Marcus?" says Accalon, still watching Emily. His voice is old and intelligent. It is slow and practiced—suited to calming courts and cities.

"Come on," Adam whispers soothingly, gently pushing Emily forward and pulling out a seat for her.

Marcus stares determinedly ahead, not acknowledging the Emperor. Why is he not as stunned as Emily?

Adam and Cazimir take their seats, and at last, the table is full.

"Together, at last," says Accalon. "I thought the day

would never come . . ."

"I *prayed* the day would never come, Accalon," Marcus snaps, though his eyes are still glued to the wall opposite him.

"*Enough*, Marcus," Mason scolds.

Emily cannot believe Marcus' behavior towards the Emperor, but it only intensifies her fear that what Scott was saying is true. She clenches the rim of the table.

"That's all right, Mason," says Accalon slowly, eyeing them both. "It is good to see you, too . . ."

Mason swallows.

The ship's floor sways beneath their feet, and the room is very warm. "Your highness," Emily chokes, but regrets it immediately. Adam winces at the sound of her speaking out, and Accalon's attention snaps to her. She is white. She cannot complete the sentence.

"Forgive me . . ." says Accalon. "I owe some of you an explanation. Others . . . others know why they are here." Accalon adjusts a gold amulet that got stuck in the fox fur of his coat. "What is your name?"

"Emily Byrnes."

"Emily Byrnes." He straightens. "*Byrnes*. What a name you have. Well, Ms. Byrnes, I bet I could tell you, right now, something about every person in this room you don't know."

"I bet you could, too. My lord." She adds this at the last moment, her mouth very dry.

Accalon studies her, and she can see several thoughts wave through his lamp-like eyes. "And still, you have no idea why you are here, do you?" There is a note of sympathy in his voice.

"I know why I'm here," Emily manages to breathe. Accalon tilts his head. "I'm here because I love Adam. I don't care about anything else."

Accalon's thick eyebrows are furrowed. He examines Adam next to her. "Ah," he says uncomfortably. "I see. Adam . . . *Flanagan*."

There is too much emphasis on Adam's last name, and Adam, who had been watching the surface of the table solemnly, shoots his eyes up at Accalon and fidgets. Accalon lets slip the merest trace of a dark smile.

But when Emily reacts to this with an inquiring look at Adam, Adam avoids her.

"Accalon," Marcus rumbles, pulling their attention back to him. "I said I would help you. *For her, Accalon.* I said I would help you *for her.* And now I *know* you lied to me. And *Scott—*"

"Scott will be left out of this, Marcus," says Accalon.

"He has done his job. He has brought me *exactly* who I needed to fix my problem."

"What are you talking about?" Emily speaks up. Scott is looking at her, but it is no longer that peculiar, intense look. It is smug.

"I need to tend to our other guests, Marcus," says Accalon. "Give me a moment, please."

"Your Highness, how could Marcus light the flame?" Emily blurts. "He was in Darson's Ford the night after it—"

"I never said Marcus lit the flame, Emily," says Accalon reasonably.

Emily stops. "You . . . but then why—?"

"May I explain?"

Emily is a statue, but he takes this for a yes.

"A flame has been lit in my Empire. One that could uncoil everything I have built. My people are in terror—and at great risk of breaking the terms of the treaty with Asht Vendar. Druids are dying. Forts are burning. If left unattended, the very foundation of this Empire will burn. Afterwards . . . ashes. This is something I am not prepared to let happen.

"They planned my evacuation to the islands offshore—the sea, the 'holiest entity.' I ordered before leaving that Marcus and his followers be summoned into my service against the flame as the Council argued and refused to act. But while I was being evacuated underground, a young man intercepted me in the tunnels. I halted the arrows of my guards because the man stayed in shadows . . . he simply told me to await letters. Then he disappeared. I later learned this young man was Scott. As he promised, I received mysterious missives at my hideout. Somehow, he knew my whereabouts. And he explained everything . . ."

"Hold on," says Emily, who too late realizes she's just given an order to the Emperor. "What I don't understand is—"

"Why you didn't run," Adam speaks now, flat, but his eyes are on Marcus. Marcus just breathes deeply.

Accalon answers for Marcus. His voice is slow and measuring.

"Marcus didn't run, Adam, because he is my brother."

Adam sits back in his seat at the same time Emily and Cazimir do.

"What?" says Emily, breathless.

Accalon smiles. And suddenly, she knows why Accalon looked so familiar to her. The dominance, the leader, the strength and size—despite old age—are all mirrors of Marcus. Accalon's features are just a little sharper. His face a little thinner. They share green eyes.

That explains why Marcus has so much wealth.

"I swore to gods I never wanted to see your face again, Accalon. And your filthy, gold-plated hands tricked me," Marcus seethes.

"Marcus hoped," Accalon raises his voice, ignoring Marcus, "amid his *falling out*, that we would never see each other again. But he also knew that if I were ever to call upon his help, ever to draw him back to me, it would be for the dire sake of my Addie."

"Don't you *dare* call her that!" Marcus slaps the table.

"Marcus . . ." Mason whimpers.

"She is my wife now, Marcus," says Accalon smoothly.

"And yet you sent *me* to deal with the flame! *Me,* so she and you could be protected. Your guard told me her life was at stake!"

"And how grossly you have *failed* me, brother," says Accalon.

"Where is Adrienne?" Marcus says. "Is she safe?"

"That is none of your concern."

"IT IS MY CONCERN!" Marcus stands, and as he

does, Adam stands as well. Accalon's two royal guards draw their blades.

"At ease," says Accalon hastily, raising his hands. "Do not be goaded by my brother's temper. And *Flanagan* . . ." Accalon looks at Adam, amused, his hands still raised. "Sit."

Adam swallows, but there is true worry in his eyes as he studies the peculiar tone of the Emperor's address. He sits slowly.

"Now that we understand Marcus' actions . . ." says Accalon. "Let's move on to why I changed my plans for you and listened to Scott's advice to have you lured to me instead."

"You got lucky we decided to head for the ocean," says Marcus. "There was no luring."

"I was on your tail the whole time," says Scott. But there's an adolescent shake to his voice that tells Emily he might still be trying to prove something to Marcus. "I was making sure you headed here."

"Scott," Accalon interrupts, as if it's been too long without him at the center of attention, "is first and foremost working for me because he is smart—he's shared much information with me through his letters, and I've excused his poisonous-plant smuggling crimes for his services. But there's another piece to the fire puzzle."

They wait.

"The water," whispers Accalon. "If you can control the water, you can control the flame . . . and if you control the flame . . ."

"You control everything," says Scott.

"Accalon," Mason squeaks. "What are you saying?"

"I'm saying," says Accalon, "I don't wish to destroy the fire. Yet. I wish to use it."

"That's madness!" says Marcus, still standing.

Scott rises. "What's madness is not exploring our capabilities!"

"So we can what?" shoots Marcus. "Burn down the provinces?"

"Maybe the whole globe," taunts Scott. "You have no idea what's out there. What's past this Empire. None of us do."

"The provinces are shaky," Accalon agrees with Scott, now meshing his fingers together. "Darvica is too strong. Fellvren too distant. The fire will bind them."

"What will bind them is your wisdom to *extinguish* the fire," Mason declares, outraged. "Accalon, cousin, this is preposterous. The provinces love you. They're relying on you to destroy the flame, not bring it back." Mason attempts to use his diplomatic talent. Flattery galore.

"And I *will* destroy the flame. But not before I've mastered its use. In war. In peace. In everything. I *will* bring order back to my Empire, and I *will* protect my people. Asht Vendar will fall to me at last and join the Empire in safety. This is the best way."

The Emperor's true motive revealed now: Asht Vendar. Scott sits, his eyes glinting, as if satisfied with the Emperor.

"But here's the catch," says Accalon. "I need to be the *only one* capable of extinguishing the fire. I need to be the *only one* harnessing that power if I am to mold myself to this throne. Once the people see that I and I alone can extinguish it, they will all bow."

Emily swallows.

"There is only one water that can destroy the fire." Accalon leans in to Emily, and she is startled at being fixated on.

"And it's not seawater."

The room is taught with silence.

"Let me tell you a story, Emily. One you'll never find in the history books."

Has he been watching her? Does he know of the

books she reads, the classes she teaches? Or is paranoia seeping in already?

"The Vicar is a dear friend of mine. You'd be surprised the stories he can tell you over tea. But a few months ago, I came across a peculiar tale of his . . . one about a druid, causing controversy in the church by playing with—now isn't this ironic?—lightning."

Sakole. Emily freezes.

"The young priest had meddled in some sort of experimentation. Trying to find water that would purge the lightning's power and thus, he hoped, extinguish fire, if the horror ever were to happen."

The visions of Sakole's story come flashing back to her, and she can hear the clink of the herbal jars on the table.

"To make a long story short, the young druid made his round to several villages, performing death rituals and burials . . . and one day, he performed a burial for a man in a very famous little town. The man's wife was a pretty renowned fisherwoman, I think. Lynne, is her name?"

The widow from Darson's Ford. Lynne. Emily doesn't dare look at Adam.

"And after performing that burial, he left this famous town . . . and shortly after bought water from a local merchant heading back to it . . . can you guess the rest of the story from there?"

"Oh my God . . ." Emily whispers. "It's Darson's Ford. The water that can extinguish the fire is in Darson's Ford."

A smile creeps over Accalon's face. Marcus and Mason are immobile in shock.

"Precisely," says Accalon. "The only water that could ever extinguish the fire is from your hometown. The very place you *left* in order to find it. And the reason for this leads me to my next story . . . do you know why the waters of Darson's Ford are so special? Holy enough to remove fire?"

Emily's eyes are scanning back and forth over the table's surface but seeing nothing, trying to stay ahead of, or at least with, the Emperor. She feels she is in a battle of wits with him, one historian against another.

"Because," Accalon answers for her. "Many, many years ago, there was a famous General, falsely accused of treason . . ."

"General Darson," says Emily.

Adam is tense next to her, and he still will not look at her. She can feel the instability of his breath, the tremor of his hands. She imagines she must look no better herself.

"General Darson, yes. And this poor man was sentenced to certain death, banished into the Darson's Ford woods. Inches from perishing, he stumbled into a clearing and found a mere handful of water in its center. The water reconciled an innocent man, who fell to the grass and drank it . . . and the next anyone knew, in the place of his body, a clean pond filled the clearing. It became the entity of sacrifice . . . of redemption . . . the embodiment of humanity's purity . . . or so the Vicar predicts. Now, it is all good and well if no one knows this little secret of Darson's Ford. I can still hold the power to destroy the fire alone if I take a healthy stock from the Ford, drain the rest, and no one is any the wiser.

"But here is my problem—here is why I heeded Scott's suggestion to bring you to me. General Darson created the holy water that lies beneath your village. He perished . . . but few people know *why* the innocent General was accused in the first place."

"They feared there was a spy for the Vendari among them," Emily spars. But Accalon is a challenging historian opponent. She knows her breadth of knowledge is outmatched by his decades and by his ears around every corner of the Empire.

"Yes," says Accalon. "And they were right—there was a traitor of sorts. But the traitor was not General Darson. The General was taking the blame for someone. Someone he loved very much . . . and someone who could, in turn, because of the General's sacrifice, inherit his ability to create this holy water."

The ship gives a small lurch as it is lifted by a wave. The lanterns filled with blue light swing above them.

"And the only person who can create that holy water now is sitting in this room."

Emily stares at Accalon, but something deep within her thinks it knows what he will say.

"He adopted his mother's maiden name . . . never left the home named after his father . . ."

"No," says Emily. She cannot turn her eyes away. She will not look at anyone but Accalon right now. She can't.

Accalon nods.

"Yes," he says slowly. "Turn, Emily, and meet Adam Darson."

CHAPTER 26

Adam's arms are crossed on the table. His head is hung, and moments pass where he does not move. They breathe, silent, and Accalon's sharp, inquisitive stare is upon him. Emily is hyperventilating. She watches Adam, desperate for him to speak. Desperate for his eyes to meet hers.

But he sinks his face into his hands, and that is all the confirmation she needs.

It is true.

"Adam." Her voice frightened, hurt, and confused.

"Do you deny it, Adam Darson?" says Accalon. His voice is not cruel or mocking. It is genuinely interested.

Finally, Adam lifts his eyes to Emily. Her heart sinks. His gaze is etched in sorrow, shame, and regret for a history she has never known. A history that has never been written in her books. Or taught in her class. A lump is welling in her throat that she cannot quell.

"It's true," Adam breathes.

It is Marcus' turn to fall back into his chair, disbelieving. So, this is not the secret Marcus was keeping for Adam—he looks too surprised. Mason shifts and wrings his hands, but Emily doesn't care about anyone's reactions. In fact, their presence means nothing to her now. This is about her and Adam. About his lies after all the days they've spent together.

"Will you enlighten us?" Accalon presses diplomatically, clearing his deep, ancient voice.

Adam ignores Accalon. He is still watching Emily. Every moment that she does not speak causes him pain. He twinges every time Emily gives her head the shadow of a shake, or swallows down the burn in her throat.

"I'm so sorry," he whispers, as if they are the only ones in the room.

"Adam?" says Accalon.

"Yes," Adam says, louder. "I am Adam Darson."

"And tell us, Adam Darson . . . what did you do to cost your father his honor in the military?"

Adam inhales a deep breath. He turns from Emily finally and focuses on the surface of the table again, knowing he will have to speak.

"I defied my orders," he murmurs.

"I'm sorry?" says Accalon.

"I defied my orders," Adam repeats louder.

"You defied which order?"

"About the Darvicans."

Cazimir bristles at the sound of his country, listening more keenly.

"Go on," says Accalon in a lower baritone. This time, it is an order.

Adam pauses to remember.

"My father was General Darson. He got me accepted into the military, despite any recruiting requirements." Adam's throat seems to be dry, for he is swallowing a lot. "I was young. Seventeen. I served a ten-month tour in the Sunlight Wars in Asht Vendar under the command of my father. When we returned, they stationed us at Fort Pull on the Darvic border, and we were ordered to treat the Darvicans as enemies if they came near us. *You* were afraid of them." Adam looks up at Accalon almost accusingly. "You thought they were forming an alliance with the Vendari."

"A mistake I now accept. Go on."

"One night, I overheard my father say you wanted

him to annex Kroikcher, even though they're citizens of the Empire." The Darvic town closest to the northern border. "I argued with him. He told me to wait and see. But I couldn't. I didn't want to kill Darvicans."

Cazimir is steadily fixated on Adam, listening to every word about his country.

"I abandoned my post," Adam goes on. "I went into Darvica, thinking I might warn Kroikcher. But before I could arrive, I ran into a band of mercenaries. I thought they might be what you were so afraid of." Adam speaks now to Accalon. "They were not. They were just . . . mercenaries . . ." Adam shakes his head now. "I was so stupid."

"What did you do?" says Accalon, but at this point, it sounds as if Accalon already knows.

"I gave them a message to send to Kroikcher. They agreed to relay it, and I believed them—partly because of my naivety, and partly because I was tired, and lost, and had taken on more than I could handle. It was a relief when they nodded at me, but now it's clear they were nodding in mockery. Seeing I was a soldier, they offered me work—enough money that I could quit the army and run away. I took a job tracking down enemies for them and dragging them back to their camp. I left Darvica with enough money to start a new life."

Accalon actually scoffs, but he is enthralled.

"Although I only spent a few weeks in Darvica, by the time I got back, my post was in chaos. Not because I deserted—only my father knew that. The others would not have known my absence was not because he'd sent me on orders somewhere. No, the chaos was from everyone talking about a traitor. I thought I might have actually missed a big event . . ." Adam sighs darkly. "And then I realized the event was me. Someone from the Darvic mercenaries sold me out. Went to the post ahead of me and, for a bagful of coin, pledged he knew who was working as a spy for Darvica and the Vendari . . .

"Darson. That's all they said."

"You did all this, too, Adam?" says Marcus snappishly. Emily's stomach plummets at the sound of "*too*." Again, this story must not be why Adam joined the Brotherhood, or else Marcus would be familiar with it. "You're just full of surprises, aren't you?"

"Let him finish, Marcus," Accalon scolds. He nods for Adam to continue.

Adam pauses, eyeing them both, as if unsure whether Accalon's manners are genuine or not.

"Darson. That was all the Darvican said. All he really

knew how to say. Your punishment for treason, Accalon, was death. So Fort Pull was pressured to distribute the punishment quickly. Darson could only mean one of two people in the military. Me, or my father. The renowned, acclaimed General. And all the odds . . . all the evidence . . . leaned towards me . . ."

Adam shakes his head and bows it. "And it was me," he says. "I did sell out yours plans to the Darvicans. I wasn't working for the Vendari, but I deserved the punishment. And the things I did for the mercenaries . . . I deserved the punishment even more for. Then . . . then everyone was shocked when my father took the blame. He took the death banishment into the woods to protect me.

"After that, I disappeared from the world, took my mother's maiden name. I just . . . couldn't . . ."

He swallows.

"So the sins of the father, in truth, belong to the son . . ." says Accalon musingly.

"Adam," Emily says, ignoring Accalon. Adam turns to her sadly. "This happened decades ago. And Marcus said . . ." Emily blinks and drops her gaze from Adam, fighting the tears. It's all about to end, though. She needs to know. She needs to know everything now, or else the pain, the secrets, will continue to grow like a cancer until she cannot stop it. "You were a kid, Adam. Kids make mistakes," she manages. "But the Brotherhood . . . why are you in the Brotherhood?"

Adam begins to shake his head in grief, but Emily stops him.

"Adam, please," she says, but her voice finally breaks. "I can't bear any more of this. Please. Just tell me now."

"I'd quite like to know myself," Accalon interjects.

Adam's eyes actually well with tears. Marcus and Mason watch him—Mason with sympathy and Marcus with a hint of that sly amusement Emily had seen in him the night they met. Like he is curious as to how Adam will confess what the Brotherhood already knows he's done.

"Four years ago . . ." Adam begins, voice tighter than ever. "Four years ago . . . I met someone . . . a woman who I thought . . . thought loved me, but . . ." He shakes his head dismissively. "She needed money. Needed it badly. She lied to me, said she was dying, that she couldn't afford the medicine. And so I returned to the Darvic mercenaries. I went back to sell myself as an experienced soldier to them . . . and they gave me another job."

He pauses, swaying as the magnitude of emotion hits him.

"They needed an innocent man killed."

Emily can barely breathe, looking at her Adam, thinking of a life being ended at his hands.

"They had a tip that this man was going to report them to the Rovercaul . . . that he was planning a bust . . . so they sent me to deal with him. In the winter, one of the coldest nights . . ."

"To the sopping Rovercaul?" says Accalon, his tone raised an octave with superiority. "What in light's name would he care about in the business of the mercenaries?"

"Nothing, brother," says Marcus. "Adam was fooled. What did they have, some personal strife with the guy?"

"Stop," is all Adam says. His voice cracks. There's a pause before he goes on. "Midwinter. In Darvica I went after him . . . under orders to torture him first . . ."

Something beyond the obvious feels wrong about the story, and Emily stiffens. Cazimir has leaned in very close to listen . . . something in his eyes flashes like a dire wolf smelling blood . . .

"The man was camping in the woods. I took him from behind with a knife against his back. Walked him half a mile into an abandoned shelter for questioning . . ."

"What was his name." Cazimir's voice—loud, shaking—startles everyone. He does not care this time.

Adam looks up, surprised at his interest, but his eyes are still swimming.

"His name?" repeats Adam cautiously.

Cazimir rises slowly.

No, Emily thinks.

Cazimir speaks every word slowly and with emphasis, now towering over Adam.

"*The name. Of man. You tortured.*"

Everyone is tense. Adam looks up at him, and his mouth opens and closes again and again. He thinks before answering.

"Hawcaff," Adam says.

Cazimir lunges across the table. He grabs the scruff of Adam's shirt and hurls him over the table and into the wall of the ship. The chair clatters to the ground. Adam hits the wall and slides to the floor.

Everyone except Accalon stands now. The two royal guards draw their blades again, but Accalon, too entranced by the turn of events, raises his hand.

"No!" Emily cries. "*Please!* Cazimir—"

Before Emily can reach Adam, Mason moves behind

her, grabs her by the shoulder, and reels her in. He locks his arm compassionately over her chest. She is too late to help Adam, as Cazimir already moves with power.

"You killed him," Cazimir slurs, approaching Adam. He yells a curse in Darvic.

Adam holds his head with one hand as he tries to pull himself up. "No," he moans. "I didn't kill him . . . I let him go . . . I . . ."

Cazimir grabs Adam again by the shirt, pulls him up, and punches him across the face so hard that Adam's head bangs back against the wall, making the glass lanterns shudder on their ropes above.

Emily has to turn away with a sob, covering her eyes.

"My brother!" says Cazimir. "There was little boy with him! And you took my father! You left boy to freeze!"

He throws Adam onto the floor again. Adam gasps a broken, ragged gasp. His eyes end up on the wall and he closes them in shame and sorrow. "I'm sorry," he says, as if he now remembers the little boy with the older Darvican.

It is not enough for Cazimir. As soon as Adam says it, Cazimir reaches the ground and smashes another punch over Adam. And another.

Emily's heart is ripped across. Seeing the two men she loves—for she loves Cazimir, yes, or else this divided, excruciating pain would not be apparent—causing the other such misery. She sobs again and begs for an end.

"Please," is all she can say.

And Accalon agrees. He nods at Cazimir and Adam, giving the order for his Black Guard to restrain them.

They pull Cazimir off Adam, but it takes both soldiers their full might.

"Take him outside," says Accalon. "Go."

Emily sees a tear run down Cazimir's face as the guards shove him out the door, finally letting a wave of cool air relieve the small, hot cabin.

Mason releases Emily and she rushes to Adam's side, hugging his bloodied body to her.

"Adam," she murmurs into his shirt.

He rests a trembling hand over the back of her head.

Accalon allows this for a moment. But then, when his guards return and close the door behind them, he stands at last.

"Emily," says Accalon. "There is a small problem."

Emily wipes her nose with the back of her hand and looks up at Accalon.

"Adam can create the holy water. Any water he

simply drinks from—anything that gives him *life*, the life his father sacrificed to give him—becomes sacred as the Ford. And thus . . . becomes capable of destroying the flame. Since I must be the only one with that power . . ."

"What are you saying?" says Marcus suspiciously.

Accalon gives him a long look, and then resolve hardens his eagle-like features.

"I'm saying he needs to die."

Panic, hysteria, confusion—everything hits her like a tidal wave. Like the one that knocked Adam off his feet in her dreams. But she cannot do anything to stop it. She is bloodless as she watches it all go down, sitting up instantly.

"I'll die before that happens!" Marcus hisses through grated teeth.

"I'd hate to see that, Marcus. It will be humane and quick tomorrow morning. An honorable soldier's death. This is the way it has to be." The Emperor sounds truly regretful, but Emily doesn't care. "Goodnight, everyone," Accalon finishes as a fresh pair of guards in black armor joins the others. "I hope you'll find your stay tonight comfortable."

Two of the guards force Emily off Adam.

"No!" she screams. But they are too strong.

Adam keeps his eyes on her as one pulls him to a stand and ties his hands behind him. The other drags her back farther. Tears stream down her face, and she cannot breathe—how can she, when there is no oxygen in the air? How are the others not choking, too?

I love you, Adam mouths, a tear trickling down his own face.

She tries to pull for him, but they usher him into the back door of the cabin, where Accalon has disappeared to. At the last second, Adam lifts his eyes to the ceiling and then back to her as if trying to communicate something.

And then he is gone.

Emily is shaking her head. The walls are melting to blackness around her.

And since she cannot reach Adam, she turns and breaks free of the royal guard and runs into Marcus. She buries her head against him and convulses with sobs, feeling as if her heart will give out.

Marcus wraps his arms around her and exhales sharply.

"We won't let this happen, sweetheart," he says in his rough, deep voice, but it is shaky.

And then she realizes what Adam was trying to tell

her as he looked to the ceiling.

The stars.

His soft, promising voice comes back to her.

They're not going anywhere.

CHAPTER 27

She lies on the hard floor of the ship, pressing her hand flat against the smooth uvarde wood, and sobs. The ground rolls and raises the ship, and the darkness of this bare, cold room is absolute.

They had been herded below deck, into separate cabins, and black-armored guards had sealed the hatch leading back up. Marcus had hissed "*Stay,*" in her ear as they'd clunked down the steps to the underdeck. Emily had glanced into his eyes and saw the resolve in them, the strength and authentic caring, beckoning her to trust him. Emily knew what he had meant. He needed time to work out a plan, and any radical interference from her, in a desperate ploy to save Adam, would make things worse for Marcus and Mason.

The waiting feels like forever.

A scratchy, wool blanket is over her, and it had taken every ounce of willpower to lie on the floor and attempt to rest.

But there is no energy. Her body is sucked of all life, leaving only a limp, weeping form on the floor. Inside is darkness, a black even deeper than what blankets the room now. The only sound is the occasional creak of the ship as it rises, relaxed in the port, and the hysteric gasps of her grieving.

It wasn't Marcus Accalon was after. It was Adam. Adam the entire time. The Adam who those nameless, faceless guards will never know. The Adam who Accalon cannot see, even through his eagle-like green eyes. The Adam who kneels to pin a carved flower on a girl's shirt. And the Adam who has nothing in this world—no family, no wealth.

That person who has nothing is everything to her.

She holds the tiny flower gently in her hand, hoping that somewhere on this ship, Adam is holding the token she carved for him.

One thought of his face, his body, poised for the death strike, and the sobs return in new vigor. The wool blanket has no warmth. She is cold, shivering, and exhausted from the tears, but still, they come.

The door to her tiny room opens with a soft click, allowing the dimmest of light to sneak in. She doesn't bother to turn and see who enters as it clicks shut. They can take her if they want.

She reins in her tears as best she can, but still finds her breath escaping far too quickly, her eyes tightly closed.

He does not say a word as he lies down next to her—above the blanket, so as not to make her uncomfortable. The second she feels his weight next to her, hears the deep exhale of his breath, she knows who it is.

Cazimir.

She allows her tears to continue and he wraps an arm around her, moving closer in the complete darkness and reeling her into his warmth. She clutches his arm and recognizes the dark hairs, the sword-arm muscles. He tightens his hold around her. Still, he says not a word. He just holds her as she cries in his embrace, and he does not move from his spot.

Hours of restless sleep pass, fading in and out of nightmares. And still he is there—awake, she is sure, for he responds to every distressed fidget, every whimper of renewed sorrow, with a tighter squeeze.

There is no imagining what it takes for Cazimir to be

here. He knows Adam's fate, and knows what Adam is to her. And yet Adam is responsible for Milo's death. Emily has no anger towards Cazimir. Just sadness, for everything. For all of it.

When, in the refusal of sleep, she is stabbed with another deep return of the pain, Emily turns towards Cazimir abruptly, and his reaction is instant. He kisses the top of her head. And his right hand—the one not wrapped around her—slides into hers. She clutches its fingers weakly, and he presses their entwined hands to his chest, the way she had done in the woods, to feel his heartbeat.

With his body next to her, his heat, she can finally fall into an exhausted, heartbroken sleep. He stays awake, breathing evenly, and her fingers finally relax in his.

Not an hour passes before the door opens again.

Cazimir props himself up instantly, squinting in the light of the open door. Emily is stirred by his movement and shivers. She registers the light at the open door and allows a swell of hope in her chest that it is Marcus, prepared with his plan. Or better—Adam, escaped, collecting her and Cazimir for their breakout.

But as she turns backwards, Cazimir stands slowly. He takes a slow, hostile step towards the figure at the door.

It is Scott.

Emily sits, startled, but Cazimir holds a hand out behind him, urging her to stay.

"You . . ." Cazimir begins, low and dangerous. But Scott is not the least bit intimidated.

"Sorry, miner. Am I interrupting something?"

"Get out."

"I'll take that as a yes."

"Now. Leave."

"Can't, Darvica. I'm here for Emily."

Whether Scott meant this as wanting to simply see her, or something graver—more in line with Accalon's execution plans—doesn't matter. The second he speaks Emily's name, Cazimir jumps for his throat.

Emily is on her feet, drawing her knife, but it happens too quickly.

Cazimir manages to pin Scott against the wall once again, grunting beneath the other's protests, his hand pressed against Scott's throat. But Scott wriggles his arm free and punches Cazimir in the stomach, who doubles over.

Scott comes forward for another punch, and Cazimir swings out a fist and knocks him to the floor with one hand and a *thump!* of falling limbs.

Retching, one had still on his stomach, Cazimir straightens and limps forward for Scott, but Scott jumps to his feet in one smooth motion, and Cazimir stumbles backwards in alarm. The second's weakness is all Scott needs. Knowing the Darvican is much stronger than he, Scott relies on dexterity. He twists Cazimir's arm behind him and throws his other arm around Cazimir's neck, locking him in a choke hold.

Emily is approaching them with the point of her knife directed at the pair.

Cazimir huffs for breath, sweating and turning his head away, eyes tightly closed. But when he opens them to see Emily standing alone, with just her knife, against Scott, he shakes his head "no" with all the strength he can muster.

Emily ignores him.

"Let him go," she says.

It is all Scott can do to raise himself on his tiptoes and peer over Cazimir's shoulder and meet her eyes.

"I just want to talk to you," says Scott. "Without your boyfriend trying to kill me. Not that he's having much luck."

Cazimir gives a valiant jerk at these words, nearly

breaking free, before Scott twists his arm harder in response. Cazimir winces.

"All right?" Scott presses.

"Okay," Emily says. "Let him go. And you can talk. But after tonight, Scott, I let him maul you. Unless I can do it first."

"Tell him," says Scott. "Tell Cazimir not to attack me."

Emily meets Cazimir's eyes, which are hard with disapproval.

"Don't hurt him, Caz. Just for tonight. Okay?"

He doesn't waver his gaze.

"I mean it, Caz. Trust me. All right?"

Cazimir looks away stubbornly, staring into the corner of the empty room. But his silence—perhaps slightly fed by embarrassment—is the best confirmation they will get.

Emily nods at Scott, and Scott releases him—not before throwing him to the ground first as if discarding a sack of potatoes.

Cazimir hits the floor with a thump and jerks onto his back. Scott brushes himself off nonchalantly, and Cazimir, panting, allows the adrenaline to die down.

"That was pathetic, Darvica. Maybe next time we

fight, your girlfriend won't be here to save you."

"You've got one hour until I lift the deal," says Emily. "Start talking."

"Fine. In my room. You can bring the mountain bear."

Scott turns and leaves for his cabin.

Cazimir, still catching his breath and propped up on his elbows, eyes Emily sharply.

"What?" she says.

He exhales and looks away dully.

"I'm sorry," she whispers. "I didn't want to see him hurt you."

As if in defense of his pride, Cazimir sits forward and hops onto his feet in a swift motion. He stands, regaining every inch of his towering height, which seems to restore some of his dignity.

Some.

He slinks out the door, ducking his head under the doorframe, and heads towards Scott's cabin.

"Make yourself at home," says Scott, closing the door behind them.

Scott's den is as dreary as Emily's, but not nearly as desolate. Barrels are stacked high around the cramped room, mostly covered with nets. It reminds Emily briefly of Mr. Robutan's basement, filled with the barrels made by the cooper.

The blankets for Scott's bed are carelessly rumpled at the only free wall, and in the center of the room are three crates around a rotting, rocky table. Dull, soggy playing cards are strewn around the floor of the room, suggesting many nights of gambling and drunk crewmen.

Scott sits on one of the crates and Cazimir, as if accepting a challenge, sits across from him.

This leaves only the crate next to Scott available for Emily. She takes it, wary, and Scott actually smiles cockily at how close she is to him.

"Start talking," she repeats.

"Fine with me. I like a decisive woman."

Cazimir gives a warning growl. This seems to amuse Scott, but he goes on in a determined voice.

"I thought you two might like a few questions answered . . . and maybe I'll coax your common sense into agreeing with me."

"I doubt it, Scott. You sold us out. If it weren't for you, Adam—" Emily cannot finish the sentence.

"I'm sorry about Adam. But we'll get to him later."

"So what are we getting to right now, then? Your rendezvous with the Emperor?"

Scott pauses.

"Sure," he says. "Let's start there. But before you say anything else, I'll tell you this right now. The Emperor is working for me. Not vice versa."

"That's believable," Emily scoffs.

Scott gives her a dark look. "Isn't it?"

She hesitates.

"The Emperor is a good man, Emily. He sincerely believes this fire will protect his people from bloodshed, and just as sincerely believes the provinces will disintegrate without his guidance. And he's right. Which is why I'm going to kill him."

Her heart jumps against her chest. Cazimir straightens.

"Hear me out . . ." says Scott cautiously.

It is a brilliant position Scott is in. Emperor Accalon is ordering Adam's execution. The thought of the Emperor's death does not immediately horrify Emily. In fact, it may be her only way of saving Adam.

"Speak," she says.

"I came to the Emperor after the news of the fire. In the escape tunnels. Then I raced back to Darson's Ford and my people brought him my letters . . ."

Emily let's that "people" comment go and just tries

to keep up.

"In those letters, I convinced him that the fire could be used to his benefit. Like I said, the Emperor is a good man. And good men are easily manipulated. When I told him of the water and Adam's ability to create it . . . he knew he needed Adam killed. He needed someone to either lead Adam to him, or kill Adam themselves. As long as Marcus was around Adam, we knew I wouldn't be able to kill him myself. But I offered to shepherd Adam here. I followed you. Ever since you left Darson's Ford."

"It was you," says Emily, the blood draining from her face.

The cult attacking them. Ravaging their rooms in Welshire. Clogging the Glens. All along, they were after Adam. All along, it was Adam who was the target. She remembers how that arrow hit Mason—but he'd been standing behind Adam. It was Adam they were aiming for. And if they couldn't kill Adam thanks to Marcus and his party, they at least needed to bait him to Endraft. Scott had the Glens clogged so they could not get the seawater there; so they'd have to keep going. If only Emily had chosen to follow the dry river and find the dams . . . maybe none of this would have ever happened.

"You sent the cult after us," says Emily. "To kill Adam. You were trying to kill Adam, Scott."

"I doubted they'd get past Marcus—and then your boyfriend, Darvica, an unexpected addition —but it was worth a try."

"You had our rooms ravaged in Welshire looking for the water."

"I didn't care about the water," Scott corrects. "They were looking for Adam."

"You killed Druid Parr, too," says Emily. "I know you did."

"Yes," says Scott. "I poisoned Druid Parr. We killed many druids that night, but Parr was a unique priority I had to take care of myself. He suspected too much."

A memory flashes back to Emily—one she's surprised she held onto, for it seemed inconsequential at the time. "*The water here will do,*" Parr had said, referring to why he filled his church's water basin with Darson's Ford's silky, murky water rather than seawater like the other churches in Galeduen.

Even the ultimatum of Scott helping Emily to save Adam is starting to wane. She is sitting next to a murderer, and she knows it. Her mouth hangs open as all the pieces start coming together. There is only one conclusion to this.

"So you're a part of it," she says, disbelieving. "You're part of the cult. The one that brought the fire back."

"Of course I am. I sent them after you, didn't I? I ordered them to clog the Glens so you'd have to go to Endraft."

"Who are they? And *why*? Why do you want the fire back?"

"Some are of Brotherhood roots, wanting to reemerge with the might of the flame behind them. Others . . . others just want the end to ignorance. Ignorance that this weak, powerless blue light is all we're capable of."

"But it *is* all we're capable of," says Emily.

Scott pauses, giving her a long, evaluating look.

"I'm going to ask you both, right now," he looks at Cazimir, "to listen to me. And make your decision. After tonight, we're either allies . . . or enemies."

Cazimir is watching Scott with suppressed aggression, every line of his body pronounced, perfectly fine with these conditions.

"There is a connection between the fire and the blue light. Right now, fire's been summoned back after centuries of having been banished from the world. As long as that log burns at Fort Myrth, fire can be created. But any fire besides that one can only remain lit for a short amount of time, as its energy doesn't survive very long in this realm. We're too ensnared by the force of the blue light—this is its domain. The fire can't compete energies with it for long."

That explains the immediate disappearance of the fire after it swallowed Fort Myrth. And the black, burned markings on Hopskip, the pack horse, after the flaming arrow ignited him. The horse survived because the fire died on its own before it could become fatal.

"In order for fire to return permanently, others have to succumb to its power. The more who choose to create it, the more who wish for it to burn—to *explore its potential*—the more it establishes its presence against the blue light."

"What do you mean create it?" says Emily. "Something brought it back—something you know about, I'm sure. Something you probably *did*, even. But humans *can't create fire*, Scott!"

"You're wrong, Emily. How else would I have lit the flame at Fort Myrth?"

Freezing cold waves over her. Cazimir releases a shocked sound, and Emily feels like she may fall off her crate.

"Yes. I lit the flame. Right before I caught the Emperor in the tunnels." Scott speaks with odd, obsessive pride. It is like he thinks his enthusiasm will be infectious.

It is anything but.

Emily considers how greatly Scott has been underestimated. He must have ridden to Darson's Ford afterwards as unceasingly as Wes had done to make it back in time for Marcus' Brotherhood meeting.

"Now—Emily, Cazimir—you can join me. We can do this *together.* Us, as a new generation. You don't understand how many agents I have in this burning Empire—*they* can find your parents, Cazimir. And Emily, if Adam is on our side, he can live. Empires rise and fall . . . it's your decision whether to fall with them or stand amidst the ashes."

"You're . . . you're not . . ." says Cazimir, swallowing and shaking his head. He cannot understand the concept of man creating fire—just as Emily can't.

"Scott . . ." she says. "If we do this . . . are you certain that—?"

"How." Cazimir swallows again, interrupting her. "How do you create . . .?"

Scott's voice is low and entirely, terrifyingly sincere. "You can create it, too, Cazimir."

Cazimir's eyes are no longer hostile. They are stunned, nervous even.

"I could never . . ." he says.

"You can," Scott presses. "Right now."

Emily watches Cazimir as he stares, incredulous, at Scott.

"Do it," says Scott. "Now. Hold out your hand."

Cazimir places his forearm on the table.

"Caz!" says Emily.

"Think of Milo," Scott instructs, dark and far too eager. "And then think of fire."

"Caz, stop!"

"See the flames in your head."

"What are you doing to him?!"

"Now think of Milo, Cazimir. He's dead. Someone *killed* him." Scott stands slowly. "Someone heard your cry and wouldn't *listen* to you! He is a skeleton somewhere, Cazimir! *He's dead!*"

Cazimir shakes and grips his forearm with his other hand. He is growing whiter . . . his hand clenches and trembles.

Scott smiles now, and whispers, probably to himself:

"Sing forgotten words . . ."

There is a whooshing sound.

Cazimir opens his hand.

And from it—red, glowing, crackling at the air . . .

Sparks.

They emerge only for an instant and then recoil. Gone, as if nothing had happened. The silence and terror are deafening. And when Cazimir, stricken, finally looks up from his hand, it is not Scott's eyes he meets.

It's Emily's.

CHAPTER 28

A crash outside their door interrupts the dead silence. Scott turns to it, but Cazimir holds his gaze on Emily just a second longer before tearing it away for the door.

Cazimir is breathing raggedly, unsure of himself, scared of what he has just done.

"Go ahead and check that out, if you want," says Scott. "We're done here." He seems self-satisfied, and he eyes the Darvican with measuring interest. "Tomorrow . . . I'll know where each of you stand."

Still in a daze, Emily slides up from her crate as the noise in the other room lures her, and the mist of information fogging Scott's cabin becomes smothering.

She stops at the doorway as she senses Cazimir has not followed her.

"Cazimir?" she says tentatively, turning.

Cazimir has not risen from his crate. He looks up at Scott. "You can . . . find my parents?"

Scott gives the merest smile. "I can do more than that."

"Caz," says Emily, firm. "Come on . . ."

"How?" says Cazimir, still fixated on Scott.

Another ruckus is heard in the room across from them, and two voices rise with it—Mason's and Marcus'.

Emily abandons Cazimir and makes for the door.

"Will you please stop destroying things?" Mason moans through the door. He sounds despairing, high-pitched. "For heaven's sake . . . This isn't helping."

Emily pauses outside the door. She wants to hear what they are discussing, but she is afraid they'll stop if they know she's there. The night must be approaching dawn by now. She estimates the sun will be rising within the hour, and then Adam . . .

She moves closer to the door and listens in on Marcus and Mason.

"I can't!" Marcus shouts.

"It may be the only way, Marcus! We have to think of everyone else!"

"I won't let it happen, Mason!"

"Marcus, listen. If they execute him, it will serve as a diversion and give us a chance to take her away from here. We need to warn the Vicar, and we need to get water from the Ford *immediately.*"

Emily's throat closes. Is Mason suggesting . . .?

"He's all she has, Mason!" Marcus snaps. Emily hears something else tumble to the floor.

"She'd have me, too, Marc. And you. We all care about her."

"He loves her," Marcus pants, seeming to have stopped attacking things and sighing as he sits somewhere. "Adam loves her. And I love her, too. I won't do this to her, Mason. I can't. It's her greatest fear."

"What is?" Mason prods gently.

"Losing Adam," says Marcus, although the rage has leaked from his voice, leaving only exhaustion. They'd been up all night scheming. "She told me. It's her greatest fear. I can't let them execute him. I'll die in his place if I have to."

Emily gropes the wall. Sadness weighs her down like metal. Would Marcus sacrifice his life for Adam if it weren't for Emily? Is he offering this because of her?

"There'd be no way for you to do so," Mason sighs, although he seems to agree it would've been a considerable option. "We need to get out of here, Marcus," he sounds distraught. "We need to, either way."

"It's almost dawn," Marcus mumbles. "I'm going to wake her."

She can hear him rise, and she springs aside as the door opens.

Marcus is startled to see her, but a flash of regret is just apparent in his eyes before they harden to normal.

"Emily," he says.

She inhales deeply and then an urgent idea jolts her.

"Marcus, let me in. I need to talk to you."

○ ~ ○ ~ ○

They hear footsteps above—crew and Black Guard preparing for the day.

"Go," says Marcus, opening the door of his and Mason's cabin once more. "Find him and tell him the plan. I'll stall them if they come down."

Emily doesn't look back. She hurries through the musty ship's quarters and passes the open door of her cabin. From the corner of her eye, she catches him look up to her, and she doubles back.

Cazimir is in her bare cabin, the wool blanket folded neatly under his arm. She fears, for an instant, that she will see embers in his eyes. But she doesn't. He is the same man. He looks at her questioningly, and even though he is much better at Galeduan now, she is reminded of the expressive eyes and meaningful silences that were his only communication just a few weeks ago.

"Caz . . ." she says softly, very aware that he is in her room, very aware that she abandoned him with Scott after he'd produced the sparks.

As she nears him, he holds out a hand. In it is the tiny, carved flower Adam gave her. She must have left it on the floor when she drew her knife in haste to help Cazimir against Scott.

She takes it, blushing, and replaces it in her pocket.

"Thank you," she says.

"Emily . . ." He clears his throat.

"Cazimir," she whispers.

He studies her tenderly.

"Cazimir, I . . . I need to ask you . . . ask you a favor." Her palms are sweating, and she already feels the guilt in the magnitude of what she is about to ask of him. He listens patiently.

"Marcus and I . . . we think . . . we think the only way to save Adam is to—"

She suddenly thinks better of the sentence she is about to say and turns on the spot, closing the door.

Cazimir's eyebrows are raised when she turns back to him. She sighs, a little embarrassed.

"We think the only way to save Adam is to let Scott kill Accalon at the execution. Or try to. Since you . . . since you can create the fire . . ." She speaks carefully, watching his reaction, which has abruptly become guarded. "We need you to offer to do it. Ask Scott if you can light an arrow and shoot it into something that will catch fire. It—flame—is the only diversion that will get us out of here alive, unless the Emperor really is killed . . ."

"What would catch fire on beach, Emily?" says Cazimir.

"What?"

"Scott say the execution will be on beach. What would I target that would catch fire?" he says darkly.

She pauses, uncomfortable at the conclusion. He'd have to target a body. There will be nothing else that could catch fire. Her responding look begs him not to make her say it. He returns the gaze with stern, knowing eyes. The answer to his question had already been known before he asked it.

"Caz . . ." Emily continues, now growing meek. "We need you to stay with Scott when you light the arrow for him and let Marcus and Mason get the horses. They'll ride in and grab Adam. Scott would never trust us to leave him for the horses unless one of us stays next to him."

It sounds even more horrible than she imagined. It sounds like she wants to use Cazimir as sacrifice for Adam.

He swallows and watches her, as if hoping there is more she is leaving out.

"They'll come and get us right after they get Adam on his horse and—"

"Us?"

Emily pauses. "I can't let you do it alone," she says. "But I can't light a fire, either. I'm going to stay next to you when you do it."

Cazimir inhales deeply. His eyes are on the floor, cloaked in the dim atmosphere of the room.

"No," he says.

"Cazimir, please don't argue—"

"I will not do it if you are with me." He looks up at her with firm resolve.

"Caz, no." She shakes her head, already feeling the burn in her throat.

He places his hands on her shoulders and leans in to her height.

"Emily," he says, slowly and clearly, looking into her eyes. She will not meet them. She is looking around the floor of the room, fighting back tears.

Cazimir steps forward and turns her head up to him with his hand. "Emily," he repeats, and she is forced to look up at him.

He shakes his head slowly. "I love you," he breathes.

A new guilt, and so much emotion, washes over her. A tear slides from her eye, but the sound she makes is almost happy.

"Please," he says. "Do for me. Save Adam. You cannot come back for me. I do not want to go with Scott . . . but he can find parents. His cult can find them for me before something bad happens to them. I am all they have left, Emily. But you . . ." He places his hands on either side of her face. "I have you."

She is crying now, because she knows what this means—Cazimir will not be escaping with them.

"I can't let you go, Caz." She chokes. "I can't."

"I know, *valsera*," he breathes, but before she can protest more, he kisses her. She wraps her arms around his neck. Her feet step over his shoes as buries her in his arms and draws her higher up to him so he doesn't have to stoop as much. He steadies her weight on his shoes.

There is longing and desperation on his lips.

All too soon, he pulls back. This is their goodbye.

She clings to him, clutching both his arms and looking up at the tall Darvican, whose eyes are reddening as well.

"Cazimir," she finally manages to whisper, gulping down another swallow. "*Ahm cara . . .*"

He searches her eyes with tenderness and a distinct touch of sadness. Slowly, he pries her hands from his arms and steps back.

Emily thinks he will not answer her, but as he steps for the door behind her, head down, he whispers in her ear.

"Soul mate."

○ ~ ○ ~ ○

Streaks of yellow and pink paint the sky in the east as greenish, foamy waves lap at the beach. They walk with Scott by their side, who holds himself high and proud. He wears a quiver of arrows and carries an elegant Fellish recurve bow, which thankfully draws no unusual attention. The guards, thinking he is on their side, expect him to be armed, after all. That is also how he arranged for Cazimir's sword to be returned from custody—and Emily asked him to retrieve Adam's short sword as well.

It is at her back.

Emily's stomach is tighter than ever. Endraft remains in lockdown; they are the only ones walking along the shore—the only ones in sight besides guards, who appear by the glint of their black or silver armor in the morning sun.

Ahead are four figures, facing them, standing just where the uprush touches the wet, heavy sand. Two reflect the blinding shine of sun—the Emperor's black-armored royal guards. One is tall and broad—Accalon. And the other . . . the other . . .

Adam's hands are still tied behind his back, and Emily prays they hadn't kept them like that the entire night. She can just make out the sorrowful expression on his face as he sees her before Scott stops them.

Scott looks at Marcus and nods. Worry suddenly pierces Emily. What will Scott do to Cazimir once he realizes Marcus and Mason aren't returning to pick him up? She watches a tiny crab scamper sideways over the sand at her feet to control her expression from revealing her thoughts.

Marcus and Mason cut away from the group instantly and make for the horses at the back of the inn.

"Mr. Osborne!" one of the guards calls as he sees this.

Has Scott gained such allegiance with the Emperor that the guards address him so properly?

"It's okay," says Scott. "They're with us now. I've talked some sense into them . . ."

The guard nods hastily, as if acknowledging a previous understanding.

Emily hesitates. She is supposed to follow Marcus now, but Cazimir . . .

Cazimir gives her a hard, demanding look.

Go. Now.

She exhales shakily. When she pauses again, Cazimir raises his hand to his chest. He clutches his fingers over it, and there is a pang at her heart. Her hand belongs there, too.

But she knows what the gesture means.

Emily chokes down her heart for what she needs to do. She follows after Marcus. The fine sand sinks under her feet, making her pursuit slow, and Scott can be heard behind her.

"I knew you'd join me, Darvica," says Scott, and she thinks she can hear him select an arrow from his quiver. She glances to the side and sees Adam at the shore, watching her worriedly and glancing back at Scott's drawing of an arrow. Adam is the only one who notices the tiny action, as the two royal guards behind him aid Accalon in signing a document approving Adam's death.

Marcus and Mason are already invisible behind the buildings of Endraft.

And Emily decides she cannot bear it. If something went wrong . . . if Cazimir missed the shot . . . if Adam was killed before the diversion was set . . .

She turns in time to see it all happen.

The Emperor's voice booms out at the same time Scott is insidiously handing his bow to Cazimir. Cazimir does not see Emily has stayed behind. He looks straight ahead, stiff but composed.

"Adam Lawrence Darson . . ." Accalon's deep voice can be heard against the gentle lapping of the low tide. One of his royal guards draws his sword and hands it to him. "Kneel."

She sees Adam kneel in the waves and hang his head. It breaks her heart, and her knees wobble. He is clutching something in his hand . . .

Scott's voice intermingles with Accalon's in her ears, giving soft instructions to Cazimir.

"Think of Milo, Cazimir. His shivering. See the fire leap. And do it. Now."

It takes a moment. There is a soft whooshing sound,

and then the smallest flicker of fire emerges from Cazimir's hand. With extreme skill, he holds it down to an arrow in his left hand, so it looks as if he's adjusting the leather bracelet on his wrist. He draws the arrow slowly, bow down, so he will be ready to fire.

"We are men of the Empire, Adam Darson." Behind Adam, the Emperor raises his sword, point down, as he speaks. The blade glints. "Your death now—"

"His heart, Cazimir. Aim for his heart. On three."

"—will ensure peace for many—"

"*One*."

"—in this era—"

"*Two.*"

"—and the eras to come . . ."

"*THREE!*"

Cazimir raises the bow and the arrow soars into the air, whooshing against the sea wind. Scott grabs Cazimir and tugs him away, into a run, as soon as it is fired.

"Look out!" one of the silver-armored guards shouts when he sees it, but Accalon is too late. He looks up, still holding the sword aloft, just in time to see the arrow gliding down and burying itself into his ribs.

Cazimir is not a skilled archer. The injury would not be fatal—or perhaps Cazimir hadn't intended it to be—

but the fire catches Accalon's robes. Adam jumps to his feet as guards draw their swords and Accalon, flame swallowing up his clothes, plunges into the seawater, thrashing and howling in pain.

Adam looks down in shock at the burning man. The shallow water does nothing to the fire. The flames lick even through the frothy water, and as Accalon squirms, another strong wave rushes in.

Emily freezes. Just like in her dream, Adam, not expecting the impact, is swept off his feet and into the wave. He disappears beneath the white water and she screams for him.

"*Adam!*"

But the second she takes a step towards him, a horse thunders by her and she springs back.

It is Marcus, riding towards Adam and his scorching brother.

"GET ON COPE!" he yells without looking back.

Copenhagen gallops up next to her and she dives for him, just gripping enough of his saddle to haul herself upon him as the ground escapes her feet. Wind rushes over her as Copenhagen flies, and she can hear Mason jogging behind them and leading Folk Tale, Adam's white stallion in one hand and his own painted horse in the other.

The guards are in chaos. The black-armored ones have thrown themselves over the Emperor and stripped him of his burning robes. Others sprint along the town, yelling, "*Fire!*" to warn the townspeople and search for the culprit.

But they've yet to see Scott and Cazimir.

Marcus gives a roar of exertion as he leans far down from his saddle, nearly tipping over, and grabs Adam from the water. Adam had been sucked into the undertow, and now water is fleeting down him as he coughs and gasps. Marcus embraces him against his horse, and Adam clutches to stay on, water still dripping down him in streams.

Marcus wheels his horse around, back towards Emily, Mason, and the horses.

Reaching over for Folk Tale's rein, Mason pulls the horse to a stop as Marcus thrusts Adam into the sand. Mason quickly undoes Adam's hand ties.

"Get on the horse and run!" Marcus yells. "You and Emily! Go to Darson's Ford and warn them! Go! *Now!*"

"Where are you—?" Emily begins.

"We're going to the Vicar! GO!"

Adam climbs his stallion just as a silver-armored

guard confronts Marcus with his sword drawn. Marcus' horse rears and Marcus gives a mighty kick in the soldier's chestplate, knocking him into the ground.

"Let's go!" he shouts at Mason, and they flick their horses into a run.

"Come on, Emily," says Adam, shivering, following their lead. Relief floods at the sound of his soft voice, shaken, but alive. "It's all right; come on."

Copenhagen, without any real guidance from Emily, pulls away from the shore, turning towards the north, where Marcus and Mason had gone.

The agonized cries of Accalon still ring in her ears, and it's like her vision is spotting in and out, even though it is broad daylight.

Cazimir. Where are Cazimir and Scott? Is he safe? Did the guards see it was them who sent the arrow?

But her questions are never answered. For already, the grey shacks of Endraft pass beside her and Copenhagen climbs the sandy incline with ease into the grassland. Already the shrill cries of the guards are fading.

Already she is leaving.

Marcus and Mason are nowhere in sight, but Adam rides alongside her. She thanks heaven for Copenhagen, who carries her on his own accord as she bows forward and buries her face in her hands, balancing on the saddle with her knees.

Already she is leaving . . .

And already, she's left her *ahm cara* behind.

CHAPTER 29

It is a blur, every mile. The sun swoops across the sky too quickly, the grass rolling on forever, and Emily feels she'll be sick.

The weight of the past twenty-four hours sinks through her like glue down a bottle until there is nothing left in her body but a tight pain in her stomach. Adam is safe. She has him. And she prays her thanks again and again, but each time, the prayer is interrupted by Cazimir's face, his hand lifting to clutch a fist at his chest.

"Just a little longer, Emily," Adam croons beside her. And she hears him say this over and over as the ground is eaten away beneath them. "Hold on . . ."

By the time they reach the woods—accomplished only by Adam's stout leadership—it is nightfall, and Emily is swaying. Her stomach churns and she feels hot, hotter than natural as heat comes in flashes over her skin. Perhaps it is the lack of sleep, the fact that she hasn't eaten since morning, that her stomach aches and she's caught something in the air. Her immune system has no doubt been weakened.

She tilts in the saddle and nearly slides off Copenhagen when Adam catches her by the shoulder.

"It's okay," he breathes. "I got you. We need to keep going."

"Just . . . sleep . . ."

"I'm sorry," he whispers, and he truly sounds anguished. "We can't stop. We have to get to the Ford by tomorrow night . . ."

And so the dark trees arch over them. Night creatures scurry beneath their horses' hooves, and Emily registers the deep, slow hoot of an owl as she tries not to fall asleep in the saddle. Adam's voice continues to guide her.

"Hold on . . ."

○ ~ ○ ~ ○

She is shaken awake to find herself in a familiar room.

It is circular, with polished mahogany floors and stone walls, but is otherwise dusty.

The guardhouse posted at the Emperor's gong they encountered, just through the woods, seems to have allowed them board once again. Emily and Adam have outraced the Emperor's forces from Endraft by at least half a day, so no one at the guardhouse could be wise to what just happened.

And once again, Adam has placed her in the bed. He is kneeling at her now, gently prodding her awake. Emily is so tired, her eyes seem plastered closed. She vaguely questions how she got to this bed—did Adam carry her all the way up those narrow, winding stairs? Or did she somehow sleepwalk up here? She hopes the latter.

"We have to move again. I'm so sorry."

She tries to say he shouldn't be sorry, she tries to thank him, but her voice doesn't want to vibrate any sound to her throat. Instead, she rises mutely, and Adam gains the rest of his stand heavily, weary as well.

They scurry down the steps, and even the large, blonde, female guard doesn't have the nerve to bid them goodbye as they reach the front door. She has obviously taken note of their diminished number of party members—perhaps also of the purple blotches on Adam's face from Cazimir's hand. She'd even let Adam keep his short sword without objection this time.

Emily's fever persists. She is shaky as she mounts Copenhagen, and even the sun—unusually hot for the autumn day—cannot warm her. She suffers waves of heat and then freezing, shivering cold, but does not comment, does not speak, as Adam leads them into a gallop.

It is as if the weakness in her body has transferred to her mind, making it numb, and she struggles to identify landmarks, gauging where they are and how much farther they have.

Has Accalon been killed, or did he survive the burns as the fire died out against the blue light's energy?

And Cazimir.

Still she knows not why Marcus' hand had been burned. Marcus left with Mason—but why did they go after the Vicar?

She bobs on her saddle, feeling the ground pound beneath Copenhagen's hooves, as the sun resumes its fast-forward loop over the sky.

This new era of Scott's may already have closed in.

○ ~ ○ ~ ○

"I recognize this," says Emily. It is the first time she has truly spoken. "We're almost here, Adam. These trees . . ."

"We're back," Adam sighs in exhausted agreement. "This is the road we took from the Ford." They had entered a path through the forest nearly thirty minutes ago, and Emily has only now picked up on its familiar characteristics.

Rather than the greyish, thinner trees growing near the gong, these are strong, with ragged, reddish bark and green ivy and moss twining through their branches. But that is the only green remaining—all else has succumbed to autumn. The bluebells are gone. The leaves are brown, orange, and red, and the ground is laden with dead foliage and dry twigs. There is a distinct chill to the night air, but the movements of the woods at night, the evening sky hidden from view, do not frighten Emily. It is all familiar to her. It is all home.

A certain peace stills the emotion inside her. Soon, she will be home, where the familiar Darson's Ford waters carry fallen leaves like rowboats. The black trees will stand tall, nestled like sentinels around the opening of the tiny village, the wooden houses untouched and warm inside.

Those waters have so much more meaning now.

The smell is apparent long before she notices it. It is a faint, woodsy, almost sweet smell, at first so gentle that it seems to mingle with the forest air and doesn't interrupt her thoughts. But then it becomes more powerful. Something shifts in the trees as she inhales another strong whiff.

Adam and Emily look at one another.

"What is that?" says Emily, nervous but determined.

Adam holds her gaze for a moment, equal with uneasiness.

And as their horses lead them closer, they can hear it.

A faint, unbroken rumble.

"No," Emily whispers.

"What?" says Adam.

"No!"

"Emily, what?!" Adam demands.

But she doesn't respond. She urges Copenhagen into a sprint, and he shrieks and obeys, dodging through the roots and thickets of what's left of the beaten path.

The sound grows into a roar.

She breaks the tree line, jumps off Copenhagen, and runs down the decline into the small clearing that is Darson's Ford.

That was Darson's Ford.

The inferno engulfs wood and deck. Millions of embers stream up into the stars. A menacing red flicker dances over the black waters, which catch burning beams and posts with a seethe of smoke. The waters extinguish the flames.

Emily stumbles backwards, away from the heat, away

from the roar. The surrounding trees are black, merciless bystanders as she falls into the grass, an arm over her eyes.

Mr. Robutan. Lynne. Can anyone survive this?

The heat hits her like a wall, preventing her from going any closer, and the roar sucks away all other sound.

A strong hand grabs her shoulder and forces her up to her knees.

"*Adam!*"

He is kneeling before her, trying to collect her, but she gropes for him unsteadily, his arms, his hands, anything, and breaks down sobbing.

"Please don't go!"

Don't disappear. Don't fade. Don't burn like the rest of them.

"*Hey,*" he says, voice thick but forcing her to look at him. Wood collapses behind them in the fire. Sparks billow into the night. The smolder is intoxicating. Smoke pinches her lungs. She sways on her knees, tears flooding her stinging eyes, trying to comprehend Adam's voice floating to her.

"*You see that*?" Adam speaks with vigor and points to the sky.

The stars.

"*You see them*?" he demands. "They're not going

anywhere! And neither am I!"

He seizes her in his arms and lifts her, eyes tightly shut, until they're both off the ground.

Darson's Ford crumbles before them.

END OF BOOK ONE

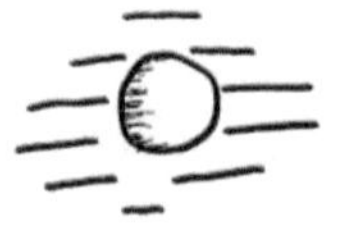

The Braelian Dynasty

Emperor	Years of Rule	Additional Information
Myrril Braelius	T.M. 0–74 (Born R.M. 19)	Many of the stories of Myrril's life are legend and unsubstantiated. Some believe he split an ocean and walked onto Galeduen from another continent. Some believe he was a fallen god. Historical evidence supports that he was a warrior responsible for beheading Gennan, the last High King of Galeduen, ending the era of the fire-rulers and ushering in a dynasty of light. No one knows the shade of blue belonging to Myrril's light—many accounts conflict. Myrril married a Galeduan commoner who asked him to withhold her name from the public as a means of protecting her. He also had a lover, Kyara Sille, from a powerful family in the highlands. He produced heirs with both women. The

		Sille Family would carefully carry on his lineage in the background while his legitimate bloodline claimed the throne. But soon it became customary that the Council would appoint the Sille bloodline to the throne as alternatives when the legitimate heirs seem unable to govern. Typically, Sille emperors may not have a direct successor. Myrril warred with Darvica, Fellvren, and Asht Vendar at the same time in a single year in the War of Four Armies. His successes in each campaign preserved Galeduen and made it the powerhouse of the continent. Some sources say he banished giants from the continent—most believe this is a metaphor for keeping back the Darvicans in the war, but some interpret it literally. To avoid a succession war, Myrril declared that his rightful heir would be blessed with a black light (a shade of blue so dark it is only one shade away from absolute black) called Midnight Light.

		Myrril is said to have died in a flash of sudden light while sitting on his throne.
Euris I "the Beloved"	T.M. 74–83 (Born T.M. 51)	The favorite grandson of Myrril. His light turned to Midnight Light after Myrril's death. Beloved by the people, Euris I has over fifteen statues throughout Galeduen, second only to Myrril himself. The statues usually depict Euris I in compassionate poses, embracing a derelict woman or surrounded by children, etc. There are more than a dozen sources claiming a different shade of blue for his light, ranging from sapphire to almost white, leading some to believe he could change his light color according to the preference of others. This is likely just a myth, and it is therefore uncertain what the real color of his light was. He is sometimes called Euris the Beloved.
Lurio	T.M. 83–110 (Born ?)	The second eldest son of Euris I. He began construction on Cathair Mór.
Ilegard	T.M. 110–129 (Born T.M. 84)	Son of Lurio. Oversaw the completion of Cathair Mór.

		Signed the Darkwing Pact, officially making Darvica a province of the Braelius Empire.
Euris II	T.M. 129–178 (Born T.M. 107)	Son of Ilegard. Originally named Ilegard II, Euris II changed his name on the throne when the Southern Rebellion occurred in T.M. 175. He hoped the name change to the beloved second emperor would inspire unity. He failed to quell the uprisings before his death of pneumonia.
Euris III	T.M. 178–180 (Born T.M. 127)	Son of Euris II. Continued attempting to contain the civil war. Had to move from Cathair Mór to the Shrine as rebels occupied the capital. Killed in battle trying to retake the capital.
Euris IV	T.M. 180–225 (Born T.M. 158)	Son of Euris III. Managed to retake Cathair Mór and execute the top rebellion leaders. After evidence revealed their involvement decades later, Euris IV ordered the eradication of a fire-worshipping cult known as the Brotherhood of Rain and Cinder. It is written that Euris IV came face-to-face with the kinfather (leader) of the cult during his

		execution. The cult leader looked Euris IV in the eyes and delivered his final words: a promise that the Brotherhood would assassinate the following three emperors in retribution before eventually ending the dynasty by fire. Euris IV died mysteriously the next day of unknown causes.
Plegiatic	T.M. 225–228 (Born T.M. 187)	Son of Euris IV. Restored peace to the empire. Unified people with poetry, visits to rural villages, and a kindness to animals—he outlawed animal cruelty. He was popular among women, who admired his pinkish blue light—the blue of sunsets. His assassination, presumably by the Brotherhood, is one of the reasons the Galeduan people began to despise the cult.
Rieles	T.M. 229 (early months) (Born T.M. 204)	Son of Plegiatic. Rieles was assonated by the Brotherhood while praying in the temple of Cathair Mór.
Luthore	T.M. 229 (later months) (Born T.M. 206)	Brother of Rieles. Assassinated by the Brotherhood while praying at his brother's tomb. Their

		double assassinations in the same year came to be known as "The Year of Two Emperors."
Brachlian Sille	T.M. 229/230–277 (Born T.M. 191)	The first Sille emperor (a distant half-cousin of Luthore) to be appointed to the throne by the Council after the assassination crises of the past three emperors. Witty and fond of speech. Referring to the past two assassinations, he is famous for saying at his coronation, "I shall not pray." Brachlian is remembered for making the controversial decision not to intervene in Darvica during a Darvic civil war over the Darvic title of Rovercaul. It rang a heavy death toll. "Let them fight it out" Brachlian Sille is remembered for saying. "The Empire shall respect the victor." Died of natural causes.
Theros "the Wide"	T.M. 277–291 (Born T.M. 238)	Grandson of Luthore. Remembered for moving the seat of the Vicar to Cathair Mór and signing the Treaty of Windsong, making Fellvren a province of the empire. Widening the empire is how he got his namesake. Died of a tick bite

		possibly contracted by his contact with the immune Fellish.
Ducato	T.M. 291–301 (Born T.M. 256)	Son of Theros. Said to have woken the Black Guard nightly with screams and nightmares of fire engulfing the Empire. He built the flowing aqueducts of Cathair Mór in an attempt to drench himself in safety and wash away the nightmares. Died of heart failure.
Ardonius Sille	T.M. 301–346 (Born T.M. 282/3)	It is not perfectly clear why the Council elected to appoint a Sille emperor after Ducato, who kept the empire stable enough but seemed haunted, perhaps made mad, by dreams of fire. Ardonius Sille packed the Council with Sille aristocrats. He was poisoned by loyalists to the legitimate bloodline, who favored Theros' brilliant grandson, Winhelm, but ended up with Malchor instead when Winhelm died by suicide only days after Ardonius Sille's murder.
Malchor	T.M. 346–369 (Born T.M. 313)	Grandson of Theros. Said to have been so obsessed with his own light that he forbade all other light in Cathair Mór but his own, which

		floated in every streetlamp. This resulted in several men moving east and populating the villages. Died in a room full of his light.
Ordo I	T.M. 369–399 (Born T.M. 329)	Son of Malchor. Known for sending an oceangoing expedition in search of another continent. The expedition did not return. Died of natural causes.
Ordo II	T.M. 399–428 (Born T.M. 361)	Son of Ordo I. Ruled from a wheelchair, which made him especially ruthless. Cause of death unknown.
Cintarron "The Forgotten"	T.M. 428–448 (Born ?)	Grandson of Ordo II. Little else known about Cintarron, sometimes spelled Sintarron in Fellvren. He was so hated by his son, Magentioch, that records of his rule were destroyed when Magentioch ascended the throne. However, scholars suspect Sintarron was a moral and gentle ruler as there is little evidence to the contrary. Likely he was poisoned by Magentioch.
Magentioch	T.M. 458–491 (Born T.M. 429)	Despite his violent rise to power, Magentioch was an effective statesman. He created the rank of Supreme General, a position generals jockeyed for. Magentioch

		likely intended this to prevent generals from gaining too much local following. He died while challenging the first Supreme General, Graccus—his own appointee—in a duel.
Polontius	T.M. 491–522 (Born T.M. 475)	Son of Magentioch. Claimed to be a seer and revelator, and saw visions of great dangers ahead in the dynasty, especially involving fire. For this reason, he built the Emperor's Alarm gongs throughout Galeduen. His death in T.M. 522—ironically of drowning, not fire—was the first time the alarms were used.
Vernidad	T.M. 522–524 (Born T.M. 501)	Son of Polontius. Vernidad was remembered as a handsome and charming Braelius with much potential. Unfortunately, he was assassinated by an unknown organization.
Dralus I	T.M. 524–573 (Born T.M. 500)	Nephew of Venidad. Crowned when he was only nine, the Council ruled until he came of age in T.M. 531. Dralus I was fascinated with astronomy and hired rural astronomers to teach him how to predict the annual

		Celestial meteor shower. He declared three bright stars, lined up next to each other, to be named after himself and his yet-to-be-born descendants, Dralus II and Dralus III. Together, these three emperors are known as "The Star Emperors."
Dralus II	T.M. 573–616 (Born T.M. 524)	Son of Dralus I. Remembered for attempting to arrange a marriage between himself and Princess Shalanarok of the Vendari. He sent an orb of his light to her with a convoy, assuming it would impress her. The Vendari used the light as a sports ball until a female Galeduan dignitary finally had it extinguished. Died of natural causes.
Dralus III "The Dog Emperor"	T.M. 616–660 (Born T.M. 597)	Son of Dralus II. Known as "The Dog Emperor" for always having four or five dogs around him. Decided to make his mark in transportation by building roads across the Empire. Was the first sitting emperor to reach the far coast of Fellvren. He planned to board a ship and visit its islands—the farthest point of the Empire—but fell off

		his horse and hit his head, dying to the howls of his dogs.
Rhenvar	T.M. 660–705 (Born T.M. 642)	Son of Dralus III. Said to have stood around six feet five inches. His light was well-recorded to be the "Midnight Light," of Myrril Braelius' mandate. Because of this, the mandate to rule skipped his older brother, and he was crowned emperor instead despite his bastard status. Rhenvar was born out of wedlock and raised in the Highland of Kings, where the capital of the old High Kings is thought to have resided. The Highlands are known for producing warriors of incredible skill for governance. Rhenvar was a respected and feared ruler. He frequently threatened invasion and occupation as a way of keeping the continent in control. When news reached Cathair Mór that the Fellvian potentate authorized the murder of an entire village accused of fire-worship for the Church, Rhenvar ordered the Fellish Vicar's staff brought to him

		in front of the Council. He had a soldier hold the staff in front of him. Then, Rhenvar stood from his throne and urinated on the staff in front of the Council to cries of outrage. The clergy wing threw things at him, but he did not stop, and then, when done, he left without a word, leaving only a large puddle on the floor—and a ten-year sanction on Fellvren.
Larede Sille "The Farmer"	T.M. 705–724 (Born T.M. 665)	Ascended the throne after Rhenvar's sons killed each other in succession wars. Known as "The Farmer" for his love of country life. He ceded immense power to the Council and lived most of his days in the Calder Glens, returning only to Cathair Mór in the winter months. His reign is marked by years of peace and increased food security, but, perceiving him as weak, the surrounding provinces and Asht Vendar emboldened themselves, raising stronger armies in Darvica and Asht Vendar and entertaining oppositional social movements in Fellvren.

Euris V	T.M 724–725 (Born T.M. 665)	Great-grandson of Dralus III. Crowned in his bed while deathly ill. He reigned only one year but accomplished his dream of building a theater in Cathair Mór—it's unparalleled musical reverb achieved by including echoing pools of water in the theater. While insignificant as a statesman, he is elevated to almost saintly status by musicians.
Grendolven	T.M. 725–735 (Born. T.M. 700, died ?)	Son of Euris V. Religious fanatic. Greatly expanded the power of the druid class by making the empire a financial benefactor of the Shrine. In T.M. 735, he abdicated to his nephew, Clovan I, and left to become a druid in an undisclosed monastery.
Clovan I	T.M. 735 (Born T.M. 670)	Nephew of Grendolven. Quickly disposed by his son, Clovan II, after the Black Guard tipped off Clovan II to a mass-assassination order Clovan I tried to enforce on all his male relatives.
Clovan II	T.M. 735–757 (Born T.M. 688)	Son of Clovan I. First sitting emperor to visit Darvica. Alleged to have a Darvic bastard, which created rumors of an undisclosed

		third Braelian bloodline in Darvica. Clovan II, perhaps influenced by Darvic culture, authorized women to join the clergy. He fortified the Galeduen borders, building four directional forts which came to be known as "Clovan's Cross." He alienated the Council with greater fidelity to absolute power until his death of age-related complications.
Freyon	T.M. 757–772 (Born T.M. 711)	Son of Clovan II. Frustrated war-desiring generals by ignoring the military and at times even juvenilizing it. Instead, highly interested in economic diplomacy. Placed an embargo on Asht Vendar when it (again) refused to become a province. Pushed to change the material of the coin from gold and copper to trithium, an unattractive ore found in Galeduen. Several prominent councilmembers were against this idea, believing trithium currency would collapse in value. Convenient accidents at the trithium deposits prevented the transition from happening before Freyon

		died of suspected blood cancer.
Accalon	T.M. 772–Present (Born T.M. 748)	Grandson of Freyon. Took the throne at a young age—councilmen expected him to be a scholar-ruler after two decades of classical education. Surprised many with his invasion of Asht Vendar following years of political tension and an alleged assassination attempt that many have come to doubt ever occurred. Two wars, separated by three years of attempted negotiations, came to be known as the Sunlight Wars.

ACKNOWLEDGEMENTS

I'd like say a bit more on the book's dedication to John Flanagan. John, author of *The Ranger's Apprentice* series, is my cherished friend. My love for fantasy grew while reading his books as a teenager. Through emails and the special occasions where his tour took him from Australia to within driving distance, we formed a close relationship. He's helped me in the literary world pursue my dream of being an author. Eventually, he dedicated one of his Ranger novels to me. With my love, John, we are even now in print. You have held a special place in my heart for a very long time, and I want you to know you always will.

Thank you to my beta readers, among them: Kelsey Nieves, Regina O'Shaughnessy, Mackie Thompson, Renee Erickson, Kelley Megale, Rebecca Earhart, Jasmine Renee Brown, Meagan Morrison-Crabill, and Bear Champion. Thanks as well to John H. Matthews for formatting the cover and to Madelyn E. Dulle for copyediting and offering thought-provoking suggestions.

Thank you, Mom. Thank you to Pop, my grandfather (Joe Megale), who I presented this manuscript to and who appreciated it despite the genre not being familiar to him. Another early reader was Larry Megale, whose love, of course, influenced this work profoundly.

Thank you to Matthew Baldacci. When he was a St. Martin's Press executive, he admired this book and tried to get it published there.

Finally, thank you, Matt. This trilogy may not be here had you not decided to buy *The Elder Scrolls: Morrowind* all those years ago.

I really hope you haven't gone anywhere.

ABOUT THE AUTHOR

S.C. Megale is an agented and award-winning author first traditionally published by Macmillan at the age of twenty-three. An American born in 1995, Megale's many life adventures include walking through Stonehenge, scuba diving the Great Barrier Reef, serving as flotilla commander in the U.S. Coast Guard Auxiliary, receiving a knighthood in the Order de San Luigi, meeting Pope Francis, shadowing on *The Hunger Games* movie sets (and attending the premieres in Los Angeles), directing prize-winning short films, being a beekeeper, ringing the NASDAQ opening bell, graduating from the University of Virginia with distinction and from Georgetown University with two master's degrees, adoring many dogs, and performing weddings as a marriage officiant. When not doing all that, Megale can be found in the woods. For more information, contact details, and love from a friend if you need it, please visit www.scmegale.com.

MORE FROM S.C. MEGALE

Fantasy/Humor
(Tannhauser Press, 2023)

Young Adult Romance
(Wednesday Books, 2019)

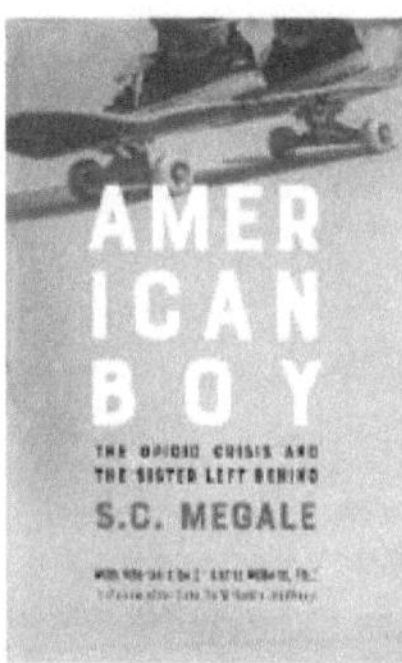

Memoir/Addiction (Bluebullseye Press, 2019) 1st Place IPPY Award Winner and 1st Place Reader Views Winner

Children's Literature (Night Song Press, 2024)

Inspiration/Historical (Rowman & Littlefield, 2022)

MORE FROM NIGHT SONG PRESS

IF YOU ENJOYED *THE BROTHERHOOD OF RAIN AND CINDER* . . .

Please leave a review on Goodreads and Amazon, Barnes & Noble, or wherever you made your purchase. It really helps!

And look for the second book of the trilogy, FATHERHOOD OF ORE AND DRAGON, coming out soon!

Thank you.

www.ingramcontent.com/pod-product-compliance
Lightning Source LLC
Chambersburg PA
CBHW020556310726
48979CB00008B/1240/J

* 9 7 8 1 9 6 4 7 1 5 0 3 2 *